SUMMER'S EDGE

ALSO BY DANA MELE

People Like Us

SUMMER'S EDGE

EDGE

DANA MELE

SIMON & SCHUSTER BFYR

NEW YORK · LONDON · TORONTO · SYDNEY · NEW DELHI

SIMON & SCHUSTER BFYR

An imprint of Simon & Schuster Children's Publishing Division
1230 Avenue of the Americas, New York, New York 10020

For information about special discounts for bulk purchases, please contact Simon & Schuster Special Sales at 1-866-506-1949 or business@simonandschuster.com.
The Simon & Schuster Speakers Bureau can bring authors to your live event. For more information or to book an event, contact the Simon & Schuster Speakers Bureau at 1-866-248-3049 or visit our website at www.simonspeakers.com.
Interior design by Hilary Zarycky
The text for this book was set in Berling.
Manufactured in the United States of America
First Edition
2 4 6 8 10 9 7 5 3 1
Library of Congress Cataloging-in-Publication Data
Names: Mele, Dana, author.
Title: Summer's Edge / Dana Mele.
Description: First edition. | New York : Simon & Schuster Books for Young Readers, 2022. | Audience: Ages 14 up. | Audience: Grades 10-12. | Summary: When five estranged friends return to a summer lake house on the anniversary of their friend's death, unexplainable events begin happening, old betrayals rise to the surface, and the group suspects a killer among them is intent on revenge.
Identifiers: LCCN 2021045657 (print) | LCCN 2021045658 (ebook) | ISBN 9781534493117 (hardcover) | ISBN 9781534493124 (paperback) | ISBN 9781534493131 (ebook)
Subjects: CYAC: Murder—Fiction. | Secrets—Fiction. | Ghosts—Fiction. | Revenge—Fiction. | Haunted houses—Fiction. | Space and time—Fiction. | LCGFT: Novels. | Thrillers (Fiction) | Paranormal fiction.
Classification: LCC PZ7.1.M4692 Su 2022 (print) | LCC PZ7.1.M4692 (ebook) | DDC [Fic]—dc23
LC record available at https://lccn.loc.gov/2021045657
LC ebook record available at https://lccn.loc.gov/2021045658

To Chris, an excellent brother and better friend.
And as always, for Ben.

1

The lake house hasn't changed in the ninety-one years of its distinguished existence. Solid, stately, a relic of the Rockefeller and Durant era, it has survived three hurricanes, countless termite infestations, and a flood. It's survived death itself. A bold claim if you can make it, but in this case, it happens to be true. Last summer, it burned to ashes with Emily Joiner trapped inside, and it was simply resurrected in its own image by its benefactors. It's indestructible. Impervious to death and all that nature and beyond can summon. I've always thought of the lake house as a special place, but as I stare up at it, risen from ruin a year after its demise, the word that comes to mind is *miraculous*.

Has it really been a year?

To the day.

I pull the stiff, custom-made postcard from the pocket of my faded army-green capris, a pair that Emily designed herself. On the front of the card is a gorgeous snapshot of the house. It was built in the Adirondack architecture style—a million-dollar mansion with a rustic stacked-log-and-stone aesthetic, a wraparound porch featuring delicate columns of hand-carved trees with branches winding up to the roof, and a sculpted arch of briar framing the door. Out back is a killer view of Lake

George, a serene little corner exclusive to the handful of neighbors scattered sparsely along the coast. Completely secluded by majestic pines, the lake house is something out of a fairy tale, a lone cottage in a deep dark forest.

I do think it gets lonely. I would.

The house is in its own little world, buffered from civilization by the wilderness and a strict back-to-nature philosophy— no internet, no cable, no Netflix, satellite, or cell service; just peace, quiet, sun, swimming, boating, and plenty of misbehavior. It's been our summer haven for the past ten years. Me; Emily; our best friend and my ex-girlfriend, Kennedy; Emily's twin brother, Ryan; his best friend, Chase; and as of two years ago, Chase's girlfriend, Mila. Last year should have been *the* last year because that was the year of the fire. The year we took things too far. The Summer of Swans. The year Emily died.

But then, the postcard came.

I flip it over and read it again. It's a hot day, and my car is like an oven. It only takes the interior of a car about half an hour to reach a deadly temperature when it's in the mid-sixties outside. The gauge on my dashboard reads 81. I pull back the dark frizzy curls clinging to my neck and twist them into a bun on top of my head, yank the keys out of the ignition, and kick the car door open. A cool breeze sweeps off the lake and touches my face, fluttering my T-shirt against my skin. It's like a blessing from the lake gods. The sound of wind chimes rings softly, an arrangement of notes both strange and familiar, like a music-box song. I imagine the sound of my name in my ear, a whisper in the breeze. I am home. I take my sunglasses off and close my eyes, shutting out the light, and allow the delicious air to wash over me. The scent of pine and soft earth. The promise of cool, clear water on my skin. The taste of freshly caught fish, charred on the grill; gooey marshmallow, melted chocolate; Kennedy's lips, sweet with white wine. Our voices, laughing, swirled around bonfire smoke.

Jesus. I open my eyes, and the bright sunlight makes me dizzy. *Charred. Smoke.* Just thinking the words gives me a sense of vertigo, even now. My mouth feels bitter, full of bile, and the phantom smell of smoke stings my nostrils and makes my eyes water. How could I think about fire in that way, here of all places, today of all days? Where Emily died. Where her bones were burned black.

I don't know that for a fact. She may have asphyxiated. The rest of us were assembled on the lawn, in shock, immobile, separated from Emily. My parents wouldn't let me know the details. I haven't been allowed to find out for myself. It's been a nightmare of a year. A year without my friends. A year without *any* friends. Any fun. Of seclusion, doctors, fucking arts and crafts and therapy animals. Which, yes, they're cute, but it's insulting. Five minutes petting a golden retriever before he's ushered away into the next room does not repair an unquiet mind.

And witnessing your best friend die because of something you did—or didn't do—is as disquieting as it gets.

You're asking, okay, yeah, why go back, then.

The answer is opening the door.

"You came," Kennedy says. She lingers in the doorway, holding a frosted glass with a lemon wedge stuck on top. Her long, copper hair hangs loosely around her sunburned shoulders; I can see a navy swimsuit strap underneath her pale blue sundress.

I hold up the postcard wordlessly, then glance down at it again.

One last night, before we all go.

The Hartford Cabin.

June 17th.

Or what was it all for?

The card stock is thick and creamy, the kind they use for wedding invitations. Expensive-looking. The words are handwritten in a deep, watery blue; a practiced, whimsical scrawl so light and airy it seems to dance off the postcard. I recognize it instantly. It's Marilyn Monroe's handwriting. More accurately, it's Kennedy Ellis Hartford's best imitation. Kennedy, in some bizarre, ironic twist, has been inexplicably obsessed with Marilyn since we were in kindergarten.

I haven't spoken to Kennedy for a year. I shouldn't be grinning at her, my body filling with lightness, the soles of my feet starting to bounce involuntarily like this is the reunion I want it to be. I have so many questions. Why did she leave things the way she did? What the hell was she thinking, inviting me back to the house that burned down with Emily trapped inside? And is this a private party, or was everyone else invited?

I think in the end, I had no choice. I had to come. There was no other way to get closure after how things ended. And I need that. After a year of mantras and painting and snuggling with furry animals, I need closure like a motherfucker.

"Chelsea." Kennedy waves me over.

I resist the urge to run to her, and open the car door, taking my time retrieving my bags, then walk the gravel driveway slowly, pebbles crunching under my sandals. "No Beamer. Are your parents on a supply run?"

"They couldn't make it." She presses the glass to her forehead. One luxury the lake house does not have is air-conditioning. Her parents insist on some semblance of authenticity, of getting back to nature, hence the lack of technology. A whole summer of it would be torturous. But it's a weekend home. And it was always worth unplugging now and then to get away from the noise and politics of high school and my summer job at the mall, peddling fast food along with half the rising junior class. Until now. Now, I have the awkward task of plugging back into my friends' lives.

Kennedy sets her drink down on the porch railing and gathers me into a hug. It's odd. I expected a burst of emotion, an apology maybe, some swelling moment of . . . something. Like maybe we'd broken up suddenly in the midst of a horrible tragedy and hadn't spoken for an entire year. This should be a poignant moment in the story of us. Instead, it's like we just saw each other a couple of days ago, around when the last day of school would have been, and now here we are, where we'd be every year, first weekend of the summer, always the first to arrive.

I press my cheek into her hair and close my eyes. Any other year, this time, Emily would have been standing behind me, politely waiting her turn, Ryan faded somewhere in the background, digging their luggage from the car. Emily was never one to pack lightly, even for a weekend trip. Kennedy's parents would be inside, her father strutting around in a too-tight swimsuit, juggling a craft beer and fishing pole, her mother mixing up ice-cold pitchers of lemonade and sangria.

A cloud moves over the sun, and I lift my eyes to the single window on the third floor, the attic window. I picture Emily inside, and for a moment, I see her pale face looking back at me. The sun returns from the cloud cover, and the sudden blaze of light burns spots into my eyes. I press my palms against them, blinking hard against the aching sensation and the momentary panic fluttering in my chest. When my vision clears, she's gone. Just a trick of the light.

"Come in," Kennedy says, but her voice is drowned out by the sound of a second car winding its way down the long gravel driveway. I turn to see who's here. Chase's jeep screeches to a halt and he bursts out, beaming like a supernova, and before I can even get a word out, I'm swept up into a crushing bear hug.

"It's been too long, kid," he says with affection. Chase smells like summertime, salt and sunscreen and slushies. His attention turns to Kennedy before I've caught my breath. Chase is warm, genuine, a true friend, but his attention is difficult to hold.

So it won't be just Kennedy and me this weekend. That makes sense. The lake house isn't a romantic getaway. Any romance by the lake is as private and intimate as the secrets told here: kept among friends, and you're never truly alone. There's nowhere to hide in this house. Still, I can't help a little sigh of disappointment. I want to talk about what happened. Not just with regard to Emily, although I want to talk about that, too. Someone needs to talk about that. But I also want to talk about what happened with *us*. It wasn't fair to leave things the way Kennedy did. Silence is worse than the cruelest words, because it leaves room for hope, even when logically, there is none. Goodbyes are messy, and Kennedy hates a mess. But I needed her this past year. I would have assumed she needed me too. But Kennedy doesn't need anyone. She's made that clear with her radio silence. I just thought I was different. I know I was. Until the night of the fire.

A shiver runs through me at the thought, because seeing Kennedy and Chase again in this place, in the shadow of the lake house, surrounded by the whispering pines and under the watchful eye of the summer sun, feels too familiar. Like nothing has changed, Emily is still here with us, and we haven't learned a thing.

2

Can you hear me?
I hope so.
I've been so lonely this past year.

3

By the time everyone has arrived, it's nearly sunset. I've settled myself into the old hammock with the rusty chain on the screened-in sundeck with a dozen pillows and a battered copy of *Murder on the Orient Express*. Chase is off in the game room playing Ping-Pong with Mila, who arrived in a lime-green barely-there bikini and is still wearing just that, although the temperature has dropped considerably. Kennedy is whipping up some spaghetti and pesto with fresh basil from the herb garden, and Ryan has just arrived, uncharacteristically late. I see Kennedy's shoulders tense as he passes through the kitchen before he reaches my side. He settles down in a beach chair across from me, silhouetted against the screen panel, a shadow figure against the brilliant painted backdrop of pink and purple sky over the dark, still water. I struggle to raise my eyes to look at him. Emily's twin, her other half. The guilt I feel just thinking about him is overwhelming.

"Am I interrupting?" he asks.

"Of course not." I put the book down and struggle to sit up. It's easy to sink into the ancient hammock and get impossibly tangled.

He hugs me awkwardly. Ryan is all angles and few lines. It's hard to find a comfortable spot to hug. There's always a sharp bone jutting out, a shoulder in my throat, a hip in my thigh. I don't know how he manages to arrange himself in that way. He's skinny, but so was Emily, and she was a great hugger. A clinger at times. Ryan never quite got the hang of it.

"How's things?" He relaxes back into the chair, and I hover over him for a moment, directionless. I'm not going to sink back into the hammock.

"You know." It's hard to casually talk about the past year I spent in a psych hospital. Or his, mourning his sister. The one I left behind to die. All the words we haven't said, paperweights. There are few casual details among us. But I can see how hard he's trying to make this all *normal*, and I appreciate it. "Hanging in there."

He studies the hammock, the intricate tangle of rope, and the rest of the room. "They did an excellent job."

They did. The whole building burned to ash, and Kennedy's family took pains to recreate it almost flawlessly. It's difficult to find even a single detail out of place. But that's the Hartfords. Stubborn, perfectionist, traditional. They wouldn't let a fire, not even a tragedy, ruin the vacation home built by Kennedy's great-grandfather. One terrible memory of an event that Kennedy's parents didn't even witness doesn't outweigh four generations of pleasant ones. I wasn't surprised that they rebuilt the house. It's perfectly in character for the Hartfords.

It does make you wonder if there's more to the restoration than appearances—if there were some things the Hartfords wanted to stay buried. The demolition and reconstruction of the house left no evidence, no trace of the fire. And although they weren't at the lake house that weekend, it *was* their house. I'm sure of one thing: If there was some code violation or structural flaw that contributed to the fire in the slightest, it *will* stay buried. Because Mr. Hartford, distinguished attorney, senior partner at Weston Hartford, would never admit to even the passing appearance of fault.

It's where Kennedy gets it.

"How are things going at home?" I ask tentatively. "I'm sorry I haven't sent a card or anything."

"I understand. I know it hasn't been an easy year for you, either."

"It hasn't." Such a delicate way of putting it. But I'll allow it. Ryan is the only one who doesn't make me feel like a weirdo. That means a lot these days. "How are your parents doing?"

He sighs. "I honestly have no idea. They're so completely closed off it's pointless trying to talk to them. But the truth is, they were that way even before the fire." He glances at me out of the corner of his eye. "What about . . . your situation?"

I laugh. "Smashing."

"You don't have to talk about it," Ryan says. "I don't mean to bring up bad memories."

"Other people have it worse, you know?" I really can't complain to Ryan after all he's been through. I had the same issue in group therapy, where I'd sit frozen to the tiny cold plastic chairs, lips sealed, silently waiting out all these horror stories about lives way worse than mine. I felt like I didn't *deserve* to speak. All I did was get out of the lake house alive. After the tragedy, I was afraid to sleep. I drank vats of caffeine. Stood for hours in icy showers. Walked around our basement in endless loops, blasting the air-conditioning. Eventually my parents loaded me into the car, drove me to the hospital, and left me. The nurses stuffed me with pills, and I slept for a thousand years. And all I did was leave a friend behind. I can't imagine how devastated Ryan must have been losing his twin. I can't imagine ever being the same. I steal a glance at him. "Nothing to write home about."

"At least you had someone to write to, right?"

"Word travels slow. Kennedy and I broke up."

"Oh?" He's staring at me so intently that it immediately irritates me.

"Yeah, well, it's kind of hard to keep up a relationship with someone who never answers the phone. But you didn't either, did you?"

Ryan looks taken aback. "I would have picked up if I'd recognized the number," he says. "Why didn't you ever leave a message?"

"What was I supposed to say? 'Hey, Ryan, it's Chelsea from the psych hospital. Sorry for leaving your sister for dead.'"

He recoils at the words, and I see something flicker in his eyes. I'm drowning in shame. Then the moment passes like clouds moving over the moon. "I see your point," he says softly. "But just so you know, I would have picked up."

"Thanks." But the mood is off now, tilted all wrong, and I feel naive for thinking this weekend could be anything but disaster. "Maybe it was a bad idea to come back so soon."

Ryan sighs. "It was messed up to come back at all. But I always do. And I always regret it."

"Then why do you?" I study his pale face, his reserved jaw and delicate lips. His eyes, set on mine, always so difficult to read in between smiles. There was a reason I fell for him once.

He smiles faintly, flushing pink in the embers of the sunset. "Aw. Don't make me say it."

I hear Mila scream in the other room, and Chase bursts through the sunroom door carrying her over his shoulder. The new girl. I don't know why I still think of her that way—Chase has been dating her for a while. She pounds her fist into his stomach, and he deposits her on the floor, his amber eyes gleaming.

"You're such an asshole, Chase." She carefully combs her long, black hair until it falls in a perfect sheet down her back. Then she smiles at me, ignoring Ryan. "Chelsea, it's so good to see you." She doesn't mean it. She leans in and taps my shoulder blades with her palms. Her hugs are ten thousand times worse than Ryan's. Her brows crease in a display of concern, her big brown eyes wandering over my face. "You look rested."

"Thanks, Mila. I'm all sane again." It's what she means by *rested*. It grates on me when people use those little euphemisms. *Rested*. People should say what they mean, or shut up. I know what they're thinking. That it's not okay to *say* that they believe I lost my grip on reality, but it's perfectly respectable to treat me like it. Like a girl made of glass, poised to topple and shatter. Like I'm a different person now somehow. I thought long and hard about words like *sane* in the hospital. Some of the girls in group didn't like words that aren't precise and clinical, words that aren't *depression* or *anxiety* or *bipolar* or *post-traumatic stress disorder*, but some of the others thought the messy words like *sane*, and the others, the *not sane* words, were important too—because those are the words other people use like weapons against us, like sharpened scythes, and the only way to make them feel dull and blunt is to allow *ourselves* permission to use them. I like that idea. It feels naked, armorless, to have certain words hurled at me, and have my own mouth sewn shut against them. So I will not allow my mouth to be sewn shut. Not against the word *sane*. Not in reference to myself. I am as sane or not as I have always been. But I am not rested.

"Great!" Mila smiles at Chase and disappears back into the living room, like she did what she promised and she's done with me.

Chase rolls his eyes. "Sorry. Mila's a little . . . awkward about . . . personal stuff."

I wave my hand vigorously. "Stop. None of that. We're not here for me." I flick my eyes over to Ryan. His pale eyes are fixed on the lake, the last rays of sunlight bringing out ginger highlights in his sandy hair, his hands shoved into the pockets of his beige shorts.

Chase flips the back of Ryan's collar up to get his attention. "You all right, bro?" Chase says playfully, but there's a gentle undercurrent of concern in his voice.

"Just thinking." Ryan draws the words out, his eyes faraway.

Chase shoots me a troubled glance. I don't know what to say. I wasn't expecting this weekend to be easy. Part of me really was hoping for it to just be me and Kennedy, a chance to work out what happened between *us*. But the invitation said all of us, and I guess that's only right. It's always been all of us. The Summer of Eagles, when we first came to the lake house. The Summer of Flickers, when Kennedy and I first kissed on the Fourth of July. Every summer a bird, named for Emily's peculiar obsession, even at age eight. Our teacher had encouraged her and named our class the Eagle Eights. That's how it started. Eagles for eight. Nightingales for nine. Thrushes for ten. It strikes me that this summer will go nameless, and the weight of it, the sadness, is unbearable. We aren't in sync anymore. Emily's gone. I'm a year behind. We should all be seniors now. Together. Emily always had the most marvelous birds at her fingertips. Flickers. Firecrests. I imagine them like little cinders swooping through a starless sky, sparking light in the darkness. I owe her a name. It's the least I can do when I can't do anything at all.

"Summer of Egrets," I say suddenly.

Chase shakes his head.

"What?"

"You never explain your thought process. How you get from A to B. I can never keep up with you."

I twist the left corner of my mouth into something like a smile. "Isn't that the fun of it?"

"*Egrets* is perfect," Ryan says. He grins ironically. "It sounds like *regrets*."

Chase's eyes linger on him for a minute, and then he smiles. "I'm glad you came, Ry. I have a good feeling about this year."

Chase always has a good feeling. Even when things are going spectacularly wrong. Maybe that isn't always such a good thing. Maybe sometimes a bad feeling is a gift. A warning. A red flag on dangerous waters. And too many good feelings rise like a fog and swallow those little red flags up until it's too late to act. We do need to talk about what happened between all of us. Because if things hadn't gone so wrong in this house, if each of us hadn't played our own part in the destruction of our happy little family, then Emily would probably still be alive.

4

It's odd, being back together like this.
Horrible and odd and revolting.
They shouldn't be here. It's a sacred site. To ignore that is a special kind of violence.
They should know better.

5

We eat outside under a shroud of stars. Chase digs out a set of candles, bundled in shrink-wrap. I flinch as Mila ignites them with a metal Zippo and then lights a clove cigarette. She leans back in her chair, stretching her long legs out under the table. The fire doesn't seem to bother anyone else. But I can't take my eyes off it. I haven't really been around fire since *the* fire. It's a restricted item at the hospital. We have to make do with the other elements. Soft earth in the courtyard when it's time for outside exercise. Cold air in the exam room, lying on a hard metal table, waiting. Tepid showers and water that tastes faintly like blood.

"May I help you?" Mila looks at me expectantly, and I realize that I'm still staring at the lighter in her hand.

I blink to snap myself out of it. "Highway hypnosis."

She gives me a look like *Why are you so weird?* and the conversation drifts on without me. Chase launches into a story, and I take a sip of the wine Kennedy has selected for dinner. I never drink except at the lake house, and I especially don't like red wine. It tastes richer and thicker to me than white, and since I was just thinking about blood, it has extra strikes against it now. It also reminds me of church, and church reminds me of funerals, and funerals remind me that we're not here to have fun. "I'm sorry I missed the funeral," I say abruptly.

Everyone freezes and stares at me, Chase trailing off mid-sentence.

Kennedy always says I have a talent for silencing a room, like, I'll be half listening to a conversation in the cafeteria and suddenly blurt out my tangential contribution and everyone will just quit. It's not a compliment, because, well, when Kennedy talks, people agree. But I like it. It's okay being the weird one. It suits me. What would bother me would be contorting myself to try to guess the right things to say all the time so that when I spoke, people would nod and agree.

How do you even do that?

Now, though, is not one of the times when I speak and everyone laughs or nods philosophically, or just *hmm*s politely. But I *am* sorry. I should have been at the funeral. I feel awful. There's a strange hollow ache in my stomach, and I cross my arms, dig them into my abdomen, and lean forward.

"Sorry," I say again more quietly, this time to Chase.

He was mid-anecdote when I interrupted him, and his hands are still spread wide in illustration. Shadows dance on his skin as he furrows his brow and tilts his head toward Ryan. "Go easy, Chels."

Ryan waves it off. "You didn't miss anything."

"But I am sorry." I take another awkward sip. "I think maybe we should just remember why we're here." I flick my eyes over to Ryan. "Not you."

"We're here to have fun," Mila says. She takes another drag and exhales slowly, watching me with glowing eyes. But that's not true. It couldn't possibly be true. Not anymore.

Kennedy takes a bite of her food, refusing to acknowledge

the tension of the moment. "We're here for each other. And for Emily."

"Sure we are," Mila mutters.

"And because Ryan asked us to come," Kennedy adds.

"Hold on." Ryan coughs violently into his napkin, his face turning bright pink, and for a second I think we're going to have a second tragedy on our hands. But he grabs the wine bottle and takes a long swig. "Sorry." He coughs one more time and clears his throat, then turns to Kennedy. "I didn't ask you to come here. Did you think I invited myself over?"

She darts her eyes to me. "Chelsea?"

I raise an eyebrow. "Yes?"

"Back me up." She nudges me with her foot.

Ryan looks at me expectantly. The last thing I want is to get dragged into an argument. I don't blame Ryan for being emotionally raw, and Kennedy can spar with the best of them. If things got ugly, they could get ugly fast. But I can't say no to Ryan. Not today. I pull the card out of my pocket. "I assumed it was from you, Kennedy. Your house, your handwriting."

She grabs the postcard and scrutinizes it. "That is *not* my handwriting."

"It's Marilyn's," I say, feeling incredibly silly. It's true that she's obsessed with Marilyn—but it seems like a leap now to assume that she would make out invitations in a dead movie star's handwriting. It's a strange thing to do, and Kennedy is not a strange person.

She squints at it. "It's not." But she says it haltingly.

"Look, honest mistake," Chase adds apologetically. "I mean,

who would make up invitations like this? It has you written all over it, Ken."

"Holy shit, who cares?" Mila says. "We all got one, and we all showed up. Anyone could have ordered them off the internet, and no amount of arguing is going to make someone admit it if they don't want to."

Kennedy frowns. "But I didn't make the postcards."

"So you just assumed I did?" Ryan reaches for the card, and Mila peers at it over his shoulder. I badly want to ask for it back at this point, before someone gets it all pesto-greasy and wine-stained. I meant to keep it. This weekend may have been an annual tradition, but it won't be anymore. Whether this was a reunion, a memorial, or just a farewell to childhood before we go our separate ways next year, to finish high school for me, and to college for everyone else, the postcard was a memento. I was going to ask everyone to sign it. Silly. But something to keep. To remember. People always say it's hard to say goodbye, but after last year, I think it's probably harder *not* getting to say goodbye.

"She was your sister." Kennedy winds a lock of hair around her finger. Tighter with each spiral, until her fingertip turns blood red. "And you're the photographer. I thought you might have taken this photo."

"I might have," he admits. "But I gave you all a scrapbook at the end of each summer."

"A collection of weekends." Chase grins. It fades.

"So anyone could have done it," Ryan finishes, crossing his arms over his chest stubbornly.

"Personally, I don't think it matters whose idea it was." I

gently take the postcard back and slip it into my pocket. "I think it's a nice way to honor Emily."

Kennedy sets her jaw. This is going to eat at her like acid all weekend. It *does* matter to her who sent the invites. She hates being wrong. But she'll swallow it because she has a rule against fighting at the lake house. "Fine. Agree to disagree."

Ryan tosses his plate onto the table, and I can feel Kennedy cringe as the ceramic hits the stone. A chipped plate means an unmatched set, which will bother her more than a clean break. "Sorry, Ken," he says flatly as he pushes away from the table. Kennedy waves it off with a long sigh as Chase shakes his head at her and follows Ryan into the house.

Mila remains behind, smoking away. "I believe you about the postcards," she says. A lick of flame, a puff of smoke.

Kennedy smiles across the table at her like she's drowning and Mila's thrown her a life jacket. "Thank you." She shifts her weight almost imperceptibly away from me and toward Mila. "Can I have a drag?"

Mila lights her another clove instead and hands it to her. "I'm possessive," she says.

"That's hilarious." Kennedy dangles the cigarette near her lips. She doesn't actually smoke. She's flirting to punish me for not backing her up.

"I'm not being nice," Mila says. "Nice is a dangerous bluff." She takes another drag, tilts her head back, and watches the smoke spiral up toward the moon. "I just don't see what you would have to gain by lying."

"What would Ryan have to gain?" I sip the blood wine and

stir the pesto around my plate. It's good. Too good. Kennedy is too good at everything.

"Well," she says. "He doesn't like you very much, does he?"

Kennedy's smile falters almost imperceptibly. She's not easily shaken.

"Of course he likes us," I say. "He's our friend."

"Not you." She laughs. "No. He wants to fuck you. He doesn't like Kennedy. He could be jealous." She wrinkles her forehead thoughtfully. "Or maybe it's more than that. Maybe he blames her for Emily's death. It was her house she died in. There's a lot he could blame her for, isn't there?"

"So what?" Kennedy's friendly veneer has rubbed off. "His grand revenge was inviting my best friends over to my house?"

Mila shrugs and bites her lip. "The invitation is never the revenge, Kennedy. The revenge is what you're invited to."

"So this house is the revenge?" She stares incredulously.

"Let's see how the weekend goes, shall we? I'll make up my mind then."

6

Mila.
You know . . .
I hadn't planned on her.
But she came.
And look what she brought.
The murder weapon.

7

Inside, Chase has placed a stack of board games on the
living room table. The living room, like most of the lake house,
is a stunning display of wood craftsmanship. Chase sits on a
throne-like chair sculpted to resemble a tree with dozens of
spindly branches stretching out in a wide arc, up to the high
ceiling and loft above. He and Ryan used to fight over it,
crowns of leaves on their heads, while Emily, Kennedy, and I
pelted them with marshmallows. I smile, remembering, but it
turns into a painful lump in my throat.

"Peace offering," he says. "We're here to be together, so . . .
let's start togethering."

"I'll start togethering." Mila climbs into his lap and wraps
her arms around his neck, leaning in close to smooth down his
dark, windswept hair. Chase blushes.

"As a group. For now." He whispers something into her ear
and she laughs.

"Keep it in your pants, Chase." Kennedy tosses a throw pillow at them, and Chase successfully bats it away. She turns the
dimmer up all the way, but it's always a little dark in the lake
house at night. She sets a couple of candles on the table, and
with the pale yellow cast of the chandelier hanging above our
heads and the two mock-deerskin lamps positioned at either

side of the room, everything seems to flicker with an eerie hue, like watching a very old film. "What should we play?" she asks.

I settle into the carved wooden rocking chair in the corner, a perfect match for the old one, probably from one of those criminally overpriced hipster boutiques that make everything from dumpster scraps and then charge you as if it were sourced from a rainforest. "Monopoly," I suggest half-heartedly.

Kennedy's bright blue eyes light up.

"Uh-uh." Chase gives a big thumbs-down. "You two are vicious at that game, and I don't feel like having my head bitten off."

Ryan selects a game. "I believe a round of Catan may be in order."

"Noooo." Mila slides off Chase's lap and onto the floor. "That game goes on forever. I like something short and sweet. She lifts the lid off a box of Candy Land. "Oh." Most of the cards and pieces are missing. "I assumed the games would be new this year."

"Sorry the house isn't stocked to your liking," Kennedy says.

"Guys, please." Chase selects a hot pink box with blue squiggles and yellow triangles all over it. "I like the look of this one." He pulls it from the pile and sets it on the table. On the lid is a photo of two girls with high ponytails in perms and neon sweaters, one giggling and one looking exaggeratedly shocked. Over their heads the words *Truth or Dare!* are written in an '80s font. "Yep," Chase says. "We're playing this."

He lifts the lid and begins to shuffle and deal the stack of cards in the box.

"You don't need cards to play Truth or Dare," Mila says.

"And we're not in fifth grade." Kennedy reluctantly takes her share of the cards. "We had this one in the old house too. You never forced us to play it then."

But we did play it. Emily, Kennedy, and me. Back in elementary school when our weekends at the lake house were new. The games, the lake, the whole world of the house. We were a little young for it then, but we're far too old for it now.

"Well, bless your mom for hunting down another copy." Chase ruffles her hair and Kennedy scowls at him, carefully combing it back into place with her fingers.

"It's some special thing between her and my aunt."

There's a moment of awkward silence. Kennedy's aunt also died young, though not in an accident. One night she simply went to sleep and didn't wake up the next morning. The Hartfords almost never mention her, except for Kennedy, who sometimes talks about her almost as if she never died. One of the few Kennedy quirks she hasn't quite curated to perfection.

"We won't use the board," Chase says. "Just the cards. It's like Cards Against Humanity or Apples to Apples. Just a conversation starting point."

"That's not really what Cards Against Humanity is," Kennedy says.

"Well, shut up, we're playing," Chase says pleasantly.

"Ugh, fine. I'll go first." Kennedy turns to me. "Truth or dare," she reads in a halting, first-grader-learning-to-read voice.

"Dare."

"Call a boy and tell him you have a crush on him." She winks at me.

"Have the landlines been set up yet?"

She shakes her head.

I shrug. "No working phones."

"You have to do truth, then," Mila says, reading the rules printed on the back of the box.

"Truth. Do you have a *crush*—" Kennedy draws the word out.

"Oooh," Chase says.

"Grow up, guys." Ryan clutches Catan uncomfortably.

"—on anyone in your class?" Kennedy finishes, and looks at me expectantly.

"Really?" I look around the room. "Not to tiptoe around the obvious, but I haven't been in school for a year." There's a brief silence, blink and you'd miss it, like a skipped heartbeat.

"You'll be a senior in September," Kennedy points out. "What about your senior class?"

"Pass," I say firmly. "I can't answer without actually meeting them."

"Boo," Chase says. "Mila's going to be a senior."

"Not interested." She gives me a once-over as if an afterthought, and then a pity smile.

"Fine, but you have to answer this one." Kennedy draws the next card. "Chelsea, on penalty of permanent banishment, who was your first crush? Wow, they really went all in on crushing."

"Crushing it with crushing." Chase looks pleased with himself.

I bite my lip. We all know the answer to this one, and it's only going to make it awkward to say it out loud. "Um, obviously it was Ryan."

Mila raises an eyebrow as a tight-lipped Kennedy folds

the card in half and reinforces the crease several times. "That explains a bit."

"Read the next question," Kennedy says.

Ryan flushes uncomfortably, then picks up a card without looking at me. "Chase, what would you do if—"

"Dare!" Chase interrupts with a look of indignation. "You didn't even ask."

"Whatever," Ryan says.

"We don't have to play." Kennedy gathers her cards and reaches for mine, but I fold my hands around them protectively and hug them to my chest. She shoots me one of her *Whose side are you on?* looks, but I sort of want to see where this goes. I've been humiliated, and it kind of feels like everyone should have a turn in the hot seat before we give up. We all know exactly who feels what about who, the good, the bad, and the ugly. But no one ever says anything out loud. That might have been our downfall. I wonder now if it might save us. What's left of us.

"Let me do my dare," Chase pleads. "Ryan, I will make you laugh during the course of this game. I will make you crush on me."

Ryan forces a pained smile. "One more round. That's all I have in me." He looks down at the card. "Hold your breath for one minute without laughing."

Chase gives him a puzzled look. "Really?"

Ryan shows him the card. "It's your genius game."

"Okay. Here goes." Chase draws a deep breath and holds it as the rest of us count to sixty together. He maintains a studied Gaston-like expression of exaggerated ease throughout, flexing his muscles and spinning the game box on his fingertip like a basketball. All he needs is a set of muddy boots and a deer's head mounted on the wall behind him. "Didn't laugh," he says when the minute is up. "As hilarious as that was." He turns to Mila.

"Truth," she says immediately.

"Who's the cutest person in the room?"

Mila smirks. "You think I'm going to say you, but I'm bound by the rules to tell the truth. You're cute, but I'm cuter and everyone here can vouch for it. Sorry." She blows him a kiss, selects a card, and looks to Kennedy. "Pick your poison."

"Truth."

"Who is the last person in this room you betrayed?" Mila asks in a low, dramatic voice.

"Read the card," Kennedy says, annoyed.

"I did," Mila protests, tossing the card into her lap.

Kennedy shakes her head. "I've never *betrayed* anyone in this room." It's the strangest thing, but just after she says it, there's a gust of wind outside and one of the candles flickers out. It's coincidence, but it doesn't feel like coincidence. Nothing feels like coincidence anymore. Partly because I don't want it to. I don't want anything to mean nothing. I don't want there to be a meaningless void out there that Emily got sucked into, and that we'll get sucked into someday too, and just vanish. Not become part of or anything, just evaporate. I don't want that. I'd rather believe in vengeful spirits than emptiness that stretches on for eternity.

Kennedy kicks my sneaker. "Your turn."

I kick her back. "You ask."

"Right." She shuffles through the cards. "Truth or dare."

"Truth."

"Who did you last say you loved?"

I think for a moment. "My mom. Before I left."

She nods. "The exciting life you do lead."

It stings. She knows how isolated I've been. I turn to Ryan. "Truth or—"

"Dare."

I sneak a look at Chase. He looks as surprised as I am. Ryan isn't exactly a daredevil. With only one candle now, the room has gone even dimmer, and all of us have taken on the washed-out yellow cast of the inadequate lights, our faces flickering flames in a darkening room. "Hold your breath for two minutes without laughing."

Chase raises an eyebrow. "They really got creative with these."

Ryan draws a deep breath. Chase begins counting and Mila hesitantly joins in.

I look to Kennedy a little uncertainly. "Isn't two minutes kind of a long time?"

She shrugs but peers over to look at the card. "They probably intentionally designed it so you'd fail and be forced to answer the truth question." But when we flip the card over, there's just another dare.

Dare: Hold your breath for three minutes.

Kennedy takes the next card.

Dare: Hold your breath for four minutes.

On the reverse side.

Dare: Hold your breath for six minutes.

My heart begins to pound. We flip through the rest of the cards in my stack one by one, but the dares are the same, escalating only the amount of time without oxygen. Then, I reach for Kennedy's cards and read the one on top.

Truth: How does it feel to kiss a killer?

8

It's not that I blame one more than the others.
All of them are at fault.
They share the blame.
Perhaps if any one of them had stayed home last year, it would
never have happened.
But no one ever stays home.
They always come.
Nothing keeps them away.
Not even an inconvenient little death.

9

I grab the card and stuff it into my pocket before Kennedy has a chance to read it, then turn my attention back toward Chase, who's still counting.

129. 130. 131. 132.

"Chase, make him stop." Mila swats Chase's arm. Her usually bored, languid tone has turned tense, with an undercurrent of anxiety. Kennedy has taken up the counting in a breathless voice. I wish she would stop.

Ryan is still holding his breath, sitting stubbornly on the couch, arms and legs crossed tightly, his lips sealed, his face bright red. He stares straight up at the ceiling, concentrating, maybe counting in his head.

"You okay, Ry?" I tap his shoulder, but he doesn't break focus.

145. 146. 147.

"You win," Mila says. "You have all the penises. And then some."

152. 153. 154.

His face is growing purple. It's uncomfortable to watch. It makes me feel like I can't breathe. I punch his arm. "Enough, Ryan."

But Chase keeps counting, and as long as he does, Ryan

will never back down. It's a game to them. Ryan won't fold while Chase is timing him, and Chase won't stop timing him while Ryan can still make it further. And I know what comes next because I know them. Next, Chase is going to be obligated to try to beat Ryan's record.

179. 180. 181. 182. 183.

Kennedy gets up, marches over, and pinches Ryan's nose. He gasps and collapses onto the sofa on his back, gulping in air. "Are you trying to kill me?" he wheezes.

"You need to breathe, asshole," she says. "No more games."

Mila looks down curiously at a card sitting in the middle of the table. "Truth," she reads. "Which one of you is going to hell for killing your best friend?" She looks up, her face pale.

Chase takes the card from her. He is quiet for a long moment. "Obviously someone tampered with the cards."

Ryan yawns elaborately, extending an arm toward Kennedy. Not subtly.

"Please let's not get into this again." Kennedy raises a hand to massage her temples. "I didn't send the postcards, and I didn't tamper with this stupid game."

"So I did this?" Ryan's face is still tinged with pink, just a shade lighter than the salmon-colored polo he's wearing.

"Chase is the one who insisted we play the game," I say hesitantly. "Sorry, Chase. I'm not accusing, I'm just saying it's a weird game, and you've been bizarrely enthusiastic about it."

"Don't look at me," Chase says. "Ryan is the one pointing fingers."

Ryan balks. He stands abruptly and paces out of the room, then back again. "I didn't tamper with the goddamn game," he says flatly. "And I didn't invite myself or any of you, and honestly, I'm starting to wonder if any of you even want me here."

"No one does."

"Kennedy." I look at her sharply, but she continues to clean up the game, tight-lipped.

"What?" She looks up innocently.

"I—" I falter. I can't tell if she just said what I think I heard her say. I'm not sure it was her voice. Sometimes I think I hear things. Specific things. Sounds that can't possibly have been made here or now. Distant explosions and rapid gunfire, the tinny kind you hear on TV, except *not* on TV. Animal sounds I can't identify. Voices speaking in languages I don't know, footsteps passing over my head, little hands tapping in the walls. It's usually just in the window between the time I take my sleeping pill and the time I fall asleep. Nurse Pamela warned me about it. The lucid in-between, she called it. She was one of the good ones. "I think we should give Ryan a break," I say. Ryan touches my elbow with his and taps his palm twice with two fingers. It's the secret language we made up in fifth grade to make the others flip out. The secret is that none of the gestures actually mean *anything*. But it infuriated Chase, Kennedy, and especially Emily.

"A dead sister isn't an excuse to be an asshole," Kennedy bursts out.

We all stare at her. She claps her hand over her mouth, looking mortified.

Chase looks pointedly at Kennedy. "I think we should all go sleep this off while we still have no regrets." He storms away to his room, and Mila chases after him.

Ryan sighs. "I'm going to get some air."

Kennedy shakes her head wordlessly and heads up the stairs.

I start to follow her, then decide that I need air too. But in the one brief moment that I'm alone in the living room, just me and the expensive scrap-wood furniture and the pile of ancient board games, with the lights off, and only sharp slivers of moonlight slicing in through the windows, I hear it.

A voice whispers into my ear, so close and so tangible I can feel a wisp of breath traveling down my neck, freezing me in place, turning me to stone.

It says, *"I'm still here."*

I scream. Ryan bolts back into the house breathlessly. Kennedy rushes down the stairs. A moment later, Chase and Mila follow, Mila wearing Chase's T-shirt, Chase in his swimsuit.

"I'm still here."

This time the voice is so loud, so unmistakable, and so insistent, that I whip my head to the side, half-certain I'll see Emily standing beside me, that the last year has been one long nightmare. Because this time the voice was clear as my own heartbeat. And it belonged to Emily.

"Are you okay?" Kennedy asks, taking my arm and brushing the hair away from my face. "You sounded like you stepped on a scorpion or something."

I look from face to face. They all look expectant. Concerned. But not scared. That's not reassuring. It just makes my anxiety rise. "I'm still here," I whisper.

Chase looks to Kennedy. "We all are. And none of us are going anywhere. Can we all agree to take it down a notch?

Hit the reset button and start over? I'm really glad we're back together. All of us." All but one.

Kennedy nods. "Of course. I love you guys." She looks to Ryan. It's the closest she'll get to an apology.

"No!" I interrupt. "Someone said 'I'm still here.' Just now. And before that when I was alone in the room." I feel Ryan's eyes on me. I can't stand the idea of even him not believing me.

"Okay, Chelsea," Chase says. "It's late, you're tired, everyone is a little shaken up. Imaginations run wild when emotions are high. I get it. We're cool."

"No. We are not cool. Someone tampered with the game, and everyone claims it wasn't them." I rip the top off the game box and tear through the stack of cards, but I can't find a single one that includes a dare related to holding your breath without laughing. Or a truth about going to hell or betraying your friends. It's crush, crush, crush. I slam it back down on the table, frustrated.

Kennedy places her cool hands on my cheeks and looks into my eyes. "Chelsea. Everything's fine. This is an emotional situation for all of us. We have to be here for each other. I'm sorry I was distant. I just don't know how to handle being back together."

The words sting. The multiple meanings. I step back away from her. "We're all witnesses. She spoke, and we heard."

Chase gives me an odd look. "Who spoke?"

"Emily."

Kennedy and Chase exchange a look. "There are a lot of memories in this house," Kennedy says carefully. "Of course it feels like she's still with us in a way."

"Or maybe she's really still with us." My words hang in the air like a dare. I hate being put on the stand like this. Being forced to testify. "We were all here," I say, my eyes stinging, beginning to fill. "We all heard her."

Kennedy gathers me into a hug and strokes my back. "Of course we did. Right, Chase?"

Chase is silent.

"You've got to be kidding me," Mila says. "No. I'm not humoring her."

"Mila, please," Chase says quietly.

"No. That's not helpful. I'm not being a bitch, I'm just being honest. None of us heard shit. It was a bad idea to come back here. We watched a person die. I didn't even care about Emily. I barely knew her. But I still have nightmares, and this is like living through them all over again. Also, what ghost sends out printed invitations? Do they like materialize in Staples or possess a printing press? Come on. No ghost. Emily's gone, and we're freaking ourselves out."

"What about the game?" Ryan circles it suspiciously.

"Kennedy said it herself. Her mother dug it up somewhere. Probably at a yard sale or used on Amazon or something," Mila says. "You don't think in forty years no one had the opportunity to mess with it? None of the questions or answers are specific to us. Someone wanted to mess with their friends, and it eventually ended up in our hands."

No one speaks for a while.

"I'm going back upstairs. Chase, you can come with or spend the night telling ghost stories with your friends and sleep on the sofa." Mila looks at Chase, who avoids Kennedy's pointed stare. A challenge. Choose sides, Chase.

"We'll talk tomorrow." Chase surveys the rest of us. "Try to get some rest, Chels. Everything will look different in the morning. It always does." He flashes his signature team-captain smile and heads upstairs after Mila. Chase is the one who's always shined the brightest among us. Valedictorian, second team all-American. Nothing ever slowed Chase down. I wonder if Emily's death has. He doesn't seem drastically altered. There's something a little disquieting about that, but grief hits people in different ways, and Chase plays his cards close to his chest. Still, Ryan will be hurt by Chase's act.

Ryan glances at me and edges toward the back door again. "I need a breather. My brain is on overload."

I bite my lip and smile. "I know the feeling."

Kennedy turns back to me. "Are you going to be okay? Do you want me to make you some tea, or draw you a bath, or . . ." She gives me an impish smile, but it's half-hearted. She's as exhausted as the rest of us, the hint of a shadow forming underneath each luminous eye.

"Nope. If I don't take a sleeping pill now, I may never get to sleep."

Her smile falters and my heart aches. "I thought we could share my parents' room," she says hesitantly. "I feel like my room should stay empty this year."

I nod. "Of course. I'll see you later." The words feel awkward and wrong. Splitting up, even briefly, shouldn't feel new after a year of living entirely separate lives. But back here, in the place where we fell in love, it does. She kisses me on the cheek and hugs me a couple of seconds longer than she did this afternoon, and I smell the whole day in her hair. The lake breeze, lemonade, basil, the pines. The lake house. Cedar and wool. Cotton and beeswax. Organic. Those beautiful paper postcards. Everything that went up so very quickly in a swirl of fire and smoke.

10

The waiting.
The waiting is the trick.
I waited a year for this moment.
I waited to gather with my friends, murderers all.
The awful thing about waiting is that if you wait too long, you start to disappear.

11

I don't take my pill and I don't go to bed. Instead I take the game outside, where the whispers can't reach me. I sit on the patio in the moonlight and spread the Truth or Dare cards on the stone table and read them one by one, discarding each one back into the box after I've read both sides. The patio and table are probably the only parts of the original house that didn't have to be replaced. They're all stone, with a fire pit on one end and a cute little rock wall lining the path down to the dock. Looking at the cards spread on the table in the moonlight reminds me of Emily. Her mother does tarot readings at the mall. Emily did them too, just for us, but she didn't have "the sight." According to her mother, anyway. Mrs. Joiner used to say I was an old soul and all old souls could see a little if they opened their minds.

When I told my parents that, they told me not to accept any special teas or baked goods from Mrs. Joiner. In hindsight, I find that both hilarious and sad. Emily and Ryan were always embarrassed that their mother was the mall psychic lady. I think it's kind of neat. My father is a grief counselor and my mother is the office administrative assistant, so everyone hates and fears them.

Anyway. Emily couldn't have thought the cards were

actually bullshit, because she read them too. Maybe she was just pissed that her mom thought I had the sight and she didn't. And maybe her mom was just pissed that Emily was embarrassed of her.

I read every single Truth or Dare card and can't find the suspect ones from our game. I sigh, frustrated. None of this makes sense. In the distance, I can hear the sound of tiny intermittent splashes, little plunks of water, and I crane my neck and gaze out toward the dock. A dark figure is silhouetted against the bright moonlit water. *Splish.* Ryan is attempting to skip stones. A faint smile touches my lips. He never could quite get it. The momentum. They always start so promising and then sink. I leave the game on the table and kick my sandals off, then head down the boardwalk leading to the dock. I like the feeling of the cool, damp wooden planks beneath my bare feet. It's old wood, uneven, dangerous. Full of splinters. Another unapologetic fire survivor.

Ryan turns around, his face flushing. "Hello again," he says with his endearing nervous smile.

"Brain still buzzing?"

"Endlessly."

I take the round stone and hand him a smooth, flat one. "Try this one."

He rears back his arm and hurls my stone. It goes straight under with a loud *plop*. "Do you think some people are just fated to sink? Like sad little human *Titanic*s."

"The *Titanic* wasn't fated to sink. Icebergs are dangerous and people are careless." I sit at the edge of the dock and dangle my legs over the edge, kicking at the dark water.

"I'm glad you came out here." He eases himself down next to me and takes my hand almost absently, and I instantly feel guilty even though I shouldn't. Kennedy and I aren't together anymore, and it's a friendly gesture, nothing more. But there's something that unnerves me about the way our palms fit together, an unsettling urge to never let go. I never wanted to feel a thing for anyone in the world except Kennedy Ellis Hartford. And I don't now. But the feeling of Ryan's hand in mine, his warm skin, draws a deep, aching sadness from within me. It's been the longest year. I miss my friend. "I wanted to tell you something," he says softly.

I turn away so he won't see my face flush. I badly don't want to have this conversation. I know how he feels. It would be a terrible idea to bring it all back to the surface.

But he doesn't say that at all. What he says is, "I believe you."

I look up at him. "You do?"

"About Emily?" He nods. "People we love don't disappear. They stay with us." He looks up at the sky. "Think how lonely it would be if they just vanished."

"But the others—"

"I think they're too afraid. I was, at first. Fear makes people lie, even to themselves."

"What if it's just us? What if they can't hear her?"

He chews his lip. "You mean the sight? That shit my mom used to talk about? I wouldn't stress that. She was a phony. I think anyone who wants to see, can." He stares down at the water and I kick at it. A sudden hint of bitterness has crept into his voice. He bumps his forehead against mine and rests it there, and I feel the warmth of his skin, the closeness of him, the cloud of his breath at the edge of my lips. I close my eyes, my cheeks warm. *I have no reason to feel guilty*. If Kennedy wanted to be sitting next to me right now, she would be. She would have stood up for me when I heard Emily calling. That's the thing about Ryan. I never question myself when he's around. I know no one *means* to make me question myself. But I do.

"That's actually the real reason you haven't heard from me this year."

"How so?" I draw back and study his expression.

"What I said about people not being gone? That was the result of a year of . . . for lack of a better word, haunting." He looks at me nervously.

"Haunting?" I glance back at the house. All of the lights are off; everyone is sleeping peacefully.

"I thought it was in my head, that it was wishful thinking." He stares at me intently. "But it was Emily. *Is* her. Sometimes it's just a voice, or a feeling."

"Why didn't you call me when all this was happening?"

"Believe me, I wanted to. But I thought it couldn't possibly be real, and it was the last thing you needed to worry about. Honestly, part of me wanted you to tell me it *was* all in my head. But then at the house, you heard her too, and I knew." He falls silent.

"Because it can't be your mind playing tricks on you if it's in *two* heads." I hug my knees to my chest, and he puts an arm around my shoulder.

"Let's say it's not. What did you think of that card from the game?"

"Which one?"

"One of you killed your friend. That one stood out quite a bit."

My heart seems to slow and grow quiet in my chest. "I'm so sorry you had to see that," I blurt.

"Why?" He looks at me intently. "That card was a gift." I start to shake my head, but he continues urgently. "I have a theory. Emily read tarot cards. I think she's using cards to tell us what happened to her."

"We know what happened," I whisper.

"We know what they want us to think." He nods to the house at *they*. "An entire house burned to the ground on a windless night because of a suspected gas leak? Chelsea. Something still had to ignite the fire. Even if it was as small as someone flicking on a light switch. And everyone claims it couldn't have been them. A house that big doesn't go down by accident. Someone's lying."

"Who?"

He hugs himself nervously. "I don't know. The authorities will always believe people like Kennedy and Chase. The real reason I came back this weekend is to find out." He pulls a stiff, cream-colored rectangle from his pocket. "When I woke up this morning, this was lying next to my pillow with one of Emily's tarot decks. I swear I've never seen it before. I don't think it proves anything, but it has to mean something. And I'm sure she left it for me because she wants me to find out what happened to her." He hands it to me, and I peer down at it curiously.

Mila's criticism crashes back to me. *Ghosts don't work with paper products.* But as he presses the tarot card into my hand, a creeping chill runs through me. It's from a deck I've never seen Emily use before. It's gorgeously drawn in an eerie, vintage style, the color faded from use. The figure on the card is quirky, a little disjointed, like Emily's own artwork. But the truly unnerving part of it isn't the little details that feel off— the bloodred water of a lake, the odd stitches in the fabric of the sky—it's the fact that the figure in the center of the card looks so familiar. The card depicts a young woman at the helm of a gilded sailboat, gliding over a crimson lake. She is draped in flowing blue robes, and a crown of jagged glass shards sits atop her head of long red hair. Her eyes are a piercing blue, and even the stubborn set of her chin screams Kennedy. Scrawled at the bottom of the card, in Emily's handwriting, is *Queen of Pentacles: trust at your peril.*

I cover my mouth with my hand. "It looks so much like Kennedy."

"Tarot cards were always a mode of communication for Emily," Ryan says. "What if she never stopped?"

"How?" I turn the tarot card over in my hand.

"If I could explain it, I'd know what happened to Emily by now."

"But you don't think Kennedy could have had anything to do with Emily's death?"

"I think this card came from Emily, and it's a clue." He takes it back. "It would feel like a betrayal if I didn't take it seriously." His eyes connect with mine. "What else did she tell us?"

"If cards were her language . . . she left us clues in the game." My heart slows and quiets in my chest. "That one of us betrayed another, one kissed a killer, and one of us killed our best friend." The words wrench my throat shut.

"That says it all, doesn't it?" He catches my eye. "Chels. I know you weren't involved."

But I was involved. I was in the house with Emily, and now I'm here and she isn't. I snap my head up to find Ryan looking at me carefully.

"It wasn't your fault," he says. But the words make me flinch.

"Why would you say that?"

He gives me an odd look. "Because you have to forgive yourself." He points to the house. "They're the ones I don't trust. Especially Kennedy." He looks at me nervously, and for a second, the world skips in time and we're fourteen again. All-night phone calls, secret languages, inside jokes that the others rolled their eyes at. "We could leave them. Not look back."

I laugh. Nervous laughter. Not the real kind. "In the middle of the night?"

He moves closer, and I feel the fear radiating off him. "Do you feel safe here now? Knowing what you know?"

"Ryan, we don't know anything yet. The card could be a coincidence." My voice seems to echo in the darkness.

"Wake up, Chelsea." His voice is edged with agitation, and I feel his patience slipping away, the last grains of sand in a game timer. I'm not guessing the answer quickly enough. But his expression softens. "I'm just freaked out. I was so ready to be wrong about the tarot card. But then the game happened, and you heard Emily too, and I can't believe it's a coincidence."

"Ryan. I believe you. But . . . *murder*?"

A shadow falls over his face. "Chelsea . . . I've never

doubted you. Not once since we met. Do you trust me?" I glance back at the house uncertainly. I do trust Ryan. I trust my own senses. Emily is not gone, and maybe there was more to her death than what we think we know: an accidental fire, a blocked escape route, an unfortunate tragedy. I don't know if I can accept that one of us could have intentionally set that fire. My friends are flawed, but none of us are monsters. Who would be capable of returning to this house with murder on their conscience?

"Of course I trust you. It's the message I'm not sure of."

He stares at me. "How could it be any more clear?"

"You can't believe our friends are killers, Ryan."

"I can't?" He stares at me in disbelief. "A flick of a switch, a spark that raged out of control, panic, and then lies? You can't even imagine a scenario where *anyone* could fuck up like that and not have the guts to come clean?"

"I guess." Put like that, the world looks a bit darker. I don't want to think of a mistake as murder. But then, I guess it's not a mistake. Somewhere along the line, even in that scenario, a decision was made to let the house burn. To not save Emily. To never speak a word. I turn to Ryan. "I'm with you. But I'm not leaving. Stay. It's the only way to find out the truth."

He hesitates. "Fine. But if anything happens—"

"I said I'm with you, and I meant it. No matter what happens."

"Good," he says. "Because if I'm reading the clues right—"

I suddenly feel nauseous. "—someone in this house killed Emily."

12

Mother always used to say Kennedy was a young soul. Born from the blue, no previous lives, everything so new. An excuse for ignorance, selfishness, the mercurial lack of focus people mistake for passion.

What's Chelsea's excuse?

She's died over and over and never learned a thing.

Every time the same mistake, the cards never lie: She *is* the Queen of Cups. She *loves* a fool. She's crossed by the Ten of Swords. And she falls from the tower.

But she is not the innocent girl my brother believed.

Why was she allowed to survive last year?

Why wasn't she the sacrifice?

I don't think it's fair.

13

The words echo in my head as I make my way back to the house, pack up the game, and place it on the living room table.

Someone in this house killed Emily.

It feels impossible, but Emily's death itself feels impossible, and the impossible fact remains: she's gone. I have forced myself not to think about her death, because the parts I have failed to scrub from my memory are unbearable. But what if in sparing myself the pain of reliving the trauma, I've willingly closed my eyes to a crucial detail? I pause by the closed door to Kennedy's bedroom, a small but beautiful room with a Juliet balcony and scenes from fairy tales carved into the walls. A sense of dread settles over me in the darkness. This is where it happened. Where the fire boxed her in, trapped in the attic, engulfed in flames. There was nothing I could do, and time had run out. Everyone else was already gone. I was *forced* to be the one to leave her behind, because I was the last to give up on her.

I frown.

But my memory begins with me in the bedroom, drowsy and disoriented from smoke inhalation, the fire well underway. The day up to that point is a hazy blur, blotted out with guilt. I'm a useless witness. I don't know how the fire started. I don't know how she got into the attic. I didn't even know about the gas leak. I've been away during what might in a sense be the most crucial year of our lives, when everyone else was sifting through ash and making meaning of things, and settling on the story of what happened in this house. Healing, maybe. I missed all of it. I should start questioning. Because accidents happen, sure.

But Emily was trapped. I wasn't. Why didn't any of my friends come back for me?

Kennedy is in bed with the lights out when I get to her parents' room, a gorgeous master suite overlooking the lake. We usually share a queen bed in her room. Emily used to crowd into the bed with us when we were little, until Kennedy and I started dating the summer after ninth. This year the room will remain empty. I can't bring myself to sleep in the room where Emily died, and even though it *should* feel strange to share a bed with Kennedy after a year of being ignored, it doesn't. This is the way it's always been, since we were children. There's a tiny bit of comfort in that. When I enter the master bedroom, I find one side of the bed turned down, duvet cover perfectly aired, sheets folded under in a triangle, smooth as the placid surface of the lake. She's even laid a little sprig of lavender on the pillow and a sleeping mask on the nightstand, next to a glass of water and a note reading *For your pills*.

I strip down to my T-shirt and a pair of boxers and sit at the edge of the bed. I can't sleep with all of the questions swirling around my head. I want to talk, but I hate to wake her. I won't learn much with everyone fast asleep, though. I dig through my backpack for my sleeping pills. I'm going to need two tonight. I tap them into my palm and knock them back with the glass of water—still ice-cold—and snap the light off.

"Where did you go?"

I turn. My eyes haven't had a chance to adjust, but I imagine Kennedy looming before me, and I feel her weight shift as she sits up. "Nowhere. Outside. I thought you were sleeping."

"I was waiting for you." I hear a clicking noise, like she's biting her nails. Kennedy doesn't really have any nails. She's a biter. "Can I ask you something without you reading into it?"

Probably not. But I desperately want something, anything, to read into. "Of course."

"Do you really hear voices?"

There it is. "I don't hear *voices*, I heard *a* voice. Emily's voice," I say.

She sighs. "I didn't." Her faint outline is beginning to materialize in the darkness. Her shoulders are hunched, and her hair is wound into a bun and pinned atop her head.

"Well, you don't have the sight, do you?"

She swats my knee. "You know Mrs. Joiner was full of shit." She pauses. "I know it's stressful being back here. Just . . . don't let it get inside your head."

"Casualty of having a heart, Kennedy." I say it a bit more sharply than I mean to. The encounter with Ryan rattled me, and it feels a little like I'm sitting in bed with a stranger. But there's so much I need to know, and the tarot card pointing to Kennedy is the only clue I have to go on, vague as it is. And I don't have much time because the pills work fast. I already feel my heart beating slow and steady in my chest, anxiety seeping out of me like poison glistening on my skin. The calm comes quickly, and it brings the strange, the little lights and sounds I know are fragments of dream waiting for the fall. The lucid in-between. Little sparks of waking sleep. I can see Kennedy now in the sliver of moonlight sneaking in through the half-drawn curtains draped over the enormous windows. A radiant halo of light illuminates her, and the image from the tarot card merges with the present, the crown of glass shards glittering like knives. Outside, the full moon sinks into the lake, lighting it up like a radioactive swamp.

"We should talk about last year." My voice sounds thin and tinny.

Kennedy walks her fingers over the sheets and weaves them through mine. "You disappeared on me."

Even through the rapidly thickening fog of drowsiness, this gets to me. I can imagine how busy Kennedy was over the past year. Horse shows, ribbons, trophies. Clam bakes with beautiful people in the Hamptons. Visiting Princeton and Yale and Harvard with her parents, wearing cashmere and pearls, a matching mother-and-daughter set. I wonder if she was just the tiniest bit glad not to have me by her side for a year, skewing the picture like a single pulled thread. With my torn jeans and secondhand sweaters, handmade jewelry and untamable hair, I always stuck out with the Hartfords. And that's before I opened my mouth.

I wonder if she wasn't a little relieved.

She had to have been.

Because after the fire, Kennedy changed her number.

"I almost didn't come this weekend," I say finally.

"Why?"

"You know damn well why. I didn't disappear; you know exactly where I was. Pathetically waiting for you to write or call or show up. And you never did."

"I wanted to," she says in a quiet voice. She strokes my hand, but I withdraw it.

"My parents shipped me off to boarding school again."

"I'm impressed the uniform still fit."

She casts me a withering glare. "It was a nightmare."

I laugh. "Let's not compare notes, then."

"I missed you," she says, her voice catching. She reaches out again, and this time I let her take my hand. I missed her too. But the missing is so wrapped up in hurt, it's impossible to untangle. Every single day I waited in line in the rec room with a feeling of dread in the pit of my stomach. I dialed her number, whispering a prayer of *please, please, please*. And I listened to a prerecorded message, a hollow voice telling me that her number was no longer in service.

Kennedy had left me.

And that was her goodbye.

I stare at her in the darkness. "I missed you too. I guess I'm just used to losing you by now."

"That hurts."

"I'm sorry. It's not true. I don't think I'll ever get used to it. It just seems like you could have called if you wanted to."

"I'm here now. Isn't that what matters?" She tilts her chin up and I stare down. Her hair is damp, and she smells like lavender and honeysuckle. This is where we kiss. It is written in the history books.

But I turn away.

"What's wrong?" She sits up.

"Everything. You. You're acting like nothing happened." The drowsiness is starting to set in again. My body wants to drift away, but I can't.

She sighs heavily and snaps on the light, temporarily blinding me. "What do you want me to say?"

"That our best friend is dead, Kennedy." My words feel slow, and through the fog, I'm so frustrated I want to scream. "And maybe the fire wasn't an accident."

She stares at me, aghast. "Wasn't an accident?"

"As in, what if that game wasn't just a harmless prank?"

"The game?" Kennedy laughs, an ocean of relief in her voice. "You almost had me worried." Her face looks pale, though, and there are shadows under her eyes.

"Why?" I challenge. "Why would me suggesting that it wasn't an accident worry you?"

She pauses, seeming at a loss for words. "Because. You're talking about arson."

"I'm talking about murder." The word hangs in the air between us. Speaking it out loud feels like opening a door to a very dangerous place.

She looks up suddenly, past me, into the hallway, and places a finger over her lips.

I turn my head and stare down the dark hallway, and again I strain to hear a noise that shouldn't be there, to see a face emerging from the darkness. A long, low-pitched creak echoes down the hall, and I feel Kennedy's hand on my arm. I pull away gently, pressing my feet slowly onto the cold hardwood floor, and take a cautious step toward the door. A second creak freezes me in place, and the hair on the back of my neck stands up.

"Chelsea!" Kennedy hisses.

"There's something out there!"

"It's just Chase."

I look back over my shoulder in disbelief. "If it's just Chase, why do you care if I go after him?" I flick on the light switch. The hallway is empty. I turn back to Kennedy. "Must have been the wind."

She scoots to the edge of the bed. "You have me hearing things." She reaches for my hand, but I keep it by my side. "Look. We'll hike to the cell spot tomorrow and call my mom. I'll find out who sold her the game, track them down, and prove it was a prank. Then will you let this go?"

"It's not just the game!" I force myself to look at her. She looks concerned, but she can lie as well as anyone. "The game just reminded me that the circumstances were suspicious in the first place. But you've all avoided me so well, I've never had the opportunity to question them."

Her eyes widen. "You make it sound like we conspired against you."

"I just want to fill in the blanks about what happened."

"You don't remember?"

I hesitate. "Not everything. But even if I did, I wouldn't know the whole story. I'm just one witness out of five, and I don't know what the rest of you know. What you saw, heard . . . Any evidence that came out while I was away."

"You didn't think to ask until now? Your parents, your doctors, pick up a newspaper maybe? Did you *try* to find out what happened all of this time?"

I shrink from her accusing gaze. Of course I didn't. I didn't want to think about it. In a haze of grief and sedatives, it isn't hard to set bad memories afloat, and in the wake of the tragedy I pushed those details as far away as I could. Because thinking about it meant images and sounds like a newsreel, occupying every moment, every space in my head. No sleep. No peace. Just the attic door stuck shut, billows of smoke pouring in from the hallway, the sound of screaming, and then, almost the worst, the moment my gaze swung away from the fog of smoke and toward the open balcony doors. The terrible moment my eyes zeroed in on the sky, the lake beyond, all of the little living things outside, and I knew I was going to leave her behind. And I was never going to forgive myself.

"Why do you *want* to revisit that night?" Kennedy says.

"I need to in order to make peace with it, Kennedy! You weren't the one who abandoned her. Can you for once please think of what it feels like to be someone other than you?"

She's quiet for a moment. "What do you want to know?"

"How did the fire start?"

She shrugs helplessly. "I don't know. I was outside when Emily went in. Something must have happened while I was out in the yard. You were the last one to see her alive, Chelsea. If anyone saw anything, it would be you. But I accept that you didn't because it was an accident."

"But why was I the last? No one thought I was worth saving either?"

She flinches. "That's not fair. The doors were locked." Were they? I frown. I couldn't have known—my escape route was Kennedy's balcony. "I pounded and shouted until my voice was shot," Kennedy continues. "And no one would ever say you didn't think Emily was worth saving, because everyone understands that you had to let her go."

"Are you sure about that?" I try to ignore the guilty feeling that overwhelms me whenever I start to think too hard about last summer. I bet a lot of people would say that about me. I bet the Joiners would. How do you forgive your daughter's friend for letting her die?

"Everyone who matters, anyway."

"If you were outside . . ." The tarot card comes back to me. "Did you take the boat out?" I picture her on the bloodred water, radiant in the moonlight. There has to be some significance to the tarot card. Unless Kennedy is right, and Ryan and I are grasping at straws, searching for meaning that doesn't exist.

She looks at me oddly. "Why?"

"Just . . . I want to know."

She starts biting her nails again. "I don't recall."

"That's convenient. Is that what your dad told you to say?"

"I don't recall," she snaps.

I stare at her. That's coached speech. It's what lawyers tell guilty clients to say to avoid admitting something that could lead to their guilt, without telling an outright lie. It's a very specific phrase. Who says *I don't recall* in everyday conversation?

"Look, Chels. If you need to process your grief with this . . . game? Go for it. But I don't want to be part of it. It's not funny to me."

"Does it look like I'm joking?"

"It looks like you think one of us could have actually killed Emily. Why would I kill one of my best friends?"

"I don't know why you do a lot of things you do, Kennedy. Or don't do."

She stares at me. "If that's true, either you really have changed or you never knew me as well as I thought you did."

I stand unsteadily, grabbing a pillow and throw blanket. "Maybe I didn't." My head is swimming now. The images are floating before me, blinking in and out of dreams, the jagged crown, the golden sails, the lake of blood.

She looks at me, perplexed. "Where are you going?"

"I'm sleeping on the couch."

I stumble downstairs, and when I sink onto the couch, I feel like I'm sinking down and down and down through layers of soft, soft, earth, an endless descent, as if the world is bending inward and changing shape, all time and space destabilizing to open an eye for sleep. But I immediately regret my decision. This is where I heard Emily speak. I glance up the stairs and consider apologizing. But I'm so tired I can't think without glittering crowns, or breathe without gallons of blood, or dream without yards of golden silk, billowing in the lavender wind, carrying me through the in-between. I sink my head into the deep, downy pillow and close my eyes.

A voice whispers in my ear, "Don't think you're going to get away—"

Darkness falls.

14

Close your eyes and drift away.
I'll be right here beside you.
After everything you've done, I'm still here.

15

I wake up soaking wet on the dock.

The moon is still high in the sky, and an unnerving thought flits through my brain like a buzzing fly: I don't know how I got here. I sit, shivering and disoriented, a prickly, electric sensation humming through my body. I climb to my feet slowly, like in nightmares. The cue is run; you turn to stone. My clothes hang off me, drenched, and I hug myself, self-conscious and terrified. Because I've never sleepwalked in my life. So then how did I get here? No one at this house would do this as a prank because they know I'm deathly afraid of entering the water.

It isn't the lake itself—I love the lake. But I don't swim in it because I have an irrational fear of sharks. It's rational to fear sharks if you find yourself face-to-face with one. Maybe even if you swim in water where you might conceivably encounter one. But after watching *Jaws* as a kid, I've been terrified to go in any body of water where I could *imagine* a shark. I can dip my foot in for a bit, but if I leave it too long, the image of a shark grabbing me and dragging me under eventually becomes so intense I have to take it out. I can't even swim in the deep end of pools. I get fixated on the thought of being bumped on one side. Then the other. Then jaws, razor-sharp, folding around me. Like I said, irrational. But no less *real*.

This was no prank. And whoever did it is still here.

I glance back at the house. All of the lights are on, and the house stares at me unnervingly with rows of bright yellow eyes and teeth, a bizarre wooden jack-o'-lantern. My eyes travel from window to window, but I don't see any movement. Every room is empty, silent, still. The night is eerily quiet. No crickets. No frogs. No hush of wind through the pines. The night of the fire was windless. It saved the woods, the neighboring houses. It didn't save Emily.

"Guys?" My voice reverberates. "Hello?"

I know they haven't driven anywhere—Kennedy is strict about drinking and driving—and there's nothing within walking distance. A few other houses, but no neighbors we know. I turn back to the lake, a chill settling over me. That's the only other place to go.

The mooring line lies loose in the water. A mix of relief and annoyance washes over me. They've taken the boat out, that's all. There's a small sailboat not too far away, swimming distance for a skilled swimmer, dead on the water. It could be the Hartfords' boat, *Summer's Edge*. But although the moon is bright, I can't see anyone on deck. I gaze into the water, imagining the one rogue shark that *would* be lurking beneath, a leftover from prehistoric times, waiting, biding his time. For me.

I cup my hand around my mouth. "Kennedy!" My voice is swallowed up by the night. I try again, shouting for Chase, Ryan, Mila. No one answers. A slight breeze lifts my hair from the back of my neck, and I raise my head to gather it into a ponytail. I glance back at the boat just as a stiffer breeze picks up and swings the sail, changing the boat's direction. I catch sight of a shadowy figure propped up against the mast. I squint. The figure sways, steps forward, and stills.

"Kennedy?" I try again, louder. It stands in the darkness for a moment, then slowly turns its head toward shore. An odd sensation vibrates through me like electricity, suspending me in silence. My arms float uselessly at my sides; my vocal cords slacken and sink in my throat. My legs are melting into the dock, and my eyes are shadows, spilling into the shadow person's gaze. Though I cannot see its face, I feel its unspeakable dread as it creeps to the edge of the boat, hovers for a moment as if suspended in time, and plunges into the inky water with the sudden violence of someone who has been pushed or pulled with incredible, almost supernatural force.

I startle out of my trance with one terrifying, heart-stopping thought in my mind: It was too dark to make out a face. But I didn't see the silhouette of a life jacket.

"Hello?" I call, heart pounding, eyes frantically searching the surface of the water.

No answer. The wind continues to pick up and the boat rocks. There's some bulkiness on one side, maybe someone asleep on the deck, but no one rises to help. I shout, "Man overboard!" but no one responds. It's an ambitious swim to the sailboat—I can't be sure it even is the Hartfords' boat—and my fear of sharks is no joke. If it gets in my head, it takes over. But someone is in trouble and everyone seems to have vanished. It could be one of my friends out there in the water, and I will not abandon them. Never again. So I make the split-second decision to dive in after the figure that hasn't resurfaced.

A deep breath.

Don't think.

Two.

It's only water.

Three.

Nothing lies beneath.

One last breath, and down into darkness.

The water is bath warm, unseasonable for New York in early summer, and I have to push every thought out of my head to keep moving forward. I repeat *man overboard* to myself over and over, because if I don't think *man*, I will think *shark*. *Man overboard, man overboard, man, man, man, over, over, over. Light as a feather. Stiff as a board.* I glance up at the boat every few breaths, but the distance doesn't seem to be closing.

Man overboard. Girl overboard. Over, over, board, board. Breathe. Kick. Breathe. Kick. Breathe. Breathe. Breathe.

As I near the boat, I search for a dark shape bobbing on the surface, and my heart sinks when I don't see one. No life jacket means they've been under for a few minutes, and it may be impossible to find them. Or revive them. I grasp the side of the boat and see the familiar block letters: *SUMMER'S EDGE.* The water is almost black. And when I look down, fear rushes up and strangles me. Something is under there. Something big. Big enough to tear into me.

My throat closes up and I gulp at the air. My legs are numb from kicking. I can't see. My heart hammers in my chest. I have to go under, because if I don't, I'm a murderer for abandoning the person I saw fall in. At the same time, it's been minutes already, and my chances of finding them are slim. Every moment I spend deliberating makes me more of a killer, but my fear of submersion eats at me like acid. I have to try. Have to.

I strangle a scream, thrash with my legs, and dive down, grasping in every direction. I have never felt so isolated as I do in this moment. And then the fear clicks in and adrenaline surges through my body. I imagine it like a comic-book transformation, boiling my blood from red to green, altering my DNA. I am not the same Chelsea. I am not a rational thinker. I am prey. I am the hunted. And the only thought I can process is *escape*. I kick for the surface, lungs bursting, chest on fire, my heart ten times the strength and speed of a human specimen.

I break through the water to the air, and still I do not breathe. My numb, tingling fingers somehow find the ladder at the back of the boat, and I claw my way up and over and collapse onto the deck, sobbing, defeated. Beneath the surface of the lake, a body lies. Someone who walked down the boardwalk of the Hartford Cabin, climbed aboard *Summer's Edge*, sailed out on the lake, and plunged into the water while I watched. And as I flailed and panicked, maybe a foot or two, maybe inches, over them, they drew their last breath and died.

"Chelsea."

I remove my hands from my face, wiping away warm tears with lake water. Kennedy is staring down at me drowsily. Drunkenly? Her starlit eyes are heavy-lidded, and her breath smells sweet, sugary, like white wine and lemon sorbet. What did they do after I went to sleep? An image of tarot Kennedy with the jagged crown flashes through my head. *Trust at your peril.*

"I had the most messed-up dream," she says.

I sit abruptly. "Someone's in the water. They went overboard."

She scrambles to her feet and searches the water anxiously, then looks down at me with relief. "You scared the shit out of me." She sinks back to the deck. "Did you swim out here?" She's wearing the dress she had on earlier, and there's a bottle of wine at her feet. Empty.

"Did you hear me? Someone fell overboard and went under."

"That's not possible." She crouches down and attempts to open the shutter to the cabin.

I bend down and yank it open. Beneath, Chase and Mila are snuggled under a fleece blanket. "Where's Ryan?"

Kennedy assumes an angelic expression, the one she wears when she doesn't want me to get upset but knows I have a damn good reason to be. "He left."

I stare at her incredulously. "He just got up in the middle of the night and took off?" It's not like he was enthusiastic about staying. But he did give me his word.

"I checked the loft before we left and found the sheets folded up along with a note from Ryan thanking me for a lovely weekend." She frowns. "Sarcastic and rude."

"You were rude to him." I look to the boat's edge. "I'm telling you, I saw someone fall."

"Then I am telling *you*, you're seeing things," she says sharply.

I suck in a gulp of air. That stung. "I know the difference between real and imagined."

She looks embarrassed. "I know. I just meant I would have

seen if someone else got on the boat. It didn't happen, I promise." But I know Kennedy, and she isn't telling the truth. At least she's not *sure* she is. A sudden breeze skims over the lake and I shiver. I'm still soaking wet.

Kennedy gazes up at the telltale, the little ribbon atop the mast that monitors the wind and indicates how to navigate the boat to take advantage of it. "Now, will you stop trying to freak me out and give me a hand?"

I reluctantly help her with the sail. "Why did you come out here so late? Without me?"

"Mila wanted to see the stars, and Chase wouldn't take no for an answer. I wasn't about to let them take the boat out alone. And you were dead to the world. Those pills are no joke."

I grit my teeth to ratchet the line. "Someone moved me. I woke on the dock, soaking wet."

She barely flinches. "Don't those heavy-duty sleeping pills cause sleepwalking? Even sleep driving and sleep murdering and all kinds of messed-up shit?"

"I just sleep." I love how one sleeping pill makes me an unreliable witness, and their hours of drinking doesn't factor into the equation.

The sail catches wind, and she jumps behind the steering wheel. "They cause hallucinations, though. Don't they?" She says it lightly, but the implication is clear. I didn't see anything from the dock. It was exhaustion, it was a trick of the light, it was my *pills*. Kennedy will always find a reason not to believe. I study her silhouette, standing at the bow of the boat, hair tossed by the breeze. The resemblance to the tarot card gives me goose bumps.

"You know what? I think it's your fault Ryan left. He lost his sister and you were horrible to him. And I don't know how to get through this weekend without him."

Kennedy's expression tightens. "Well, I'm sorry for your loss."

"It is a loss! He's the only one who didn't laugh in my face about hearing Emily."

"Because he always says whatever you want to hear."

"No, because he hears her too. And not just whispers. Clues. About what happened to her. Like the cards in that game. Don't you see it?"

I don't like the way she's looking at me. A little bit of pity, but a little bit afraid.

"Don't look at me like that. Emily left Ryan . . ." I stop short of telling her about the tarot card warning not to trust her. "You're proving my point. He believes me, and you're condescending as fuck."

She presses her hands against her lips and screams into them silently. "There is no more Emily! I don't know what Ryan's going through, and I'm sorry, but it's no excuse to drag you into it, and turn you against us *again*. Against me. He is always getting between us."

"I can't believe you're making this about you." I wrench my arm away. "It's about Emily and what really happened last year. Maybe if you were honest with me, I wouldn't need Ryan."

"Wow." She stares at me. "Well, I feel a little better about the fact that you think it's remotely possible that one of us killed Emily. Because now I know who brainwashed you."

"I don't think it. I just . . . have questions. Don't you?"

"Fine," she says as we drift up to the dock. "I'll prove he's lying. If that's what it takes for you to finally trust me."

We dock and Kennedy moors the boat and stalks back to the house. I climb down into the cabin and find a couple of towels. I dry myself off with one and smack Chase with the other.

He startles awake. "What did I do?"

"Have you been asleep this whole time?"

"I mean, not since birth. I dozed off at some point when we lost the wind. Does that mean I deserve to be towel-smacked awake? Reasonable minds may disagree."

I sit down next to him with a sinking feeling. "Chase, something weird is going on. I saw someone go overboard, and they never resurfaced."

His eyes widen. "Did you send out a mayday?"

I shake my head. "I don't even know how to do that."

"Kennedy does."

"I'm the only one who saw it."

His expression changes. "Oh."

It suddenly clicks, and I can't even begin to describe how furious it makes me. These are supposed to be my best friends. "You think I'm imagining it. Like hearing Emily in the house. You think I hallucinated a person falling into the lake and disappearing under the water."

"I mean . . . How well did you see it?" He looks like he wants so hard for it not to be true, *and* for me not to be having some kind of breakdown. Why can't he just take me at my word?

"I was on the dock, and it was dark. But I *saw* it, damn it.

You know how I feel about water, and I dove in and swam all the way to the boat. That's how sure I was."

"Hey." He puts a hand on my arm. "If you're that sure, we can go to the cell spot right now and call 911." The cell spot is the one place nearby with reliable cell service—a secluded spot in the woods, about a fifteen-minute hike. A drive to town would take five minutes longer. But I hesitate. I *feel* sure. But sure enough to attach my name to a police report? Something about the thought sets off alarm bells. I can't put my finger on exactly *why* it feels like such a bad idea. But it does. I wish I didn't always second-guess myself. I wish Ryan were here.

I sigh. "I could be wrong." My eyes fall on Mila, still sleeping. "Chase," I say quietly. "What can you tell me about the fire? I'm trying to piece together what happened. I figure all of us saw things the others missed." Better not to mention Ryan's suspicions. It probably wouldn't be the smartest way to get honest answers, anyway. It backfired with Kennedy—she shut down the second I even mentioned the possibility that one of us could have been at fault.

Chase frowns. "Why?"

Mila yawns and stretches. "Why are you like this, Chelsea?" She turns to Chase. "She legitimately gives me nightmares."

"She's one of my best friends," Chase says with a warning look.

"I'll tell you what happened last year if you vow not to mention ghosts again," Mila says.

"Fine," I say. We'll see. "I know about the gas leak . . . not so much about the spark."

She relaxes. "I was asleep when the fire started. Sorry I

can't help you there. Chase carried me outside to safety." She nestles her head into his shoulder.

Chase pulls away slightly, giving her a puzzled look. "No I didn't."

She gazes up at him. "Yeah, you did."

He shakes his head slowly. "I went to try to stop the fire. By the time I gave up, there was no way to get upstairs."

Mila sits up straighter, looking alarmed. "Oh my god. Someone did. Some guy carried me out of the house and laid me down on the grass. I thought you saved my life, Chase."

He shrugs helplessly. "I had no idea. I'm glad they did it. Can we pretend it was me?"

"No, seriously—if you didn't, who did?" She looks at me.

"It had to be Ryan," I say.

"Ew." She shudders.

Chase casts her a sidelong glance. "What's wrong with Ryan?"

"Nothing," she says. "It just feels wrong. It should have been you."

Chase looks uncomfortable. There's always that unspoken rivalry between him and Ryan. But it also *does* feel wrong in a way I can't articulate. It's not because she was Chase's girlfriend. And I wish I could say that none of us needed saving. But that's not the truth. Emily needed saving. I guess the unsettling part is that Ryan came back for Mila, but left Emily behind.

"I guess I have some questions for Ryan now," Chase says, ruffling Mila's hair.

I sigh. "Me too. I wish he'd stuck around."

Chase looks at me in surprise. "What?"

"Kennedy told me he packed his bags and left a note. I guess things got a little too intense. I know he was having a hard time."

Chase looks crestfallen. "He should have woken us to say goodbye." He chews the side of his cheek thoughtfully. "I wish you wouldn't worry about whatever you saw. It was just us three on the boat—kind of hard to board without anyone noticing. You were asleep on the couch. We came out here and . . ." He starts to drift, and I wave a hand in front of his face. "Clearly drank too much," he finishes, rubbing his eyes. "Jesus, I haven't blacked out since freshman year."

Mila looks thoughtful. "Did you actually see Ryan leave?"

"No."

"Then he's probably still here."

Chase and I both turn to her. "Why?"

"I heard him, up in the attic." She eyes me. "I figured it was you at first. Insomnia and all. I couldn't sleep with the footsteps pacing back and forth all night." Mila turns to Chase. "That's why I woke you and suggested a moonlight sail. It's quiet on the water." She looks at me. "When we found you on the couch, I realized it couldn't have been you in the attic. Kennedy was with us—so it had to be Ryan. Probably creeping around, basking in the death sparkles of his sister."

I make a face and she returns it. It's comforting, in a way. It makes it feel like things are still sort of cosmically balanced. No one believes in anything, and Mila thinks I'm a loser.

"Kennedy said she found his note just before you went out," I offer.

Mila shakes her head. "I was the last to leave, and I heard the footsteps again as I left."

"But why would Kennedy lie about Ryan leaving?" I say.

Mila shrugs. "Maybe she didn't. Maybe he lied to her." That gets my attention. He *could* have left the note to fake Kennedy out and then stuck around to investigate unseen. But why wouldn't he tell me?

"I'm sure it's all a misunderstanding." Chase takes off his T-shirt and hands it to me. "You must be freezing." I strip off my soaking T-shirt and pull his on. It's like wearing a dress. It's strange how the temperature drops so quickly from day to night. The chill of the lake air hangs on your bones, seeps into you. It sucks the heat right out of every cell in your body. Chase and Mila seem calmer now, the odd events of this evening forgotten. But then, they didn't see that figure disappear under the water. They didn't wake up on the dock, soaking wet in the dark. For all they know, I'm lying about everything. It must be nice to be believed. By the time I reach the dock, Kennedy is gone. Up ahead, the lights in the house seem to glow brighter, the kind of unnatural brightness that hurts to look at, and suddenly blink off all at once.

"Did you see that?" I whisper.

"Seriously?" Mila groans.

"Blackout," Chase says with a hint of uneasiness.

My eyes travel up to the attic. I could have sworn that before the lights snapped off, I did see something. A shadow, a blur. I take a careful step onto the dock and begin to walk quickly toward the house. If Ryan is still there, I want to get to him before Kennedy does.

16

Power is a funny thing.
When you have it, you take it for granted.
When you don't, it's the only thing you think about.
I'm going to take yours before you die.
It's the least I can do.
Maybe not the least . . .
But I *can* do it.
That's the whole point of power.

17

I walk ahead as Chase and Mila linger behind to tie up the boat. By the time I reach the lake house, I can see faint candle-light flickering in the living room, Kennedy's room, and the one tiny circular window in the attic. Someone's definitely been up there. Inside, a thick blanket of silence hangs over the house, and a panicky feeling flutters through me, the feeling of déjà vu, of crushing loneliness, of being abandoned over and over and over again. Kennedy has lit a candle on the living room table next to where I was sleeping, alongside a glass of water with another note reading *For your pills*. I stuff it into my pocket, annoyed.

I flick the light switch, but the light doesn't come on. Every hair on my body stands on end. I've had a recurring nightmare since childhood where I wake up and reach for the light next to my bed, and it doesn't turn on. I go to the door, and the light switch on the wall is broken. I feel my way down the hall to the bathroom, and those lights are out too. And just as it's dawning on me that all the lights in the world are out, I wake up. It shouldn't be that scary. Blackouts happen all the time, especially during heat waves. They happen frequently at the lake house. It's not the content of the dream, it's an unspoken implication, a subtext. It's not the *what* of it all, it's the *why*.

The dread that saturates that dream flows through me now. I try every light in the living room, then the kitchen, flinging open the refrigerator in desperation. There's something creepy about a dark refrigerator that's hard to explain. I slowly close the door on the gradually expiring milk and eggs, and a light wisp of condensation escapes like a gasp of breath. I turn back to the living room. There's a circuit breaker in the cellar. I'll find Ryan faster if I can get the lights back on.

I can make out the door by the candlelight, near the base of the staircase. As I draw near, I notice the cellar door is slightly ajar, and for a split second I reconsider my circuit-breaker plan. The cellar has always creeped me out. We found a dead rabbit down there once—not a mouse, a rabbit. I don't know how it got down there. It was our first summer at the lake house all together, the summer after third grade. We'd had a class pet rabbit that year, Miss Palindrome. We all took care of her, we all loved her, and we all cried at the end of the year when we had to ceremonially hand her over to the next class.

We found the rabbit in the cellar just a week later. She had white fur with caramel-and-coffee-colored spots, just like our pet. She was about the same size, and I thought their faces looked similar. I don't think she'd been dead for very long. It wasn't like roadkill, with a stretched-out, gaunt, tortured, almost petrified look, but her throat had been torn. Chase stood staring, stuttering, while Ryan held Emily's hand, forcing her up the stairs, shouting for Mr. Hartford. But I was stuck, my eyes locked on the rabbit I was convinced was Miss Palindrome, who must have somehow found us, and been punished by some divine force for running away. Of course, it couldn't have been Miss Palindrome, and she didn't run away. But a child's imagination can make impossible things feel very, very real.

I reach for the door, but before my fingertips touch the knob, it begins to move. Slowly, so slowly that in my head I feel time grinding to a halt and beginning to move in the wrong direction, like a record player going backward, twisting your favorite song into a dark and terrifying hymn. It moves. I watch helplessly as it drifts away from me with a long, sighing creak, like a little doll's scream, and clicks shut. Every single hair on my body rises. The brass lock above the antique doorknob slowly turns, sealing the door shut. I stare at it for a moment, frozen, a strange numbness in my legs, my lips glued together. My brain begins to buzz like it's swarming with flies, and I get another shutter flash of Miss Palindrome. I force my wooden legs to bend and hinge in their sockets, and I reach for the bolt and turn it. For a moment, I rest my hand on the doorknob. The metal is warm under my skin, like someone's been holding it for a long time. I shake the thought out of my head. Absurd. People don't stand around holding doorknobs.

I take a deep breath and try to yank the door open. It's stuck. I flip the bolt back and forth a few times, but the door won't move, even when I throw all of my weight behind it. It's odd. It was ajar just moments ago, and it drifted shut softly. It shouldn't be jammed like this. I knock on it, feeling silly. "Hello?" I call through the door. No one answers. I put my ear to the wood and rap again. "Hello?" One more tap, this time with my knee. "Kennedy?" I make a skittering noise on the door with my fingernails. "Miss Palindrome?" I whisper, just to be an asshole.

There's an enormous bang against the door from the other side, like someone is throwing their entire body against it. I scream and fall away from it, slamming against the living room table and sending the Truth or Dare game sprawling onto the floor, and the candle on top of it.

I smack my palm down on it in a panic to stop the flare-up, but regret it the instant the room is cloaked in darkness. A watery rinse of moonlight filters in through the windows, but it doesn't reach the stairs. The cellar has gone quiet again. I make a dash for the staircase and feel my way up, scrambling on all fours. The rest of the house is chillingly silent. Kennedy must have heard me scream, which means I won't be alone for long. I pause at the top of the stairs and consider calling for her. I don't want her following me up to the attic, though. I hear Chase and Mila stumble into the house, something glass shatters on the floor, and Mila curses. Perfect—that should buy me time to find Ryan first.

I tiptoe past the guest room and then stop short. The door to Kennedy's room is wide open. It catches me off guard. It's been closed all day. The balcony doors are flung open, and a slight breeze flutters the gauzy curtains, princess pink, just like the old ones. Exquisite care has been taken to carve the fairy-tale scenes in the walls anew. Sleeping Beauty with her spinning wheel, Rumpelstiltskin dancing around his fire, the Snow Queen with her shattered mirror. Kennedy has placed a candle here, too, on the dresser. I shut the door silently behind me. The entrance to the attic is through a trapdoor in Kennedy's closet. I open it and climb up the ladder.

"Ryan?" I call softly. No one answers.

As always, the attic is about ten thousand degrees and smells like sawdust. I get a suffocating sense of claustrophobia just poking my head into it. Ryan isn't up here, but someone was. At the center of the unfinished, cavernous space is another lit candle and an open book. I step lightly across the floor. When someone walks in the attic, it sounds like elephants stampeding below. I bend over the candle curiously and pick up the book. It's an old library book, but all of the pages have been scribbled out in black ink. On the inside jacket is Emily's name. Under it is a short series of notes in tiny handwriting, hers and mine. We must have passed it back and forth in class years ago. I hold the candle up and squint to make out the words.

No one will believe you. (Emily's hand)
They might. (Mine)
She gets away with everything. They all do. Don't bother.
You don't know them like I do.
Yes I do. That's your problem, Chelsea. You think you know everyone better than me. They're my friends too. And they don't give a shit about anyone but themselves.

I stare down at the words, bile gathering in my mouth. I haven't thought about the incident the notes are referring to in ages. It almost tore our group apart. It was just after Kennedy broke my heart for the first time, the summer after ninth grade. After, I guess, I inadvertently broke Ryan's. Kennedy and I were barely speaking, and Ryan was avoiding me. Emily was the one everyone trusted. And suddenly things got really ugly. According to Emily, Kennedy's mother discovered a family heirloom missing at the lake house. Either she or Kennedy suggested that I "accidentally put it in my bag and took it home." Obviously I didn't do it.

But the words were spoken, and you can't un-ring a bell. People already thought I was a freak. Now they also thought I was a criminal.

I stood my ground, showed up at Kennedy's door, and politely but firmly told her mother that I was very sorry to hear about her stolen goods, but I didn't have them. She had no idea what I was talking about. Either Kennedy lied, or Emily made it up to turn me against Kennedy and earn her spot as the leader of our group. Ryan took Emily's side, Chase took Kennedy's, and I was stuck in the middle, alone. It took six months for us to even start speaking again.

I tear the page out of the book, crumple it up, and stuff it into my pocket. If Mila is right and it was Ryan up here, why would he leave this? Is it a message to me to remind me whose side I'm supposed to be on?

I flip through until a flash of white catches my eye. I thumb back, looking for the page that hasn't been inked out. It's a stick-figure drawing. I skip a few pages ahead and find another, then a couple more. It slowly dawns on me that someone has created a flip-book—that if I flip the pages quickly, it will look like animation. I go back to the beginning and slowly fan the pages through my fingers. Before my eyes, five stick figures line up on a dock. A lightning bolt flashes above, and four nooses drop. Four of the figures hang and one figure remains. Another lightning bolt, and then a sudden rush of air blows out both of my candles as the attic door is slammed shut, leaving me in total darkness.

18

Attics are places for secrets.
Attics are places to hide.
Attics are places to set traps
For creatures that creep inside.

19

I feel my way over to the attic trapdoor on my hands and knees and slam my heels down on it in an attempt to kick it open, but it won't open from the inside. The way the ladder folds up into itself and automatically latches underneath makes it impossible. My breath comes out in hot, wild bursts. It sounds like roaring in my ears. It's too hot. I scream and bang my fists on the floor, then listen. I know at least Chase and Mila are down there.

The silence seems to stretch out for an hour, and the sound of my own panicked breathing echoes in the hollow room so loudly it creates the illusion of a chorus. I squeeze my eyes shut so a stray beam of moonlight won't seep in through the window and illuminate a roomful of faces, quiet watchers sitting silently around me, breathing the same hot air in unison, still and patient as death. It strikes me that the chorus that isn't there sounds louder the more I panic, and if I hold my breath, I would have proof that it's my fear getting the best of me. But if I hold my breath and the chorus continues, what then? A quiet shuffling, dust scraping across the attic floor, a sense of sudden closeness? A rhythmic pulse of air on the back of my neck, timed to the gasping breaths? A hand on my arm, or throat, ice-cold and strong as steel, the grip of bones closing to crush?

Terror washes over me as my breath freezes in my throat, and I cover my ears and scream.

There's a sudden burst of fresh air, and I hear Chase's voice. "Chelsea?"

I launch myself toward him and feel my way down the stairs, and he grabs my waist halfway down and helps me back into Kennedy's room. "There's something up there."

He climbs the stairs cautiously, looks around, and returns. "It looks empty to me."

"There *was* something. And someone slammed the door on me."

"What were you doing up there?"

"Looking for Ryan!" I point to Mila. "You said you heard him up there."

"I said I heard *someone* up there. Everyone else was accounted for." But Ryan was accounted for too. If Kennedy is telling the truth, he wasn't even here. Mila gives me a look. "It wasn't a ghost." But as she speaks, she tugs at her hair like a child clutching a security blanket, so hard it makes my skull ache.

I hand Chase the book and hold the candle up for him to see. "Someone made this into a flip-book. Look."

He glances down at it dubiously but begins to flip the pages. As the stick-figure scene plays out before him, his face transforms, his lips going taut. When the book flips to the last page, a flash of color catches my eye and I reach for it. It's the tarot card. The woman standing on the boat. I gaze up at the attic. Wherever he is now, Ryan *was* up there at one point.

Mila takes the tarot card. "What is this?"

"Nothing. One of Emily's cards."

"It looks a lot like Kennedy. *Trust at your peril?*"

But Chase ignores us, still staring at the flip-book. "This isn't funny."

I stuff the tarot card into my pocket. "I didn't do this. Look at me."

Chase raises his eyes to mine. For the first time this evening, I see actual fear in them.

"I didn't do it."

"For fuck's sake, Chase, she's not lying. She's terrified." Mila takes the book and flips through several times, studying it without emotion. "Five figures. One is a hangman." She snaps it shut. "There are only four of us. Unless Ryan really is still here. But then where is he?"

"Unless it's Emily," I whisper. Ryan wouldn't do this. Couldn't.

"What's going on?"

We snap our heads up in unison. Kennedy stands in the doorway, holding another candle.

Chase puts his arm around Mila. "Chelsea got trapped in the attic."

He had to throw me under the bus. "I thought I heard something up there."

Kennedy's eyes fall on the book in Mila's hand. "What are you reading?"

"Some old library book." Mila hands it to Kennedy. "A ghost story." There's no mistaking the mocking undertone in her voice.

Kennedy flips through the pages carefully. "Lovely." She drops the book and slams her purse down on the dresser.

"I assume whoever made that masterpiece is responsible for this, too."

Chase reaches into the purse and pulls out a handful of cards from the Truth or Dare game—blank ones. "These are templates. Someone used these to make the messed-up cards."

Mila glances at me but doesn't say a word. Someone with a beating heart.

"The question is, who planted them in my purse," Kennedy demands.

Mila folds her arms over her chest. "You have unrestricted access to this house and everything in it. It would take a ridiculous amount of planning for anyone else to pull this off."

Kennedy looks taken aback. "The only one who has the slightest reason to mess with any of us is Ryan. Emily was his sister. He blames us for her death."

Chase shakes his head. "No. No way."

Kennedy looks to me. "Tell them."

I avoid Chase's anxious gaze. "He doesn't *blame* us—he just has some questions, that's all."

Mila groans, and Chase and Kennedy immediately start arguing.

"What is so wrong with that?" I shout above them. They quiet down. "I agree with him. Last year was messed up, but the worst part is the feeling that everything we think we know is a lie because the truth is, maybe one of us did start the fire. Maybe it wasn't outright murder, but it didn't just happen, either. This house did not spontaneously burst into flame, no matter how good a lawyer Mr. Hartford is. Am I really the only one who isn't afraid to admit that? I know there are things that don't make sense to all of us. Like why were you outside, Kennedy?"

"I don't recall," she says quietly.

Mila looks at her sharply. "You don't recall taking us out on the boat?"

Kennedy sighs, frustrated. "Sure. Yes. Fine. We went on the boat. Why does it matter?"

"Everything matters," I explode. "Why were all the doors locked? Why did Ryan come back for Mila? Why did no one come back for me? Or Emily? How did the attic door break? How did she get in there if it was broken? She climbed up, closed the door behind her, and it spontaneously broke in that precise window of time?"

The others are looking at me meaningfully, and my face flushes. I know what that look means. I was the only one in the room. I'm the only one who can answer that question. "There's more to the story," I say finally.

"Maybe all that's left of the story is the end," Chase says gently.

"No." Kennedy pushes the Truth or Dare cards across the dresser, away from herself. "Someone is trying to make it look like I did this. It's obviously not over."

Mila rises. "It is for me. I am officially opting out. It doesn't matter who's doing this. Just why. Maybe it's a creepy revenge game. Or maybe there really is a killer. Maybe someone decided to lure us back to the crime scene, figure out what we know, then bam. Sharp, shiny things at high velocities. I tried to stick it out for you, Chase, but I am not waiting around to find out which one of us dies first. This is not going to end well." She spins on her heels and runs down the stairs to the front door.

Kennedy runs after her. "Wait!" The front door slams behind them.

"Mila!" Chase calls after her. He turns to me reassuringly. "She's not going anywhere without her bags. She's just freaked out."

I glance up at the attic. "She's not the only one, Chase."

"Yeah," he says under his breath. "You're not kidding."

I follow him downstairs, but as Chase joins the others outside, I stop short. The cellar door is ajar. I reach out hesitantly to close it, but pause when a flash of white at the bottom catches my eye. Another tarot card. My heart pounds against my rib cage. I should be completely alone in the house. Unless.

"Ryan?" I call out.

Silence.

I close my eyes, draw a deep breath, then open them and run, taking the steps two by two, skidding across the dusty cellar floor as I collect the card. I gaze back up to the door beginning to close, almost imperceptibly slowly, and my heart is bursting in my chest as my shoes pound against the wooden stairs, dust in my lungs, just a sliver of light, an inch of space until the door clicks shut and seals me in. I throw myself against it with a scream that comes from deep, deep within me, from a place of childhood fears and forever anger, of the unfairness of time, of one inch left and closing.

And I make it. I barrel through.

Gasping in disbelief, I gaze down at the tarot card. It's a dark-haired girl on a starlit wooden path lined with tall trees that looks very similar to the path leading to the dock, beckoning, her long hair lifted by the wind in ribbons, her eyes glowing in the darkness. The caption reads: *Queen of Wands: follow not into the dark*. It looks a lot like Mila. I look out the open front door with a sinking feeling and join the others.

I follow Mila into the dark.

20

They say letting go is hard.

That it will come with time.

That forgiveness is key. Forgiving the others for surviving, and most of all, forgiving myself. For remaining.

But I don't buy it.

Because the others didn't just survive.

Survival is passive.

It implies clean hands and a clear conscience. It implies innocence.

It assumes that survival is something they earned, or were destined for, or just happened upon.

That they deserved life more.

And that would be a lie.

Survival is something they stole.

Because Chelsea and Kennedy and the others created the tragedy they survived.

They're killers.

And I can't wait any longer.

21

When we reach the driveway, Mila is sitting in her car, her face ashen, violently yanking at the ignition and slamming on the gas pedal. The car is still, lifeless. Kennedy drifts to her car as if in a trance, opens the door, and flicks at the headlights. Nothing happens. She slides the key into the ignition and turns it, then shakes her head. Both cars are dead, and Ryan's is gone.

"Holy shit," Chase murmurs under his breath. He tries his own car, with the same result.

"What does this mean?" I try to avoid looking at my car. There's something sinister about a dead car at a dark house. Like a warning. We should not be here. The headlights stare like lifeless eyes, like that shot in *Psycho* of the dead woman in the shower. I blink and turn away.

"Someone either drained the batteries or removed them," he says.

"*Someone?*" Kennedy gets out of the car. "Well, fuck Ryan and his horrible, no good, very bad year."

I glare at her. "There is zero evidence that this was him."

"There is plenty of evidence." She ticks the reasons off on her fingers. "He shows up and disappears. He stalls us with a note, allowing him to tamper with the lights and the cars without anyone noticing. He probably got that creepy book from Emily's room."

"Not necessarily," I say. "Emily wrote the last message. Which means it ended up in my hands."

Kennedy looks at me, irritated. "Well, did you do it? Because unlike you, Ryan has a motive: we didn't save his sister. According to him, we killed her with our own bare hands."

Chase cringes. "Come on. Negligence, maybe."

Kennedy stares at him. "I'm glad you're warming up to the idea."

"I'm not," he protests. "Just . . ." He looks uncomfortable. "You don't feel guilty at all?"

"Oh my *god*." Mila jumps out of the car, slamming the door behind her. "Emily died. It was a terrible accident, and granted, the circumstances don't look good for any of us. I don't even blame Ryan for being suspicious. We all have *excuses* for not knowing how the fire started. But they're not alibis. And Kennedy." Mila looks straight into her eyes. "I think you know more than you're saying, and I don't want to know what you're hiding." She whips her phone out of her pocket.

Kennedy sighs. "No cell service."

"Shit." Mila drops her hand to her side and looks to Chase desperately. "What do people do around here when their car breaks down?"

He scratches the back of his neck. "There's usually a landline. When it's busted, hike to the cell spot or walk to town. Preferably in the morning."

She shakes her head. "No way. Something is happening, and you know what? I'm the outsider here. I have the most unbiased perspective. And it could be any of you torturing us right now. Chelsea says she wants the truth. How far would she go to push her friends into confessing? Kennedy won't talk about what happened last year. Maybe she really does want to find out what we know and eliminate whoever knows too much. Chase—sorry, babe—you make mistakes, and you don't like to be called on them. What would you do to cover them up? And the elusive Ryan? He didn't even try to save Emily. Maybe we were never supposed to know about that. And now we're being punished for it." She shrugs. "It could be any of you. And I'm not going to be next. Two dead girls don't make a right. So I'm out." She walks toward us briskly, and I have to jump aside to avoid being knocked over. And then she walks right back into the house.

"Did she say *out?*" Kennedy's forehead creases.

I turn to Chase. "Do you know what she has that the rest of us lack?"

He stares at me, speechless.

"Spirit." I can't help it. I don't know why I am the way I am. I need to joke when I'm fizzing with fear. To smile sometimes when the world is crumbling. I need to silence the room. I wish I was a better person. But I'm not. I survive and let my friends fend for themselves.

Chase sighs and launches himself after her.

Kennedy pauses at my side, looking beaten down. "You can't even entertain the idea that it might be Ryan, can you?"

"I can entertain it. That's what makes me sure it's not him. He's our friend."

"What if he wasn't the person you thought he was?"

"You really believe he would do all of this? Trap me in the attic, kill the car batteries?"

She shoots me a wary look. "Do you really want to know what I think?" I study her. Kennedy wears a hard, polished exterior. But it isn't the real Kennedy. Not the one I fell in love with. I may have always been in love with Kennedy a little, but the summer between ninth and tenth grade was when I fell, and kept falling, and never really stopped. She'd been whispering about her secret crush for weeks, building it up to be the revelation of the year. And then one night after a fish fry, Kennedy and I took out a boat to watch fireworks, and out of the blue, she told me it was me all along. I was the secret. I was stunned, she was nervous. That made her so much cuter—she was carelessly oblivious to the fact that half of the class had a crush on her. I'd never kissed anyone before and I was too scared to do it, so we just agreed that we liked each other, and sat there awkwardly in the boat with all these explosions startling the fish and forcing us to shout at each other. You think, middle of the lake, starlight, fireworks, first kiss, how romantic. But it wasn't. It was scary and awkward and important.

But eventually we agreed that kissing is customary in these situations, so she promised not to laugh, and I squeezed my eyes shut and clambered over the emergency gear, and we found each other. It was too short. Every kiss with Kennedy was always too short. We kissed all weekend, in every private moment. She laughed every time. I always opened my eyes before the end.

But when summer was over, she showed up at my doorstep and said she wanted to make sure we were still best friends, and Emily too. And my heart shot itself to pieces, because I understood. Emily felt left out. And starting high school with a girlfriend would be "limiting" in a lot of ways. We were back together by the end of the year, but I was still devastated, and it stuck with me. It still does. Kennedy always held all the cards.

"I want to know what you don't recall," I say finally.

"You don't trust me," she says, looking disappointed.

"Like you trusted me when I told you I heard Emily's voice?"

She looks torn. "I do . . . but I can't believe in something I don't see. I just can't. And when I think about everything that's happening right now, it doesn't say revenge from beyond the grave. It doesn't even say random serial killer. It says guy with a grudge. Everything is too personal. The cards ending up in *my* purse. The words—one of us kissed a killer, one betrayed a friend, one killed a best friend. They're each obviously meant to refer to one of us."

"But there are four of us, and only three cards."

"I thought of that. But then I thought of something else. Mila wasn't invited."

I look at her in surprise. "Then you did send out the invites."

"No. But when we were discussing them at dinner, Mila *said* we all got one. But she also said maybe they were ordered off the internet or something, remember?"

I nod. I do remember her saying that.

"Mine was written out *by hand*," Kennedy emphasizes. "So was yours. She didn't realize her mistake until she saw your invitation."

"Shit." It was such a small moment, it flew right by me. But

Kennedy's right. Mila's suggestion wouldn't have made sense if she'd actually *gotten* an invitation.

"So Mila isn't one of the three. And she's not the one behind all of this. She's the wild card—the one who wasn't supposed to be here. That narrows down the three to you, me, and Chase. Traitor, kisser, killer. Of the group, I've only kissed you, and Chase has only kissed Mila, and we know Mila isn't guilty. At least, it's pretty unlikely since she isn't connected to this whole clusterfuck. You, on the other hand, have kissed both me and Ryan."

"You're actually enjoying this, aren't you?"

"No!" Kennedy blushes. "If they're going to make us play games, at least let us choose the game, though. No one in this house is going to beat me in a logic puzzle. So look at the facts. None of the three of us has kissed Chase."

"You're going to argue that he's not the killer based on a logic puzzle?"

"I'm going to argue that none of us killed Emily, but you're not going to listen to that."

"Fine." I'm quiet for a moment. "Well, by that logic, Chase is the traitor and one of us is the killer."

She slow-claps. "That's what Ryan wants us to believe."

I shoot her a look.

Kennedy sighs. "What *someone* wants us to believe."

"Okay. Chase is the traitor. One step closer to the truth, I guess. The question is, what did he do?"

She pauses. "You don't know?"

I shake my head. "Should I?"

"Emily and Chase hooked up." Kennedy makes a lock-and-key symbol over her lips. "After he and Mila started dating."

I stare at her, stunned. "So which friend did he betray? Emily or Mila?"

She looks thoughtful. "That's a good question."

"Especially when one of them is dead and the other turned up uninvited to the weekend from hell." I pause. "If not both of them." I eye the front door nervously. The mist is settling in more thickly, and I'm cold. "Chase and Mila have been gone a while. Do you think they're okay?"

Kennedy pushes the door open cautiously. "Of course." But she sounds uncertain. I haven't heard a single sound from within the house while we've been outside talking. It's unnerving.

"So what if Emily did return? Do you think she could possibly be the one behind all this?"

She glances back over her shoulder at me. "That assumes ghosts exist."

"For once, can you just consider it?" I try not to think of the cellar. The door opening and slamming, the feeling of being trapped. That *something* was closing the door on me.

Kennedy steps inside the house and looks around slowly. "Okay. But even assuming ghosts exist, Emily hasn't risen from the grave to avenge her own death. Flaw number one—and I will die on this hill—her death was an accident."

"Okay, now I'll assume *you're* right. What if she *thinks* we did? Can't a ghost be wrong? Why would crossing over make a person omniscient?"

She considers. "If it were me you all left behind that night, I'd need more to go on than the fact that you were all there.

That's just not enough to motivate me to concoct a psychological torture scheme against my own best friends. *We were there* to *We killed her* is a huge leap."

"But you'd believe Ryan would do this."

"Because he *has* a motive. He's always wanted to get between us."

"It would be seriously messed up to try to convince someone their girlfriend was a murderer just to win them back."

"Ex-girlfriend," Kennedy corrects. I think I hear sadness in her voice. But it might be wishful thinking. Our eyes connect for a moment, and it almost all comes rushing out. Even tonight, even in this house, there are a million things I need to say to her that have been kept beneath the surface for far too long.

She reaches for my shaking hand. "I wish we could go back in time." She looks into my eyes, and my heart rips down the middle. Two asymmetrical pieces, the larger one for her. It's automatic. We never had one of those fancy friendship necklaces with the charms. It's impossible to make three equal and identical pieces of a heart that fit together. And it wouldn't have been right to exclude Emily. She *was* the third. She mattered just as much. And it was everything in threes or nothing. When Kennedy and I were dating, for real this time, after the heirloom incident had been buried under six months of silence, I made her a secret heart. I spun it of yarn unwound from my favorite sweater, cotton candy from the carnival where she won me a purple elephant, starlight I scooped into a jar the night of our first kiss, and my own silver blood. I gave it to her on a scrap of paper and she swallowed it, and we shared that secret. Not that she and I were dating. Everyone knew that. But that I loved her. Love changes things. It redraws the map.

Kennedy never said it back. Now we stare into each other's eyes, and I will her to tell me. *Say it, Kennedy.* But instead, she glances up the stairs. "Chase?"

"Mila?" he calls back in a muffled voice.

"It's just us," I say, a bad feeling settling over me. He should have found her by now.

Kennedy looks at me, worried. "We'll finish this conversation later. I promise." I nod and she heads upstairs.

I glance out the front window at the cars, feeling strange, like I'm being watched.

My eyes travel around the living room. The single candle on the table is burned almost halfway down, and wax is pooling on the antique wood. Kennedy and her mother are going to have twin heart attacks. I retrieve a wet paper towel from the kitchen and try to wipe up the melted wax, but only succeed in burning my fingertips and somehow melding the towel into the wax. Shit. I flatten it against the table and pick up a candlestick.

And then, something catches my eye that makes my breath hitch in my throat. A third tarot card placed face-out on the bookshelf next to one of the candles. It's a dark-haired young man in a clearing, shadowed by a circle of foreboding pines, his hands folded around something that emits a bright, eerie glow. He has Chase's broad shoulders and amber eyes, and below is written *King of Wands: keeper of secrets and lies.* I know with one glance what it's supposed to be. Chase in the cell spot. I lunge for it and stuff it into my pocket, my hands shaking, as I hear Chase's and Kennedy's footsteps hurrying down the stairs. I could swear the card wasn't there moments ago, before we went outside. I wasn't looking for it, so I can't be sure. But that sinking feeling is back, the sensation that I'm falling through the floor, through wood and dirt, through solid ground, into a dangerous nowhere, an infinite lucid in-between, and it's more sinister than sleep because I am not alone. I turn to the others and try to make my voice work, to warn them, to let them know that something *is* stalking us, pushing us into the darkness, something enormous and heartless and real.

Kennedy tosses me a sweatshirt and pair of warm flannel pajama bottoms, and I take them gratefully. I've been shivering in Chase's dress-sized T-shirt half the night. "Suit up," she says, unsmiling.

"What's wrong?" I look back and forth between them as I change.

"Her things are missing," Chase says grimly. "Mila's gone."

"No one was supposed to leave," Kennedy says, pacing back and forth, biting her nails. "This is not good."

Chase shoots her a suspicious look. "What do you mean, 'supposed to'?"

"I mean, splitting up is the worst possible thing we could do right now!" she shouts back, then composes herself. "No. Fighting is the worst thing. We need to stay calm. Stick together."

"No," I say suddenly. "We'll never get anything accomplished unless we split up. We have to find Mila."

Chase looks at me with relief. "Thank you."

Kennedy turns to me desperately. "Chelsea, don't."

But I do. It's time to trust me for once. To trust my plan. Because I think I know exactly where Mila went and why. "Kennedy, you stay here. In case she comes back."

She stares at me for a moment and then slowly nods. "Fine. I should be the one to stay here."

"Chase." I turn to him. "You and I are going to the cell spot."

Mila may not know what the cards are, but she's smart enough to know that they mean something. She saw the Kennedy card, and the Mila card was within eyeshot as she ran out to the driveway. But the Chase card—that was the one that would have scared her into trying to leave without him. The keeper of secrets and lies.

Chase opens the door and steps out into the growing fog, but Kennedy grabs my arm before I can follow.

"Please be careful," she whispers into my ear.

But it isn't the world outside that really scares me. It's what I'm walking away from.

22

Here are my rules:
1. You may run.
2. You may hide.
3. You may apologize.
Oh, who are we kidding? None of you think you've done anything wrong.
4. You may attempt to escape.
5. But you will not.

23

It's like moving underwater. The gravel crunches like tiny shards of glass under my feet, but the air is thick, dense, a steamy fog coating the earth. We weave our way down the driveway, between the cars slick with condensation, feeling our way until we reach the end, where the gravel gives way to smooth pavement. Our cars are lined up neatly like they should be—all except for Ryan's. I shouldn't have questioned Kennedy. If she said he left, he either left or wanted her to think he did. But if he *did* fake a goodbye and stick around without telling even me, he had to have a very good reason. And I intend to find out why.

By now the fog has become so thick it's hard to breathe, and it's growing heavier by the minute. We need to cross the street before beginning the hike up the steep path through the trees to the cell spot. It's a pretty rocky climb at times, and it can be tricky in slick conditions. It will be incredibly dangerous in the fog. The air hangs heavily on my skin, and the sensation that something large and dark and shapeless is going to emerge out of the fog and pounce on me is so palpable, every muscle in my body is tensed.

Chase and I link arms at the edge of the street. "Ready?" He peers out into the darkness.

"As ever." We walk slowly and carefully, and I try not to let every horror movie I've ever seen play out in my mind. Only the expendables leave the cabin in the woods. The ones who didn't bother to read the script. "It's a good thing we never hooked up."

He laughs uncomfortably. "You're doing it again. Thought hopping. Help me out."

"Because like, in a horror movie, we'd be so dead right now."

He lets out a burst of laughter. "Touché. Thank god for the chastity of our friendship."

"Or lack of active serial killers in the area," I can't help adding.

He winces as we reach the start of the trail and step into the darkness of the forest. "Did you have to add that?"

"I was thinking it." I don't like this fog. It reminds me of water, the feeling of big things with sharp jaws circling unseen. "Kennedy said she doesn't think that's it, though. I mean, she doesn't think a random person hurt Emily or wants to mess with us."

Chase climbs silently for a bit. "That makes sense."

"I think so too. Why would a random person single us out? Wait so long in between attacks? It doesn't feel right. Whatever is happening right now is personal. Someone knows how to turn us against each other." We reach a steep rocky portion, and Chase nods for me to go first.

"I'll spot you."

I look around nervously for a foothold, beginning to second-guess my plan. I think Mila *did* head for the cell spot, and there's a chance Ryan is out here too. But both of them are seasoned athletes, and I'm not. I boost myself up and begin to climb. I don't talk, focusing on reaching the next flat spot in the trail. The surface is slick and muddy, and the fog is so thick at this level, I can't see above and I can't see below. But my hands eventually reach dirt, and I pull myself up and collapse onto the ground, my chest heaving in relief.

Chase easily joins me and stands and stretches, gazing up at the moon. The fog is thinner at this height. I wonder if we've clawed our way above the clouds. "Happy anniversary," he says suddenly, with a dark laugh.

I pull myself to my feet slowly. "That's not funny."

"It had to have been around now, right? Give or take an hour?" He raises an invisible glass. "To the moment all of our lives were spectacularly destroyed."

"How can you say that? Emily died. We're still here." My voice is swallowed up by the fog. It feels like cotton in my ears, dulling even Chase's voice to a soft, muted sound.

He speaks in cloudy wisps. "Yeah. We are. But we're not okay. You spent the year in a hospital, Chelsea. A year. That's extreme. Kennedy obviously went through some kind of psychological trauma, and Mila took more than her fair share of the blame. We need to find a way to make things right and move on with our lives. That's why I came back." He shrugs helplessly. "I don't think any of us can do another lap of last year. We all suffered."

"Not all of us suffered in Rome." I can't help it slipping out.

"Fair enough." His classic smile reappears, but something is a little off. It's creepy.

"They run out of pizza or something?" I try to resent him, but it's useless. Chase is the kind of guy who can spend a gap year in Europe, floating in a haze of hookah bars, sipping craft beers, and living on a steady diet of gourmet cheese and freshly baked bread, and the worst you can do is wish you were there with him. Even when he acts like it's some kind of chore.

He tightens his jaw and slows as his eyes search through the thin velvet mist. "I wouldn't know. I didn't leave my room." I try to imagine being whisked to a villa overlooking sparkling fountains and cobblestone streets. Designer shops and unbelievable food and buildings built on the ashes of a city that burned to dust.

After a brief moment of silence he darts a look at me. "My father would never risk a scandal, so there was no question of me sticking around. But every time I closed my eyes, I was back here in the burning house surrounded by everyone I let down."

"You never let me down," I say.

"Of course I did, Chelsea." Chase looks at me with an expression that makes my stomach feel tight. His confident aura rarely wavers, but tonight it's been flickering like a candle. "None of this would be happening if I'd been a little faster. Or smarter. I'm supposed to be so fucking smart. And I couldn't figure out how to save a friend. And now I find out *Ryan* went back for Mila? The only time it mattered one bit, my brain decided to sit it out." He pauses. "I failed. I deserve every last bit of the blame." He stumbles and almost pulls me over with him, but we both right ourselves and keep going. The night is cloaked in silence, stillness. I wish we could just turn around. As much as I dread the house and whatever is within, I dread that something following me into the darkness even more. A house has walls and doors and locks. Out here we are helpless. I see nothing, hear nothing, but Chase, but I feel that *it* sees me.

It might not be Emily that's been speaking to me all this time. Because it doesn't feel like Emily now. It feels monstrous, as big as the lake and as silent as the fog, as angry as the fire and as corporeal as the house. It feels everywhere, inescapable, and suddenly I want to go back to the hospital, to the place I hated, because everything was so certain there. Half hours of certainty, menus of reliability, pills of predictability. I want the last thing I remember that was predictable and sure. It wasn't good there. I was so glad to leave. But it didn't ruin my life.

"Stop." I look around uneasily. "I have no idea where we are."

"The path only goes one place," he says, his confidence returning a little.

"But the path branches." I falter. A lookout here, a picnic spot there. Dozens of adventures that we wore into the dirt one summer at a time.

"Trust me," he says, starting forward again. But even the words make me uneasy.

"Maybe you should trust yourself. About that night, I mean," I say as casually as I can. "You tried to stop the fire. What else could you do?"

He glances at me briefly. "I wasn't entirely fair to Emily, was I?" His voice is hollow, his expression flat.

"By choosing Mila over her? That didn't kill her."

"I certainly hope not."

"You did sleep with her, though?" I ask abruptly.

"We were all so close," he says in a quiet, very un-Chase-like voice. "Don't you think it started to get weird?"

"How?"

"You and Kennedy. Ryan on the periphery. Emily. Me. For years we were all like family and then suddenly—" He snaps his fingers. "Boom goes the dynamite." He pauses. "I loved Emily like a sister. Sometimes you confuse different types of love."

I wish I could have told Ryan that. Before he got so angry. "But you did love her?"

"Why are you pushing this?" He gives me an odd look.

"I just think it's weird. You had a girlfriend. Emily turned up dead."

"Jesus, Chelsea."

"Mila was here, and you slept with Emily." I look into his eyes. "You messed up. Everyone messes up and you did too. Say it, Chase."

He stares at me for a moment. "Okay. I did. *But* there was nothing sinister about it. If you want to accuse me of something, carpe diem."

"I don't. I just wanted to—"

"Ask me about my motive," he finishes. "Well, there you go. And if you're curious why I didn't run into a burning building to save my girlfriend, it's because by that point it was physically impossible. I don't know how it all went up so fast, but it did. I hope that's an acceptable excuse?"

"Yes. Sorry. Of course."

"Now can I ask you something? Why exactly do you have so many questions about the fire? I mean, I get that everyone has blank spots. We were in different rooms, there was smoke inhalation, sleep, no one exactly *sees* a gas leak. And it does seem the Hartfords did quite a job keeping the details under lock and key. But you really seem to know nothing. Like Jon Snow nothing." He looks at me expectantly. Suspiciously?

I edge around him uncomfortably. "I know what I witnessed. None of the rest of you saw what I saw. They told me I have post-traumatic stress disorder with severe insomnia and panic attacks. I have these intrusive thoughts. Like . . ." I push forward, head down, avoiding his gaze as he tightens his pace to match my stride. "Little movies of terrible things happening that just run on a loop. The theory was, the more I knew, the more intrusive thoughts I'd have, and the more detailed they would be. And the more panic attacks. And I'd think I was dying every day. And I wouldn't sleep. Which is all true. Kennedy asked me why I never sought this information out. Why I didn't ask my parents or a doctor or just read a newspaper. What happened in the fire." I take a deep breath. "But the truth is, I was in a scary place, Chase. I'm not magically better, but things were worse. They were a lot worse. And being back here . . . the not knowing is hurting me too." I stop and catch my breath.

He reaches out to me and pulls me into a bear hug. "When I say I didn't leave my room . . . I couldn't. I was so afraid something would happen. How . . . much can you handle now?"

"All of it. I have to. And then just take it one day at a time, you know?"

He puts an arm around me and we continue on. "Exactly. We don't need to hear all the details in a single night. As for me, to be honest, I might not have caught much more news coverage than you from my pizza cave. I didn't even hear about the gas leak, although I bet that makes Mila nervous."

"Because—" I mime lighting a cigarette.

He nods. "Exactly."

"You don't think she . . . ?"

"I know she didn't." He sets his jaw stubbornly.

"Kennedy thinks she wasn't invited. Do you think she would just show up?"

He looks at me. "Mila is always invited. I'm not leaving her behind ever again."

I blush. "I didn't mean to imply she isn't welcome. Kennedy didn't either. She just . . . has a theory that the person who made the game cards meant them to be about you, me, and Kennedy, because of some comment Mila made about the invitations. If she's right, it would make you the traitor by process of elimination. Which would mean neither you nor Mila is guilty."

"Oh," he says. "Well, I'm not going to argue with that."

"So if you don't know what started the fire, what about the boat?" Someone *has* to hold the key to deciphering the tarot clues.

He furrows his brow. "Yeah, some of us took the boat out earlier . . . Kennedy, Mila, and me. I can't remember anything notable happening. I think maybe we had drinks with Emily at the stone table when we got back. But you went to bed early right? Headache?"

I grab his arm. "So you do believe I was asleep when Emily came inside."

A look of understanding dawns on his face. "Chelsea, no

one thinks you locked Emily in the attic or anything. Everyone honestly believes this was an accident."

"Not Ryan."

Chase's expression darkens. "Right." The cell spot is close, almost in view. He takes a deep breath. "Look, I'm the last person who wanted to even consider this, but I don't see an alternative explanation anymore. Ryan's fucking with us. This entire weekend was a setup. He invited us here because he blames us for what happened and he's trying to scare us to death."

I shake my head. "He wouldn't do that."

"No, he wouldn't commit murder. This is catharsis. It's messed up, and I don't believe for a second that he would hurt any of us, but from everything you've said, he truly believes one of us killed Emily. Think about that. Then tell me someone else is more likely to be behind this."

I struggle to answer. "If. *If* someone did kill—"

"But who? Who would kill a friend? Who could live with themself after that? It would be like some kind of epic torture. Look at Macbeth. As humans, we're not designed to handle it. He thinks we did this thing. No one else makes sense."

I take his arm, stopping him. "But there *is* an alternate explanation, you just won't listen. It could be Emily that called us back here. Emily or . . . I don't know, a kind of distorted echo of Emily that drew us back to the lake, the attic, the cellar. It's like she's making us retrace our steps from that night."

He frowns as he starts to walk toward the clearing. "Why?"

"Because it forces us to face what we did." My head snaps up, and I run to his side just as he's reaching the edge of the clearing. "Because when we left the lake house, it got very comfortable living in denial over what happened, but we can't do that here. And she knows that because she knows us."

But Chase isn't listening anymore. He's staring into the empty clearing. "Shit." I gaze around. Soft pine needles blanket the damp earth, untouched by footprints. Up here, above the mossy rocks, we played pirates as children, painted toilet-roll telescopes and popped sunglass-lens eye patches. Later, we discovered this was the one spot at the lake house where we could call home or text a friend. Up farther, from the highest point, you could see over the rooftops, see the sun drain bloody sunsets into the lake or crack the earth to reveal a newborn phoenix rising from the depths.

Chase shouts Mila's name, but the fog seems to swallow it up. He drops onto the ground and leans against a tree, throwing his head back in frustration. "I must have missed her by one minute. I stopped to talk to you. When I went inside, I heard footsteps upstairs. I kept calling her name, but . . . I couldn't catch up. I failed her again." A chill runs down my spine. There it is again. Footsteps. Just like Mila heard earlier. He rubs his head as if to soothe a massive headache, smearing it with mud. Our hands are stained with dirt and scented with sap from climbing. We look like grave robbers. Maybe Mila's right. I do think in nightmares.

"I'm sorry," I say quietly. "She wanted to use her phone. I thought . . . It doesn't matter."

He rolls his head over to me. "What?"

I sigh. "You keep laughing at my theories."

He laughs again but not in an amused or mocking way. He laughs like it's the only sound left to make. "I'm sorry. I think my brain is broken." He eyes me. "Mila didn't think it was funny. You know, you got into her head a little bit with the ghost-whisperer stuff."

"So she *believed* me about Emily?"

"Not exactly—not about the ghosts. Maybe just the idea of haunting. I think she's spooked by the house itself. There are a lot of ways to be haunted. A place, a person, a memory."

"I don't think any of us believed in ghosts until tonight," I say, annoyed. It's the way people word things. Always so careful to separate themselves. Mila was never kicked out of school for admitting she thought about suicide. Spent a year shuttered away in a haze of pills. So she's allowed to believe whatever she wants.

He backs off. "I wasn't insinuating anything, Chels. I mean, come on. Look at what's happening." His eyes meet mine. "The invitation, the game, the attic door slamming shut. The lights and cars didn't cut themselves. We are not alone here. Don't you feel it even now?" That's the thing. Up here, cloaked in thick layers of fog, where no one could see us fall or hear us scream, I do feel it. The clearing is empty.

But we are not alone.

On the lake, too, there was someone, something. The shadow tumbling from *Summer's Edge*. The something stirring beneath. I take the tarot cards from my pocket and slowly turn them over in my hands. "Whatever Ryan is after, he genuinely believes Emily is still here, and is trying to communicate to him that she was killed, and wants him to find out how."

"Jesus," Chase whispers.

"There's more." I sift through the cards. "He thinks Emily is using tarot cards she made to give him clues. The cards are unsettling. Believe it or don't, but she *did* make them, which means she had certain feelings about us that I didn't know she had."

He looks at me expectantly. "How bad are they?"

I hand him his card. Chase in the clearing. He takes it slowly and stands, and as the moon breaks through a veil of fog, he's cast in an eerie pale blue light, mirroring Emily's sketch. And it hits me what the tarot card is showing just as he looks up, the blood drained from his face.

"It's me," he says hoarsely.

"Right here. With your phone."

He looks sick. "When did she draw this?"

I shudder. "Sometime before she died."

He grabs my hand and yanks me to my feet. "Come on."

I look up at him, alarmed. "What's the matter?"

"We have to find Mila and Kennedy and get as far away from here as possible." He stuffs the card into his pocket, and I slip the others into mine before he sees them and freaks out further.

"Can you please walk me through whatever is going on right now?"

He shakes his head as he pulls me rapidly through the trees, down into the thicker fog. "Stay close, okay? If you see Ryan again, shout." He glances back at me over his shoulder. "I don't know what he's capable of. And I don't want to know. But I promise you this—Ryan left these cards, not Emily. And they aren't clues. They're warnings."

24

Six candles burning in the dark
Find them fast before they spark
One is in the living room Chase chase
One in the garden where the flowers bloom Chelsea Emiles
One on the boat that bobs on the lake Kennedy Ryan
One in the room where we sleep and wake Ryan? chelsea
One in the attic over your head Emily Kennedy
One in the cellar where you'll find one dead. Mila mila

25

"I don't understand." I double over to catch my breath as we reach the bottom of the hill.

Chase waits for me impatiently. "Look, I don't know how she found out, but the picture on that card is between me and Ryan. If he gave that card to you, he wanted it to get back to me. It's part of the little game he's playing."

I straighten up, wheezing. "Then tell me what it means. What does it have to do with last year?"

He pauses. "It's personal."

"Not if it's about Emily," I say, probably a little more sharply than I need to. But I'm done with secrets.

"He's mad at me for making a phone call." Chase walks briskly toward the house, and I push myself after him, but I'm exhausted.

"A phone call?" I can't keep pace with him.

He whirls around to face me. "Yes, a phone call. So it's not a secret, and it's not a lie, and we can just—" He takes the card out of his pocket and tears it into pieces, tossing them into the road and grinding them into the pavement with his sneakers. "Gone." I stare at him, a little afraid. Chase isn't one to lose his cool.

"I believe you," I say.

"Good." He looks shaken. He turns back to the house and stops short. The front door is wide open. He breaks into a run, shouting for Kennedy and Mila. I walk slowly, terror creeping over me. The house, that giant wooden box full of memories and ghosts, fills me with more dread than the uncertainty of the fog. It looms, mocking, darker than the dark, seeing with shuttered eyes, a stern, unforgiving reminder of my fatal failure as a friend. Maybe I deserve to be haunted. I hear Emily in the attic, begging for help, the pounding on the floorboards. I don't want to go back inside. But when I reach the door, Chase reappears, his face ashen. "Kennedy's gone," he says. He holds a note that reads: *Took the boat to find Mila. Meet me out back.*

The house is filled with lit candles, flickering and filling the space with an eerie light, giving the odd feeling that everything is moving, even the walls, the ground beneath our feet. I look over Chase's shoulder. The back door is wide open too. I start to follow him out but halt abruptly halfway across the room. Something doesn't seem right. Like one of those drawings in the *Highlights* magazines you read as a kid in the dentist's office. A missing chair leg here, a stairway leading to a blank wall. I turn in a slow circle until my eyes rest on the walls and zero in on the thermostat, then travel down the thin wire to the dormant metal rectangles lining the walls. The baseboard heaters. The electric baseboard heaters. Ryan's voice echoes in my head: *An entire house burned to the ground because of a gas leak.* My heart begins to beat faster as I walk in a daze through the kitchen, placing one hand on the cool coils of the electric stove. I walk faster toward the cellar, the dreaded cellar, and force myself down, down into the mold and mildew, past the acrid scent of rotten eggs, the vision of rotting rabbits, to the water heater, where the access panel has already been removed. Someone got here before me. No pilot light. No flame. The water is heated by electricity, not gas. I search the room frantically. There's an electric meter. But no gas one. And on the meter is a worn sticker with a wind turbine logo and the following words in tiny print: *Thank you for using clean energy!*

There wasn't a gas leak. There's no gas line to this house.

I turn around and rush up the stairs, my heart pounding in my ears.

The cold air hits me like the slap of a wave as I rush back out into the dark, soundless night. There are candles here, too, some put out by the fog, but one flickering in the garden catches my eye, and my heart drops into my stomach. Another tarot card. I pick it up numbly, and my breath is drawn out of my lungs. It's me. My paper twin stands on the dock, mouthless, eyes wide open. She stares out at something in the lake casting an enormous shadow that stretches back to the house. The handwritten caption says: Queen of Cups: beware the girl who sees the truth and speaks none.

I crumple it and throw it on the ground. "Chase!" He turns to me. "Where did you first hear the story about the gas leak?" I meet him halfway down the boardwalk, out of breath.

He looks surprised. "From you."

"It's a lie. The house isn't powered by gas. Ryan told me that story because he knew I didn't know anything. He wanted to control the narrative."

"Why?"

"Kennedy was right. He wanted to turn us against one

another. Look for a human spark. Mila's lighter, Kennedy's candles. This house is old. The wiring is old. He won't accept an accident, so he invented a crime and he used me to plant it in our heads."

Chase examines his card. "I knew it."

I feel sick. I should have known. I should have doubted. "I don't even know if I believe Emily made those cards. He could have faked them. And he could have faked Kennedy's handwriting on the invitations. Forgeries can be very effective when they play off your expectations. I expected him to be the good guy. That's his game." And I was just a pawn. A player piece. Pathetic.

"I wanted to say I was sorry," Chase says quietly. "But he doesn't want an apology. He wants revenge. And he's still here. I know it. He could be watching us right now."

We begin down the boardwalk together, but I freeze when I see a shadowy figure ahead. Chase grabs my arm, but I find myself drawn forward. The boat is gone, and Kennedy with it, but the life raft floats just beyond the dock. Not the raft from the boat—the extra one the Hartfords store in the boathouse. Kennedy never found her. Mila stands shivering, gripping an oar to her chest, her bags at her feet.

Chase rushes forward. "Oh, thank god."

But she holds up a hand and he halts. Her long hair falls over her face in a dark, tangled curtain, her head bowed, shoulders hunched. For a second I think she's crying, but when she raises her head, her eyes are dry. "We were wrong about everything. Everything we thought. Everything we've done." Her voice is slow, and she looks dazed, almost drugged. "And we are going to pay for it."

A chill runs down my spine. "What do you mean, 'everything we've done'?"

Chase looks at her nervously. "Mila. We can talk about this later." He jerks his head toward me. Like he's warning her not to say something, not to show something.

Mila laughs. "More secrets. How could that possibly backfire?" Her voice takes on a bitter tone. "But we can't upset Chelsea. She's *delicate*."

I glare at Chase. It's another one of those words people use. It sounds pretty, but it's unbearably cruel. And it isn't true. "Secrets? What is she talking about?"

"Nothing," Chase says sharply, uncharacteristic of him. He tries to pull Mila away from the edge of the water, but she slumps back like a stubborn toddler refusing to leave a toy store.

She grins at me and hands me the slick, mildew-covered oar. "Dead things, Chelsea. Dead things." Then she looks Chase square in the eye. "And if we survive the night, I'm telling."

The tension in the air is as heavy as the fog. "Mila, Ryan's the one behind all of this," I say. "He made up the story about the gas leak. This is all his revenge."

But she barely reacts. "Great job, Chelsea. Now tell me. Revenge for what? Have you cracked the case yet? Who kissed the killer?"

I falter. None of that was real. Right? "What happened to you out there?"

"Nothing worth telling, apparently." Mila pulls her lighter out of her pocket absently, ignites it, and stares at the little dancing flame. "It doesn't matter what we do now anyway," she says. "We're fucked."

"Mila," Chase says again. "Enough."

Mila flicks her lighter shut. "Delicate."

I'm three seconds away from exploding, and that can't happen now. Not when Mila is so close to giving in. I use the old trick, picturing a glass jar, the kind Mr. Hartford builds tiny ships in, a hurricane swirling inside. Imagine striking a match, holding the flame to a ring of wax, sealing the jar airtight. Pressure within, silence without. But the words *Shut up* escape.

She shakes her head. "Have any of you ever really faced consequences in your lives?"

"Mila, please." There's pleading in Chase's voice now.

"No. No more coddling. Not for any of you. You all ran off and left me to take the fall. I was the one dealing with reporters, detectives, private investigators. No one, not a single person, believed our story."

I feel like I've been smashed into pieces. *Our story.* "It wasn't a story," I say numbly.

"People are going to remember me as a murderer for the rest of my life. And you thank me by lying to me. To all of us. "

"You're wrong," Chase says. "I haven't been lying. Maybe I forced myself to suppress a few things as a defense mechanism or something. But *none* of us is a murderer. You know that." Chase's eyes are fixed on me.

The word *delicate* vibrates through my bones at an alarming pitch. "If that's true, why is she calling it a story?"

"You're really living in a total state of denial, aren't you?" Mila says in disbelief. "Even now, surrounded by memories."

"Don't be a hypocrite," Chase says quietly. "All of us are guilty of turning a head to certain unpleasant truths."

I stare at him, my sense of horror growing. What truths? "I was completely isolated from the outside world last year. Maybe I didn't dig for the truth, but it's not like it was at my fingertips."

"What about the Summer of Swallows?" Mila says. "The year before the fire."

"How is that even relevant? Every year is the same," I say impatiently.

Chase gives me the look I hate the most. Pity. "Not exactly the same."

Mila stands and heaves her suitcase up. "It's Kennedy's fault we're in this mess. I'm not waiting for her. Chase, you can get your stuff or I can walk to town without you."

"We're leaving together," Chase says firmly. He shivers. "It's probably not a bad idea to grab our things, though. And maybe wait at the end of the driveway."

"Kennedy said to wait here," I say with a rush of panic. "Have you seen her? She took the boat to find you."

Mila casts Chase a long look. "Yeah, I saw her out on the boat. And I sure as hell didn't stop to say hello."

I stare at her, taken aback. "Why? We have to find her."

She looks exhausted. "You still believe everything Kennedy tells you, Chelsea?"

A chill runs through me. "I have to believe it."

"The only thing I have to do is go home." She turns away wearily.

I suddenly feel an even deeper aversion to the house. I grab Chase's hand as Mila walks ahead. "Tell me the truth," I whisper. "What did you see in the tarot card? It scared you. And

Mila saw something on the water. She wasn't accusing you of hiding things before. Or blaming Kennedy."

He avoids my eyes. "It brought up a bad memory, that's all. It doesn't change anything. It was still an accident. It wasn't Kennedy's fault. Or Mila's, or mine, or yours. Sometimes people just need someone to blame."

"What about Ryan?" I add anxiously.

He sighs, and I think I can detect a hint of bitterness in it. Even in a moment like this, the tension between them is palpable. "No one ever suspected Ryan."

A chill runs down my spine. "Should they?"

He doesn't answer. But as he disappears into the house after Mila, I see a flash of movement in the corner of my eye and whirl around to find myself face-to-face with Ryan. His hair and clothes are disheveled, his expression stony, and he looms over me like a shadow.

"You tell me, Chelsea," he says darkly. "Should you?"

26

There's something I should tell you, before it's too late.
I really do love you.
Every last, damned one of you.
And you are all damned.
Every last one of you.

27

I glance back desperately at Chase and Mila, but the door swings shut behind them.

Ryan stares down at me coldly. "I didn't think you'd break so easily."

"Break?" I take a nervous step backward toward the house.

"I trusted you, and you sided with them." He laughs bitterly. "Why would I expect any more from you? Kennedy says jump, and you sprint for a cliff."

I feel frozen. This isn't the Ryan I know anymore. He was never cruel. "That's not fair. You were the one who lied to me about the gas leak. Why, Ryan?"

"Maybe I did it to test you. If you bought the lie, you couldn't have known the truth, could you?"

"But why play all these games? You know none of us would have hurt Emily on purpose. Every one of us was destroyed by her death."

"Then what did happen?" he pushes.

I struggle for an answer. "The house. There's something wrong with it."

"Houses don't set themselves on fire. They don't murder their friends."

"Neither do we."

His jaw tightens, and for a moment, I can feel the sharpness of his pain. I want to be able to comfort him. To make everything okay. But things have become too damaged.

He looks up at me. "Face it, Chelsea. You picked sides a long time ago. And you chose the wrong side."

Tears sting my eyes. "There are no sides."

"There have always been sides. Long before now. Before the fire, before the boat."

I think back to what Mila said. "You mean the Summer of Swallows? I don't. . . ." I haven't thought about that summer in ages. I've been laser-focused on last summer. But before I can pick through my memories of lake-house summers to separate it out, Ryan interrupts me with a glare of impatient disappointment. "Stop testing me. What *happened* on the boat?"

He laughs dully. "Come on, Chelsea. You know this one."

But I don't. I hate sailing, the unsteadiness. The feeling of standing on a tilting, shifting earth, like trying to balance on a spinning top.

"You were there, weren't you?" He stares intently.

"No, I wasn't." I wouldn't have gone out the night of the fire. Chase said I didn't. I don't remember it because it didn't happen.

"There's a difference between not being able to remember and not being able to admit the truth," he says quietly.

"You're lying," I say. Ryan, my Ryan, is lying to me. "You lied about the gas leak."

"And it worked."

"Because I believed you?" I feel sick. "You betrayed your friends."

"Did I?" He looks at me sharply. "When did you start thinking you were better than me?" His voice is chilling, whisper soft. "You're the one who turned on me."

I search for something familiar in his eyes, but I've lost him. My Ryan is gone. "If I'm the traitor, tell me why you came back for Mila instead of Emily?"

"Instead of you, you mean," he says. "Right?"

"No." Yes. No. The guilt is razor-sharp, ice-cold. I hate that I want to be the one he came back for. Emily died, but we were both left behind. We were both left behind.

"I didn't," he says. "It was some Boy Scout fireman. I didn't come back for any of you. Feel better?"

"No," I whisper. I start to walk back toward the house, tears streaming down my face, but I hear footsteps pounding behind me and turn, fear spiking in my chest.

He grabs my arm and looks into my eyes. "Wait. Don't go back in the house." I can't read his expression, but he says it with such urgency that my heart begins to race.

My voice catches in my throat. "Why?"

"Because no matter how mad you make me, I never want to watch you die."

I stare at him, frightened. "Why would you say that? Did you do something?"

"I didn't do anything. I told you, Chelsea—you picked the wrong side."

But he's looking up at the lake house with an expression of such pure hatred that I wrench my arm away from him and run. Right into the heart of the monster.

I push the door open slowly, afraid of what I might find. "Chase?" Silence. The candle on the living room table is burned down almost to the bottom, but someone has placed more around the room, filling it with eerie, flickering light. The cellar door is slightly ajar again, which makes me shudder. I run upstairs and burst into Kennedy's room to find the candle lit and the balcony doors open, fog spilling into the room. There's a long, low creaking sound behind me. A flood of hot air. Whispers, or maybe the rustling of leaves. *But we're inside and the windows are in front of me.* I grip the balcony door handles, knuckles bloodless, heart beating so fast I lose the sensation of individual beats, a horrifying hum in my chest, and I realize I'm holding my breath. *Dare: Hold your breath for one minute.* I feel them watching, eyes on the back of my neck. *Dare: Hold your breath for two minutes.* Footsteps, slow as death. *Dare: Hold your breath for three minutes, six minutes, twelve minutes, forever.* I turn around to see the attic stairs are unfolded and clap my hand over my mouth to stifle a scream.

"Chels?"

Kennedy's voice from the attic snaps me out of it. I hesitantly approach and climb a couple of steps. "Kennedy?" She doesn't answer. I turn away for just a second, and in that blink of time, the ladder snaps up like a snarling pair of jaws, and a terrifying weightlessness surges through me. It happens so quickly I don't hear myself scream. I shoot upward, falling up the stairs, the world upside down, soundless and breathless, and then down, hard, flat on my back on the attic floor. The door slams shut behind me.

I lie there for a moment, stunned, afraid to breathe. The air feels even more stifling than before, thick and suffocating, like a gaseous form of hot wood. Terror solidifies every cell in my body. Someone has placed another candle where I took the last one, along with the flip-book, in the center of the room. And they've added another creepy touch: a chalk outline of a body in bright red with little spiky lines coming out from it like in a child's drawing of the sun. I run to the window to shout for help and freeze. Ryan is standing outside, looking up at me with an expression I can't read. He lifts his hand in a heavy, resigned wave and then turns away.

One in the attic, one in the cellar. The voice is so soft, I can't tell if it's a memory or a sound. I am in ruins. I cannot escape her twilight voice. Emily is everywhere. She speaks through me in the lucid in-between. The between that is growing. That thrives on forbidden luxuries like sharpened pencils and pulpy wood, on postcards and newspapers, old books and recipes, pine trees and tarot cards, coffins and rope and bones and skin and everything that burns. There's a sudden crash somewhere below, and I'm jerked back into the present. I shake myself. No. Not Emily. She wouldn't turn Ryan against us. She wouldn't do any of this. None of us are monsters.

There's a loud banging on the trapdoor, and then Kennedy's head pokes through the door and she stretches her arms out to me. "Quickly." I follow her down the stairs and into the master bedroom, locking the door behind us.

"Where were you?" I tiptoe to a window overlooking the backyard.

"I was searching the lake for Mila." She starts throwing clothes into a suitcase. "We're getting out of here."

"Ken. I talked to Mila. I know you're all hiding something from me."

She turns to face me, her chin trembling. "Damn it, Mila." She paces back and forth rapidly. "Tell me why you want to know the truth *so* much. What is so special about the truth?"

I stare at her, bewildered. "Because Emily deserves justice."

She shakes her head. "This has nothing to do with Emily, Chelsea. It's about you. Why do *you* need to know the truth? Do you know what I think about the truth? I think truth breaks people. It twists them in knots until they snap. It turns them against one another. Truth is a poison, and we treat it like an antidote. It doesn't change the past. It doesn't bring anyone back from the dead. It just rips open old wounds."

I back away from her. "Why are you so angry?"

"You can't even see when your friends are trying to protect you, Chelsea!"

"I don't need to be protected."

She zips up her suitcase. "The less you knew, the better. That's how it was with Emily. When the truth hurts, friends lie." Her voice keeps rising in pitch as her speech becomes more rapid. "Everyone does it."

"Not me."

She stops short. "You lie all the time, even to yourself."

"I do not."

"Please, Chels. You lie to yourself about Ryan constantly. And then you lie to everyone else."

I stare at her. "You aren't just talking about tonight."

"No."

"Well, I'm not lying anymore. So why can't you tell me the truth?" I grab my bag, heart pounding.

"Because I'm afraid of what will happen if I do." Her eyes

are glassy and vacant, and her voice is dull. She looks like a pretty zombie. It's terrifying. "You knew, deep down. Didn't you? It's why you came back. Guilt."

"Survivor guilt," I whisper.

"What do you remember?"

"Being surrounded by smoke and flames. Trying to get to Emily. I did try."

She squeezes my hand and sighs. "I know you did."

"But I still left her behind. That was my choice." I always wonder if I'm lying to myself about this part. People lie to themselves about this sort of thing. It's human nature, self-preservation. I've read about it. I tell myself that I tried to reach Emily for a reasonable amount of time. But the smoke was thick, and the ground was scorching. Flames had made their way in through the open bedroom door. I heard Emily in the attic, crying for help. The trapdoor was closed, and the string that pulls it open was missing. Missing like someone had removed it, like maybe the fire *wasn't* an accident. I panicked, shouted up at her to jump on it. Throw all her weight against it. Try anything. But I knew there was no way to open it from the inside. And from below, there was nothing I could do to open the door either. There were no chairs in the room, and I didn't have time to push Kennedy's bed or a dresser all the way across the burning floor to the closet to try to reach up. I told myself that my best bet was to get out the window to safety and tell the rescuers that Emily was trapped in the attic.

I had to.

But I didn't really *have to*.

I chose to.

I chose to save myself.

I chose to leave Emily behind.

Maybe I never really tried to save her at all.

I look at Kennedy suddenly. "I know why I feel guilty. What about you? Why does Mila think all of this is your fault? And what does it have to do with the summer before last? The fire couldn't have been an accident if it was a year coming."

"I swear to you that to my knowledge, the fire *was* an accident." Such a carefully worded sentence. What we don't know can't incriminate us.

"Kennedy. I know *something* happened. I know about Chase's phone call."

She flinches and stills. "On the night of the murder?" My heart drops into my stomach. *The night of the murder.* She called it a *murder.* "You wanted the truth."

Kennedy's words reverberate throughout my body with my racing pulse. *Truth is a poison. The night of the murder. Your friends are trying to protect you.*

"I thought I did," I whisper. Time slips backward, and I hear Ryan telling me again that I chose the wrong side.

"What if I told you that Mila set the whole thing in motion?" Kennedy says. "Or that I came up with the cover story? What if we really are guilty? Do you really want to know?"

And then, as if in response, the sound of doors slamming echoes through the house, one after another. Windows slam shut, quick and sharp as guillotines. I hear Mila scream somewhere nearby. I rush to the bedroom door and wrench it open.

28

This is how I'll say goodbye:
Not with words.
Not with a kiss.
But with a promise.
You will remember me forever.

29

Chase is standing there, his backpack slung over his shoulder. "The front door is stuck."

"We have to get out," Mila says, her voice rising in a panic.

"Together," Chase adds.

"Now we're a team?" Kennedy glares at Mila.

Mila returns the expression. "This is still your fault."

I can feel Kennedy snap. She slams the bedroom door against the wall. "You were never invited."

"Yes, I was." Mila stands in the open door, backlit by a half dozen flickering candles.

"Not by me." Kennedy sounds desperate.

"We shouldn't turn against each other." Chase glances over his shoulder nervously. "Please, let's go before something else happens. I don't know if this is just Ryan anymore."

"You think?" Mila snaps.

There's a thundering sound above us, footsteps in the attic, the trapdoor slamming shut. Kennedy's door swings open and the pounding sound of footsteps continues, straight past us—*through us*—down the stairs and into the living room. Kennedy grips my arm so tightly I go numb. There's an unsettling silence, then the unmistakable creaking of the cellar door.

"Maybe we deserve it," I say. Some more than others. Maybe not. I don't know anymore.

"No!" Mila pounds the wall with her fist. "*We* don't deserve it." She's staring at Kennedy furiously, but there are tears in her eyes. "All of this is because of her."

"It's not that simple." Kennedy turns to Chase frantically. "Chase, you know it isn't."

"He blames all of us," Chase says grimly. "It may have been an accident, but we all played some little part." That's the story. Isn't it? The lie. None of us are monsters. None of us are killers.

"Then why did Kennedy use the word *murder*?"

The others stare at me, wide-eyed, and then at Kennedy.

"Because it was murder in Ryan's eyes," Kennedy says. "That's all that counts."

"You can debate this as long as you want, Scooby gang. I'm leaving before he finishes his little revenge game. Or whatever this is." Mila takes a step toward the stairs and then swivels around to face us one last time. "We all know this was never about who's doing this to us. It's about what was done to them. Chelsea, I don't know what those pills did to your brain, but flush them and wake the hell up because your girl-friend is going to get you killed." Chase's jaw drops. Mila turns to Kennedy. "Have fun in court when the Joiners sue you for wrongful death." She turns, flipping her hair over her shoulder, and starts briskly down the hallway.

Kennedy charges after Mila, footsteps echoing through the hall, stomping down the stairs. "This was a group activity, friend. Take a good, long look in the mirror. *You* came here uninvited. You set all of this in motion because you had to see the stars, and now we have a body count." I reach the bottom of the stairs close behind Chase to find Kennedy advancing toward Mila. The candle on the living room table is down to just a flicker, and it's hard to see. I know the lake house like my own home. But Mila's only been here a handful of times. She can't walk the halls with her eyes closed. Play murder in the dark. Look for spare matches in a power outage.

And she can't see that she's about to back into the open cellar door.

I grasp Chase's arm, choking on my own voice. "Say," I whisper. It's all I can manage for some reason. "Say. Say. Say." Panic swirls up in me like a cyclone. Chase looks down at me, momentarily distracted. "Say, say." I squeeze my eyes shut. God, why isn't my mouth working?

Kennedy stands nose-to-nose with Mila, her expression hardened. "You come into my house and break my rules. Lie to my friends and turn them against me. It's time for you to go."

I part my lips and it's like a bubble bursts. "Cellar," I gasp.

Mila opens her mouth to answer, then swings her arms out. In the darkness, she's backed up all the way to the top of the tall, narrow staircase leading down to the cellar, and just stepped one half step too far. Chase makes a grab for her but comes up short, his hands grasping at air. Kennedy freezes in place. I push her aside and reach for Mila just as her weight shifts and she swings down out of our reach.

Time slows. The function of my eyes is redefined. My eardrums filter out the sounds of clocks and plumbing and blood and chemicals moving in my body, so my heartbeat is replaced by the sound of her body thump. *Thu-thump. Thu-thump. Thu-*

thump. Thu-thump. Thu-thump. Thu-thump. Then silence.

Kennedy turns, her mouth unhinged, her face ghostly. She shakes her head wordlessly.

Chase clasps his hands over his face, then slides them down to peek over the top.

Mila lies in a sprawling heap, her hair covering her face, her arm bent underneath her. An oily halo of black surrounds her head in the shadowy darkness. Not blood. Blood is bright and slow and unrealistic. It's a prop. That's all.

"She isn't moving," I whisper.

There's a sudden flare of light behind us, and I whirl around. The candle has finally burned to the bottom, and I watch with horror as the cards from the board game ignite as if made of some hyperflammable substance. A sudden wind blows the door open, and the cards go swirling into the air like leaves lifted from a bonfire. As each card makes contact with a surface, a brilliant blaze blooms, spreading with almost supernatural speed.

"Shit." Kennedy runs to the kitchen. "The extinguisher's missing," she shouts in a panic.

A sickening sensation of déjà vu floods through me. Chase takes a step toward the cellar, but the door slams shut. He grabs the knob and wrenches it, kicks the door, turns to me with terror in his eyes. "It's happening again. The fire. Exactly like before. The doors were stuck."

Before I can speak, a wave of heat rises behind us. Kennedy screams. Chase and I are separated from her and the door by a wall of fire. Chase drops to the floor and I follow.

"Someone did this," he says. "There's no way a fire goes up this quickly without a serious accelerant."

I hear a familiar, horrible, crushing sound.
Hands knocking.
Emily screaming from the attic.
Chase was right.
It's happening again.
Exactly the same way.

30

Before you ask about second chances,
Remember the Summer of Swallows.

31

The lake house hasn't changed in a lifetime at least, and neither have my friends. Chelsea and I arrive almost exactly at the same time, and the moment we pull up in my father's BMW, Chelsea spills out of the car and stretches her arms wide as if to embrace the whole of it: the enormous log mansion, the stately pines, the glittering lake beyond.

"This is home," she sighs. She flops her arms at her sides and spins around in her sandals, laughing. "Kennedy Ellis Hartford."

I step into the sun and lift my hair, feeling my shoulders begin to bake already. It doesn't take very long. My skin is so pale I tend to flash fry. A damp lake breeze infused with wood smoke and pine whips my long hair and white linen dress up behind me like a sail. It smells like heaven.

Chelsea reaches her hand out to me. "You look like an avenging angel."

"I feel like Marilyn." I stretch an arm out to her and let her pull me into an embrace and cover my cheek and neck with dozens of kisses. I'm always shy about PDA in front of my parents, but I linger for a moment in Chelsea's arms, comforted by the familiar scent—warm strawberries and old spice—before retrieving my suitcase from the trunk.

Ryan's car pulls into the driveway, and I breathe a sigh

of relief as he and Emily step out into the sun, opposite sides of the same coin. Emily bursts forward while Ryan dips back into the car to carry their bags. Even though we just saw each other yesterday, Emily and I embrace and jump up and down like we haven't seen each other in a year. Chelsea flicks a wave, and a hint of an eye roll, and I can't tell whether she feels left out or thinks we're being silly. But this weekend is tradition, the most sacred tradition of all, and Chelsea sometimes takes things too seriously. Everything is a competition, even friendship. But then I see her eyes wander over to Ryan, a secret kind of smile playing over her lips, and it's my turn to lose the magic of the moment.

I don't like the way he looks at my girlfriend.

"Hey, handsome." I wrap my arms around his neck and plant a kiss on his cheek. He flushes bright red. Emily cocks her head at me and raises an eyebrow, and Chelsea turns abruptly and heads for the house. I grab her hand, though, and she turns back reluctantly.

Ryan reaches for her backpack and slings it onto his shoulder, which is already weighed down with several of Emily's bags. She's a fashion junkie and talented artist, headed for RISD when we graduate next year, and probably New York after that. She designs and makes her own clothes and insists on several costume changes per day. She always looks fabulous, and I let her dress me up like a doll from time to time. Chelsea sometimes wears her designs too, but she has her own inimitable style. She likes to drag me out of bed to wander through thrift stores and pick through yard sales on early Sunday mornings before the church ladies have descended and mine them for vintage dresses, scarves, blouses, cardigans, jewelry, even glasses. Whatever catches her eye, she can do something with. Emily is high fashion, and Chelsea is a junkyard scavenger. Maybe not a junkyard. But certainly a yard of junk.

"You don't have to," I tell Ryan, slipping him my suitcase too.

He takes it with a forced smile. "Of course I do."

Chelsea takes back her bag apologetically. "Sorry. I've got it."

Emily selects a small duffel from Ryan and heads into the house. "Swimsuits first," she calls over her shoulder. Chelsea heads after her, waving for us to follow. But Mrs. Joiner is still hovering in her ancient pea-green Volkswagen. As usual, my parents have whisked away the suitcases and groceries and disappeared into the house. My guests, my responsibility. I'm the hostess. With all the perks it entails. Food serving, vomit wiping, friend wrangling. Usually I don't have to babysit parents, though.

"How was the drive?" I turn and wave to Mrs. Joiner, who sticks a hand out of the car window to wave back at me. My parents don't come out of the house to greet her, and she doesn't get out of the car to say hello. She just watches us walk to the porch, then backs out of the driveway and leaves.

"It was fine," Ryan says.

"Your mother okay?"

He opens the door for me. "Women and children first."

The house smells like it always does when we walk in the door, warm and wooden and inviting. My mother bustles around in the kitchen, filling the refrigerator with clinking bottles, dropping ice into glasses, and crumpling empty cardboard grocery bags. My father is already out back working on the boat. I start up the stairs just as I hear gravel crunching in the driveway again. Chelsea and Emily begin to stampede down toward me, already in swimsuits, smelling of coconut sunscreen. Emily is holding her long, sandy hair above her head, and Chelsea is running, laughing, trying to rub in a big white spot of sunscreen on Emily's back.

Ryan sighs and kicks at my insole, and I almost topple over. "Chase est arrivé."

But as we pile onto the porch and Chase parks his car, something unexpected happens. Chase bounds out of the car with his customary *Every day is summer* grin at the precise moment that the passenger door swings open and a tall, tanned girl in a tiny dress and doubtful smile steps out. She flicks her bangs out of her eyes and sticks a cigarette between her lips, and I start hyperventilating.

Emily grabs my arm with one hand and Chelsea's with the other. "Who the hell is that?" she whispers.

"Ohhhh shit," Ryan whispers back.

Chase slings an arm around her shoulder casually and kisses her neck in a way that makes me cringe. "Okay if I bring a guest, Ken?"

But it's not really up to me. The house isn't mine. It's not even my mother's or father's. The house has always belonged to others, before us, maybe even before my grandfather. I still think of them—the quiet people—by the names I first used for them when I was a toddler, which makes them seem silly, but none of them have ever spoken, and for all I know, they don't have names. They may be cross-dimensional glimpses of some parallel universe, something Chelsea would absolutely adore.

Or some record skip in the space-time continuum.

The truth is, though, they don't look like glimpses.

They look dead.

They were clearest, most tangible, when I was young. Like some cosmic transmitter was perfectly in tune, beaming them through an invisible screen, or maybe beaming me to them. I could reach out and touch a cold hand in a game of pat-a-cake or play a game of catch. They faded over time into pastel shimmers, then cool spots, like in the movies, and finally to just a faint sense, difficult to describe, but familiar as my own skin. I do still feel them. I know when they're pleased or angry or when they simply disapprove.

Well. Everyone knows when they're angry.

They just don't know that they know.

They notice the broken dishes, feel things somehow slip out of their hands, or a sudden burst of emotion as if from nowhere. Everyone notices the power blinking out for seemingly the millionth time. It's impossible to miss something like that.

But only I know why.

It's dangerous to make them angry. They're summoned by anger, and I've learned over time to keep the peace in this house in order to pacify them. They don't like it when we fight. They don't like it at all.

But they weren't always a threat.

My parents used to look at me oddly as a child when I had tea parties with the backward girl and the blue lady or chased butterflies with the crushed man. I stopped mentioning them after my parents shipped me off to that awful school, where there were silent, ice-cold faces peering around every corner. A lot of people die in older institutions. I've learned not to talk about these things. Even to people like Chelsea, people with bright, open minds and bright, open hearts. Because believing opens up worlds of possibilities. But I don't believe. I know. And knowing is dangerous. Because they don't want to be known. Because no one really wants to know about them. And because if you do say a word, sooner or later people who don't believe find out—people with the power to send you away from everyone and everything you love. And truth isn't worth losing people like Chelsea. Nothing is worth losing her. And nothing is worth losing your home. Dead people know that better than anyone. They're fiercely protective of their homes. And right now I'm extremely nervous about Chase bringing an uninvited friend, because the real hosts of the lake house are highly particular about their guests.

And they aren't pleased.

32

The attic is sweltering. It's about eight thousand times hotter than it is outside. Chelsea and Emily and I sit in our usual arrangement on layers of towels, surrounded by a fortress of suitcases. Before us are an array of cold drinks and a deck of tarot cards. We used to hide from Chase and Ryan up here when we were little. It's the only place they wouldn't follow us. They couldn't stand the heat. We were made of tougher stuff. We would spread out towels, strip to our swimsuits, sip frozen drinks, and whisper secrets about love and the future and dark truths no one else could ever find out because it might ruin us. Emily read our tarot cards, and I read scenes from my mother's romance novels. These were the topics we never discussed with Chase and Ryan. It would have been coy on Chase's part and depressed on Emily's, because she has always been into him, and he has never wanted her back. Ryan liked Chelsea, even as kids, but she was always mysterious about it. In a way, I don't think Emily would ever have forgiven her for choosing her brother over her. Not in a romantic sense. Just as a matter of fact. You couldn't spend more time with Ryan than with Emily, because we were Emily's friends first. Ryan was the tagalong. The secondary friend. The extra seat at the table.

Now Emily keeps shuffling and reshuffling the tarot cards,

insisting every time she begins to deal that she made a mistake.

"Her name is Mila," Chelsea says in a hushed tone. We have to speak quietly up here because the sound carries down to the second floor, but it's still the most private place on the property. She reaches for Emily's hand and gives it a concerned squeeze, and I feel a ribbon of warmth encircle us. Chelsea is chaos where I am order, but Chelsea is safety and loyalty and love.

This is how I fell in love with her. *After* we broke up, I told Emily we couldn't do the lake house anymore because it would be too awkward, but I didn't know how to tell Chelsea. It was hard enough breaking up with her, and I couldn't face her again. Emily said she'd take care of it. For some inexplicable reason, she took it upon herself to tell Chelsea that I said some precious family heirloom had gone missing and one of my friends must have seen it, or moved it, or borrowed it or something. Chelsea, in high-dramatic fashion, had shown up at our doorstep in the pouring rain, and informed my mother that she wasn't a thief, she wasn't afraid of our family, she didn't care what anyone said about her, I was a liar, and she loved me anyway.

The problem with Chelsea is how she jumps to conclusions that aren't there.

But the second she said the words, I realized that I did love her. Unfortunately, those words also sparked an all-out war within our group. I naturally assumed that Emily had told her I accused Chelsea of stealing from my family. Emily was furious that I was angry at her instead of Chelsea. Chase, my oldest friend, naturally took my side, and of course Ryan took hers.

Chelsea sort of folded into herself, and I died inside. I tried passing her note after note, but she refused to speak to me until finally, about half a year later, I showed up on Chelsea's doorstep in the freezing snow and, when she opened the door, told her she wasn't a thief, I wasn't afraid of my family, I didn't care what anyone said about me, she was a liar too, and I'd do anything to win her back.

You know what? It worked.

"When did he have time to get a girlfriend?" Emily's face is streaked with charcoal lines. She doesn't wear a lot of makeup, but dark eyeliner on her lower lid is her signature. It's an unfortunate choice on sad days.

"He didn't," Chelsea says. "Not that I know of. Ryan said they weren't really dating." I swallow a thousand questions. When did Chelsea and Ryan have a chance to talk about Chase and Mila? Five seconds. It only takes five seconds to look away, to stop paying attention, and secrets start spreading like rot. I blame myself for not paying attention. Things happen when you aren't paying attention. And who can you blame but yourself? Chelsea continues. "They met at an away game, and it was kind of a one- or two-time thing. That's why none of us heard about it. You know Chase. He doesn't kiss and tell."

Emily's shoulders drop. "So they . . . just kissed?"

How to put this gently. "Do you think he would have brought her here to hold hands and sip lemonade on the porch?" Another thought occurs immediately. "Oh god, do you think he's planning to use the lake house as his personal motel? He has his own weekend home. Much closer by." I doubt that will sit well. And I stand behind the quiet people. The house deserves to be respected. Loved as a home.

"Yeah," Chelsea says. "With his parents."

"Ugh, what a dick. No, that's not happening." I take Emily's hand. "Chase is not having sex this weekend. I promise you that. You have my sword."

"And my axe," Chelsea growls, imitating the dwarf in the *Fellowship of the Ring* movie.

Emily giggles. "I don't want him to not have sex. I want him to have sex. Just not with the intruder."

"Yeah. Well. Let Operation Get Rid of the Intruder begin," Chelsea says cheerfully.

"Mmm. Okay. Let's not let this get out of hand," I say. Chelsea loves projects and Emily is . . . passionate. For all I know, Mila is a perfectly sweet person, although I seriously resent the fact that she showed up uninvited, and Chase for bringing a guest without asking, although so far the quiet people don't seem to object to her. If he'd asked first? Totally different scenario. Though I would have said no. Because of the quiet ones. And Emily. And loyalty. And friendship.

Being hostess, even as a proxy for the true hosts, involves tough decisions.

Emily and Chelsea look at me the way they do whenever I say no to anything. Like I'm the boring one in the group. Like I'm the mother. The one who always ruins all the fun. "Fine," I say. "But nothing mean. No bullying or anything remotely dangerous. This operation is to be confined to tactical and humane strategies for intruder removal with minimal suffering, resulting in a happily ever after, in the fashion of the nudging-aside of Baroness Schraeder in *The Sound of Music.* Which means I think we need to focus on building up Emily, not knocking down Mila. Agreed?"

Chelsea nods. "Yes. Definitely."

"And if that doesn't work?" Emily drops the cards, and they fan out all over the floor.

Chelsea puts an arm around Emily's shoulder and strokes her hair soothingly. "It will. Or, we'll nudge her out the door."

33

After lunch, Mom and Dad take the boat out and we head
down to the dock. Chelsea spreads her towel down, takes out
a book, and begins to read. Her swimsuit is purely for tanning
purposes. She has a bizarre fear of water that she's never fully
articulated. I'm pretty sure she can swim. She insists she can't,
and at Chase's house in the Hamptons she just lounges around
the shallow end on a raft. But one time his little brother flipped
her playing Marco Polo with his friends, and she freaked out
and shot across the pool, dolphin-dove under, and resurfaced
on the other end in record time precisely at the ladder. She
knew what she was doing. I've always wondered where that
fear comes from. If there's any possibility Chelsea has seen the
dripping man, has sensed him. If deep down, she knows.

I love this house to the core of my being, the earth it sits
on, the lake that frames it, but I have an uneasy relationship
with the lake because of the dripping man. My earliest memory of the quiet people wasn't in the house. It was on the boat.
It's such a blurry memory I could easily mistake it for a dream,
except that it aligns so easily with later memories of the dripping man. It was the day of my first sail. I was around three,
and my parents took me out on the boat dressed in a cute
Ralph Lauren navy dress and leather Mary Janes. It was the

Fourth of July and my grandparents were there, along with a couple of family friends, platters of cheese and crackers, and a bottle or two of wine.

This is where my father's stringent safety rules come from.

Most drownings happen between the ages of one and four in the presence of adults, usually the child's parents. Often at a party or social gathering. Everyone thinks someone else has their eye on the child, and unfortunately, at one point or another, no one does.

My parents did everything right, or almost did. I wore a Red Cross–approved life jacket, appropriately sized. I had adult supervision. The problem, of course, was the same one that strikes in pools and on beaches across the country. I was passed back and forth from parent to grandparent so many times that eventually someone made a mistake.

Everyone did. Even me.

I was standing by the back of the boat, eating a cracker and holding my father's hand.

He had just come from the front of the boat, and his hand was wet. There were all sorts of reasons why this could have been the case. There were the drinks. We were on a boat. Water was plentiful. I didn't question it until he began to squeeze.

It was a hot day, a bright day, the kind where the water is as bright as the sun itself, and I had been staring into it, so it burned my eyes a little, and when I lifted them to look into my father's face, for a moment, I couldn't really see anything. Just the darkness that comes after staring into a very bright light.

But I felt the cold.

And then I felt the life jacket being swiftly taken off me and two hands pushing me into the water.

I don't remember the rest.

I can't say with absolute certainty that it was the dripping man who pushed me. I never saw his face. I do know I was pushed. I do know there was no one on the boat except my family. I know they didn't push me. I know I would be dead if the boat weren't anchored or if the wind had been blowing. I was lucky they heard the splash.

But I got to know the dripping man over the years, in glimpses and flashes. I know he waits for me at the back of the boat. He has always been waiting. He is always angry. And he is never going away.

I've debated with myself for years whether Chelsea's fear of water could be connected to the dripping man, or if it's wishful thinking, desperation on my part to simply not be alone in this. But Chelsea isn't like me. She doesn't keep things to herself, and she doesn't consider the consequences of showing people her hand. The only secret Chelsea keeps is a big, Ryan-shaped one. She's never been afraid to speak her mind. I admire it, but I don't wish I were the same. I couldn't pull it off. We complement each other, but that doesn't mean we have to turn into each other. I know it scares her sometimes. The quiet that I keep. But it's the only way I can bear the things I see.

She arranges herself in the farthest spot from the water, shaded by the trees. Ryan hovers next to her, and my instinct is to swoop underneath him and grab that spot, but I can't. It's more important to place myself centrally. I need to be closer to

Emily and Chase, and most vitally, between Chase and Mila. So I suck it up and take Chase's towel and arrange it on the opposite side of the dock, and fluff mine out, smoothing it down next to his. It's important to avoid conflict. I've learned that discord is one thing the quiet people don't tolerate. It draws them like insects to sweet, rotten things, thickening the air with their presence. We don't need that. So as much as I would like to stretch out next to Chelsea in the warm rays of the sun, I have an obligation to my friends to make sure I am situated somewhere between Emily and Mila. To monitor. To watch. To smooth the rough edges of my dear friend's jagged heart. Heartache can bring out the worst in people. It's a tricky beast.

"Chase." I pat his towel. "You're over here."

I sit down and spray my arms with sunscreen. Chase looks at Mila. "It's cool, just sit wherever."

But she looks uncertain and tugs at the bottom of his shirt. "I don't know anyone," she says in a very quiet voice.

Chelsea taps the space in front of her towel with her foot. "Come sit by me!" she invites with a smile. "Where do you go again? Rocky Point?"

"Central Islip."

Chelsea's face brightens. "My cousin goes there. Junior?"

"Sophomore." Mila seems to loosen up a little and lays her blanket out at Chelsea's feet.

It's a complete lie. Chelsea doesn't have cousins at Central Islip. Her entire family is from Ohio. Her lies are so seamless and out of the blue it's almost frightening. Almost. But not really. Because they're benevolent lies. Lies in service to friendship. Like the time she convinced my parents we all had food poisoning when we got drunk the first time they left us alone for the night. I wouldn't have been able to look them in the eye and do it. But she did, straight-faced. In detail. And she saved our asses. The quiet people thought that was hilarious.

Or the time she went out with Ryan for almost half a year and hid it from the rest of us because she knew I still had feelings for her, and that it would hurt Emily. It was a masterful piece of acting. Ryan rose to the occasion too. Chase told me I was paranoid. It was all in my head. Emily denied it up and down. She's convinced she's psychic and has a twin sense on top of it. But I have something better. I have Chelsea's heart. She and I are bonded in a way that not even Ryan and Emily are. And she can lie and lie about the Ryan thing, but I know. I know from the way they looked and deliberately *didn't* look at each other when we were in a group. The way they'd roll their eyes at the rest of us, make up secret languages, like they were the twins. I knew she was lying about that. And I also knew that the reason Chelsea was able to lie so well was because she forgot she was doing it. So once it was over, in her mind, it probably didn't happen. She told me once that's how you erase pain. Chelsea would know. She was the expert. And finally, I know because since Chelsea and I have been back together, Ryan has begun to slip. He doesn't look away. There is no more secret in his smiles. Or in the barely concealed resentment that shoots my way when Chelsea smiles at me. He's losing his touch.

Emily settles down between Chase and Ryan and angles herself toward Chase. Mila stands uncertainly, and Ryan glances over his shoulder at her. He's not oblivious to Emily's decade-long crush on Chase. That's begun to show too, and Ryan lets out a sharp exhale of frustration and averts his eyes, almost an overt display of disgust.

"Aw." Chelsea sits up, and Ryan leans back on his palms so her chin is almost resting on his shoulder. I stifle a frown. But she glances at me and I reluctantly stretch out on my elbow, our heads clustered together.

"It's so awkward," Ryan whispers. "She's my sister and he's my best friend. Pick literally any other guy under the sun. It's not like it's going to happen. He should tell her the truth instead of letting her hope." Oh, the irony.

"It's so unfortunate," Chelsea whispers. "Emily is so sweet and pretty and fun."

That's probably the problem. Chase is kind of a butterfly chaser. He likes quick and erratic and ephemeral. I was always kind of surprised he and Chelsea never had a fast and furious affair. Instead, she went for Ryan, who's about as exciting as a back issue of *Business Insider*.

No grudges, honestly.

But really?

He just bugs me.

And I thought when Chelsea and I got together, he would just fffffffade away. I like to say it like that. Like in that old song by the Who. But apparently, Ryan is around as long as Emily is. And now Chase comes with bonus features too. When did guests get to start inviting guests?

Unacceptable.

Ryan frowns at Emily, who's flirting unabashedly with Chase as Mila hovers uncertainly in the background. Chelsea scrambles up and pulls Mila back to her towel again. I kneel to put sunscreen on my thighs, and to allow Chase and Emily an unobstructed view of each other. "So. Any news?" I glance over to see Chelsea chatting up Mila animatedly.

"Where did Mila come from, you mean," Chase says. He lies down on his back and pulls his T-shirt over his head and sunglasses over his eyes. He refuses to wear sunscreen, and I can see the beginning of a burn underneath his hairline and on his cheeks.

Emily plays with her own sunglasses, cheap plastic frames she painstakingly covered in fragments of mirror. It sounds tacky, but it came out looking glamorous and unique. It matches her silver-and-black handmade bikini and the disco-ball pendant that hangs around her neck in the frame of a globe. "Do tell."

"I met her at a lacrosse game a few weeks ago. We've been keeping things low-key, but it's summer now, and I don't know." He shrugs. "No more games, no more studying. Time to have fun for once."

"I agree," Emily says. She scoots closer on her elbows, and I stand.

"Anyone for a swim? First of the season?" I step to the edge of the dock, but everyone looks up at me lazily. I step forward and take Mila's hands. "You haven't been initiated. First swim is a tradition."

She looks back at Chase with a helpless expression. "Tradition as in we all go together?"

He waves it off. "Lunch coma."

I pull her to the edge firmly and look into her eyes. "Honey.

I am not going to let you drown." And with me, she won't. The rules on this are clear. The dripping man came for me when I was small, when I was too young to see the warning signs. The sudden cold. The inexplicable sense of anger. A sense of confusion, a pulsing in the head, time being distorted, a knife in the fabric of a sweet summer sky. I look around for backup. "Right?"

"Trust her!" Chelsea gives an enthusiastic thumbs-up.

Ryan shakes his head back and forth emphatically and mouths, *Don't do it.*

She glances back at Chase frantically. "I'm not a strong swimmer. I really shouldn't."

Chase starts to stand up, and Emily quickly jumps to her feet and says, "Kennedy!"

Her tone is so sharp it stops me cold. "What?"

"It's not funny." Emily smiles at Mila. "You don't have to do anything you're afraid of, sweetie."

Mila's eyes dart back and forth from Emily to Chase. A breeze ruffles the boat docked nearby and goose bumps rise on my arms, and for a split second, my attention is diverted and my eyes go to the sky. It wasn't a wave of cold—not exactly. The cold from the presence of the dripping man isn't external, like a breeze. It's all-encompassing, systemic, as if your body is fighting it off like a fever. A symptom of a parasite, perhaps. The sun is blinding like it was the day I was dragged under, and I quickly lower my eyes, my heart pounding. The headache strikes fast, too fast to react, but I often get headaches from bright lights and sharp sounds—it's a family trait. I turn my head to warn Mila—it might be coincidence—but I do feel cold now, and even if it's in my head, even if it's fear getting to me, an abundance of caution demands that I stop her. But the pain in my head is so sharp, the spots in my eyes so disorienting, that it takes me a moment to focus on Mila's face. I see her step uncertainly up to the edge of the dock, turn to me, open her mouth to speak—and then abruptly fall headfirst into the water.

A chill spills down my spine, and for a moment, no one does anything. I stare into the lake, waiting for Mila to resurface, willing her back to us, but the water ripples wildly over the spot where she disappeared. Then more gently, and more, until it faded to stillness. Like buttercream slowly being smoothed over to hide an imperfection in the surface of a cake. Burying the mistake. Making it beautiful.

Chase jumps to his feet. "What just happened?" he says, aghast.

"Dripping man," I whisper. I feel numb, immobile. He never comes this close to the house. He's never followed the boat to the dock before. But he's here now. I feel, or maybe imagine, two cold spots on my shoulders, impressions the size of hands, and stumble back from the edge of the dock.

Ryan pulls his shirt over his bony shoulders and pushes us both aside.

Chase, of course, takes this as his cue to jump, lest Ryan rescue his girlfriend and make him look unmanly or something.

Unfortunately, they bounce into each other on the way in and hit the water just as Mila's head finally breaks the surface, knocking her back under.

"What the hell, Ryan?" I shake myself back into action, and

when Mila reaches the surface again, I pull her up to the dock with Chelsea's help.

"Nice save, Ry." Chase tosses Ryan a cold look as he pulls himself up out of the water. Ryan follows, glaring.

Mila is shaking and crying, and blood is coming out of her nose. I try to inspect the damage as Chase paces back and forth, knotting his arms together and muttering an incoherent stream of apologies.

"What happened?" Chelsea throws her towel around Mila's shoulders.

Mila presses her hand to her nose, her eyes squeezed shut in pain. "Someone's elbow went into my face."

"Who?" Chelsea's eyes go to Ryan.

Mila shrugs helplessly. "I don't know. It doesn't matter."

Ryan retreats to his towel, and Emily lays a hand on his arm. A weird look passes between them, and I swear just the ghost of a smile passes over her lips. Then in a blur of a moment, he yanks his arm away and marches up to where Chelsea and I are trying to convince Mila to let us look at her nose.

"Give her some space, man." Chase shoves him backward.

"Don't touch me!" Ryan throws the entire weight of his body against him, his face red with fury.

I have to underscore this.

There's been unsettled blood between members of our group before. Not bad. Just turbulent. When Chelsea and Ryan had their little secret. When Emily royally screwed up the *no more lake house* message to Chelsea and started our own little New World War I. But no one ever. EVER. Threw a punch. Or in this case, a shove.

Mila stops crying and wipes her nose on the back of her hand, smearing blood on her skin and wiping it on her pale pink swimsuit. It hasn't stopped bleeding, and I want to tell her to pinch it, but I don't want to be rude. I want to hand her a cloth, but I don't want to stain any of the linens. I want to run to the house for a first aid kit, but I don't want to miss what comes next.

Most of all, I want to tell them what really just happened. And that it could happen again.

Instead, it's Mila who speaks. "Chase, don't."

But I don't think he hears her. I don't even think it's about her. And I barely see the shock register when Ryan slaps him across the face and storms back toward the house, ending the fight almost as quickly as it started. Because my eyes are on Emily. And she's definitely smiling now.

34

It follows me inside. The wondering. Mila looks so bewildered as she slowly makes her way up the path, into the summery warmth of the lake house, glancing behind her toward the water, opening her mouth as if to form a question. I am convinced that her fall was not an accident. I'm just not sure if the person who pushed her was living or dead. And even if I wanted to tell her what happened to her, I can't. We're trained to believe certain things almost from birth. What goes up must come down. What goes around comes around. Life and death are fundamentally incompatible. They simply cannot coexist.

Consider this, though.

We all see stars after they die.

Billions of ghosts, haunting the endless infinite night. Chelsea used to say stars made her sad, because we could never see them while they lived. As if they have stories to tell or anything to do except burn. But that's not precisely true. They create and they destroy. They collapse and absorb everything within their reach. They make life possible. I'm not a religious person. I was raised in the church of Einstein and Hawking. I believe that what we know of the universe is just a fifteen-billion–light-year snapshot, as likely as not to be a relative speck in relation to the whole. As likely as not to be one in an infinite number, each moment of our lives existing simultaneously and endlessly, somewhere. As likely as not to be heading toward a bounce. An endless cycle of birth and growth and collapse and death and rebirth.

Of course we know almost nothing about the universe we live in.

And since that's true, isn't it arrogant to refuse to admit that anything is impossible?

Even ghosts?

I can't bring myself to call them that. They don't fit into my concept of the world. But I'm convinced they were living once, and I am certain they're dead. They're gone, but they're still here. They don't feel like ghosts, but maybe it's all semantics. They are possible, and they exist. I don't believe in them, I know them. We share history and a home.

They play and fight and sometimes they do bad things. Of course, that's probably not the way they look at it. To them, it probably goes something like this:

The living are possible. They exist. They play and fight and sometimes they do bad things.

And then we punish them.

I try to banish the thought in the wake of the incident on the dock. We all need to relax. That's all. After we get Mila dried off and calmed down, Chelsea and Emily run upstairs to the attic with cold drinks and tarot cards, leaving Mila alone in the loft, attempting to apply makeup to her bruised, swollen nose using a tiny compact mirror.

I watch her for a moment, feeling torn. A dark circle is forming under one eye, and the left side of her face looks like something from *Night of the Living Dead*. She needs more than a simple sweep of powder and a tiny mirror. But Emily would never forgive me for helping her. I sigh and clear my throat, and Mila raises her long-lashed eyes. She has old Hollywood eyes, dark and round, with lashes like butterfly wings. There's something comforting and familiar about it. "Come with me." I lead her into my room and sit her on the corner of the bed before the fairy-tale mirror, the magic mirror, as Chelsea and I used to call it, and pull out my makeup case.

"I can do it," she insists.

"Can you, though?" I lift her hand doubtfully. Her knuckles are swollen; she slammed them into the dock as we pulled her out of the water.

"Fine." She leans in toward me and closes her eyes nervously. "Don't make me look like a freak."

A smile bubbles to my lips. "Don't move, then." A sudden cool sensation startles me just as I'm about to touch the brush to her face, but it's only a breeze sweeping in through the open balcony doors. I steady myself and concentrate on smoothing the cuts and bruises, masking the swelling. "I'm sorry about my friends. We're all perfectly nice people, I promise."

She smirks, keeping the upper half of her face still. "Nice isn't the same as good."

I grin. She has a little bit of spark under the timid exterior. "No, it's definitely not. But none of us are monsters, either."

"I know. Rejection is unbecoming of us all." She rolls her eyes.

I pause. "What do you mean?"

She raises an eyebrow. "Ryan tried to pick me up before Chase did. But . . . I mean, who would you go with?"

"Chelsea."

She smiles one of those *I get it* smiles. "But never Ryan."

She does get it. Never Ryan. He's not unattractive. It's hard to describe why never Ryan. I do understand what Chelsea sees in him. They're both nerdy and quirky. Funny. We got along when we were younger. But he's gotten somehow darker as we've grown. There's a bitterness to his humor now, a brooding quality that hangs on him like dissatisfaction is woven into him. I have mentioned it to Chelsea, and she says I'm reading him wrong. But I can't shake the sense that he resents me, and has from the first time Chelsea and I kissed. And it got much, much worse after they secretly dated when Chels and I were broken up and then she left him to get back together with me. That didn't make him the kind of person who would turn on Chase for dating a girl who turned him down. It just makes him consistent. That's why never Ryan.

The magic mirror frames us like a picture as I work, and I try to be quick, to finish before Chelsea and Emily tire of tarot and come looking for me, but the mirror always has a little bit of a spellbinding effect on me, and I find my arms slowing. My eyes fall on a row of dolls sitting on the bed, and my mind begins to wander back to another time, when the room was new to me. The room that used to belong to my dead aunt. The dead are especially drawn to this place.

It was in this room that I saw the second quiet person I can remember meeting. The blue lady. I was four, my aunt's age when she died. It was an arrival day, and my parents were busy unpacking and settling the house. I was arranging my toys on my bed in the order I wanted to play with them—book, puzzle, doll, book, puzzle, doll—when I heard a pair of footsteps descending from the attic. For a second, I didn't think anything of it, because half of arrival day is footsteps up and down the attic ladder, suitcases up, empty arms down.

But I could hear my father outside through the open windows and my mother in the kitchen, along with the smells of buttery popcorn and simmering crab cakes. The footsteps continued, and I froze in place, kneeling at the bedside, *Where the Wild Things Are* in one hand and a custom doll in the other, one my mother had ordered to be made to look just like me.

Some strange impulse hit, a weird protective thing, and I shoved the doll under my pillow. Like, if there was a robber, they could take everything but my Kennedy doll. She only had me to protect her, after all. I guess my protective instincts did not extend to the rest of my dolls.

But it wasn't a robber.

I was never able to look the dripping man in the face, so the blue lady was the first one I really got to look at, and it stole the voice out of my throat. There was no question about it; she was dead. She didn't look horrible or anything, at least not as horrible as you could imagine. I knew what a zombie looked like. She wasn't a zombie. She was just dead. Pale, bluish skin. Purplish lips. Not alive. Just not alive.

She sat down on the edge of my bed and lifted the pillow, and I felt my eyes fill with tears as she picked up my Kennedy doll. It's weird how when you're little, these things matter that wouldn't now. You would think the dead lady in my room would be the primary trauma, but for me, the twist of the knife was the Kennedy doll. She knew where it was, first of all, which made it like a living nightmare, and she just picked it up like she could take anything away from me. That made her all-powerful, and me totally powerless. And the thing she chose to take, out of everything I had, was the one thing I chose to protect.

I peed my pants.

Then the lady started to cry. She jumped up and fluttered through my drawers until she found a clean set of clothes for me, laid them neatly on my bed, and fled back up to the attic. She left my doll behind.

I didn't see her again for a while. But before I did, she started leaving me presents. She would find lost toys and bring them back to me or do my chores sometimes. She lined up my dolls neatly and brought me old things from the attic, toys that used to belong to my mother and grandmother. A dollhouse, a tea set, a series of books. I let her know when I was ready to play. I set the Kennedy doll by the attic with a teacup.

The next evening we had a moonlight tea party after my parents went to bed.

She still looked dead, but she had a kind smile.

I always thought I was her favorite until the day of the sacrifice. I'm pretty sure she's the one who drew first blood.

"Kennedy?"

I whirl around to discover Ryan standing in the doorway, staring at us. My heart jumps into my throat as I wonder how long he's been standing there, how much of our conversation he heard, but he doesn't let on. An innocent expression is plastered on his face, but he gazes up to the attic with a sparkle in his eyes that infuriates me, one that dances as I hear footsteps thunder across the floor above. He disappears and I hear him running downstairs, the back door slamming behind him, as Chelsea and then Emily descend the ladder and tumble onto my bed, both staring at me and Mila with accusing eyes.

"What are you doing?" Emily asks bluntly.

Chelsea looks more uncertain. She has no reason to. She's the one who went behind my back. For months. It doesn't matter that we weren't together. We both knew the other still cared. At least, I thought I did. Now she looks at me like she caught me with my dress around my ankles instead of a makeup brush in my hand. I wish my friends weren't so dramatic. Everything is life and death, heartbreak and betrayal.

"Makeup," Mila says, a little more assertively than earlier. I'm glad she's feeling more comfortable, honestly. It makes me feel uneasy to gang up, not just because it riles up our silent housemates. But because it isn't *us*. It's a mask of loyalty. But it isn't really loyalty. It's a performance. It's a role. It makes me feel like I deserve the way Ryan looks at me, like I don't *get* it, like everything about us is fake and hard and posed for display.

Emily glares at me for a moment, and I feel anger beginning to swirl up like a summer storm. I have done nothing wrong. Mila is my guest too. But the guilt hits then. Emily does take precedence. Her feelings come first.

I zip the makeup back into its case and put it away. "All done."

Emily studies Mila. "You can barely tell which side is all smashed up."

Mila darts a glance into the mirror. "It looks great." She shoots me a quick smile, then turns it on Emily. "Chase wouldn't care if my skin were on inside out, anyway. I couldn't lose him if I tried." She winks and leaves the room, and Emily turns to me, her face white as a sheet.

"What did you say to her?" Emily bites her nails nervously.

"Nothing." I stare after Mila. Another wave of guilt washes over me. "I'm sorry. I just . . . felt bad." I take her hand. "Come on, we can all do makeovers. It's been a million years."

Chelsea looks at me in disbelief. "It's not the makeup. That is not the girl who walked in here this afternoon."

I consider. "Maybe she's not afraid of us anymore."

"Great." Emily stalks after her.

Chelsea wraps her arms around me and gives me a comforting kiss. "You did bad."

"We can't just be horrible to a total stranger." I glance upward instinctively. To the attic. Where they like to play. We really can't be monsters. They wouldn't like it.

35

"Do you think Ryan's cute?" Chelsea asks me later on the back porch, as Mila and Emily look on with interest.

I nearly spit out my gemonade—raspberry lemonade with a splash of gin. It's a bad habit, I know. I took my first curious sip when I was maybe around ten. I noticed that when I snuck a wine cooler from the fridge, the world around me blurred a little, and that included the quiet people. Fuzzy, like static. I asked my parents if I could drink a small glass of wine at dinner. I was careful never to have too much. Just enough to blur the edge of the world. But sometimes, in this house, that line begins to move further and further away.

Chelsea is staring at me, and I shake my head uncomprehendingly. No, I don't think Ryan is cute, and I don't think she's cute for asking when she still hasn't admitted to my face that they were together when I considered us to be on hiatus. Then I realize that the question is for Mila's benefit. The guys have gone off on a walk to "talk shit out" while the rest of us showered and settled down for snacks and decompression. My parents are busy upstairs getting ready to head up to Albany for some bar association dinner my father has to speak at. I'd hate to be important. It carries so many obligations. It's cumbersome enough being the perennial mediator. For once I'd like to be the impulsive one like Chelsea or live out one of Emily's romantic melodramas. I never get to misbehave. Even when we break the rules, I'm the one who sets the rules for the rule breaking. *Okay, guys. No sex in my parents' room. No drinking and driving. Keys in the key basket. Empties in this cardboard box. No stray bottle caps! If you're too drunk to remember your bottle cap, you've had too much. Bottle caps, guys. Bottle caps.*

"Not cute," I say with a quick look to gauge Mila's interest in the conversation.

But Emily is watching me closely. This whole conversation is for Emily. *I* know that Mila did consider Ryan and it was a definitive no. But in friendship, you commit to the part. I suddenly feel so exhausted. The lengths we go to protect one another's feelings exceeds the bounds of normalcy.

"He was cute five years ago," I add. "He's too intense to be cute now."

"True. Too mature for cute," Chelsea says, missing the ever so slight edge in my tone. "Chase is cute, though," she continues. "You know how some people are still cute even at eighty years old? Like they never grow up. Ryan is an old soul. I feel like he *knows* things." I hum a nonresponse. Ryan isn't the one who knows things. And his intensity has nothing to do with maturity.

"My mom always says he's an old soul," Emily says shortly. I raise an eyebrow at Chelsea, and she makes an *oops* face. It's a sore spot with Emily. She has a sort of inferiority complex where their mother is concerned. She'd lose her shit if she ever learned the truth about me. Emily turns to Mila. "Old souls or new souls? Which do you go for?"

"It depends," Mila says. "Is it a sexy old soul?"

"Good luck finding out. Ryan keeps his girlfriends secret. For all I know, he's a sex god." I take another sip and avoid Chelsea's eyes.

"He doesn't keep secrets from me," Emily says coldly.

Fuuuuuuuuuck. "Not from you," I say quickly. "And not because there's anything wrong with them. I'd probably choose the exact same lineup," I finish awkwardly.

Now everyone is staring at me. I finish my drink and look Chelsea in the eye, thoroughly annoyed. She doesn't look happy either. "To answer your question, I think he's sexy as fuck," I say. I shouldn't drink when there's tension in the air. There's no reason to believe it will ever make things better.

Mila looks back and forth between the three of us. "Did I miss something?"

"Not at all," Chelsea says. She pauses for a moment and then opens her mouth, and I just know that what comes out is going to lead to disaster. "Actually, no secrets between friends. You're our friend, now, right? Here's the thing. We all love Chase. He's the best. But we don't want to see you get hurt."

Mila laughs. "I'm not going to."

I eye her carefully. So far, she's presented herself as shy, timid, and kind of clingy. Now she seems pretty laid-back and confident.

"Chase and I are just having fun. You guys seriously have nothing to worry about. You're so sweet, though." She smiles and again, I feel so guilty.

"We're not at all," Emily says.

Worried. Sweet.

"Not at all," I repeat, the guilt approaching my breaking point, and refill Mila's glass with a quarter cup of ice, the rest of the tea, and a fresh sprig of mint.

Before dinner, Chelsea corners me in the bedroom. "What was that comment about Ryan the sex god and his secret lovers?"

"Nothing. It was out of line." One weekend. This talk can wait one weekend, until we're out of this house. Asking Chelsea about Ryan right now would definitely ruin everything. Because we are a powder keg about to blow—Chelsea and Ryan and me, Ryan and Mila and Chase, Emily and Chase and Mila. I am the one standing between the match and the gasoline. One wrong move, one wrong word, and boom. I feel the quiet ones watching, waiting for a mistake. There is anger in this house, and I can't contain it. But there are consequences when I don't. I've learned the hard way.

I was six the first time I angered them, when I brought Chelsea to the lake house, to her first tea party. There were more of them by then. The blue lady had introduced me to the backward girl, whose head was twisted around behind her. Then there was the woman on the stairs, who wore her hair in a long, dark curtain over her face. The crushed man rarely came to tea, but he was nice too. They all were, except for the dripping man. And we were safe from him inside the house. I thought Chelsea would see what I saw. That we could share my secret, that it could become our secret. That I would no longer be the one who knows. The knowledge was becoming heavy already. The funny way my parents had looked at me and questioned me when I talked about my "imaginary friends." The doctors and social workers they made me talk to. I learned to keep them secret. I learned that knowing was a weight to carry. I was sure that once someone else saw, when someone else *knew*, the weight would lift.

When we got to the attic, the backward girl stood by the window, her face turned toward the lake. The woman on the stairs hovered behind Chelsea. I was filled with dread. They were my friends. We shared the same spaces. They lounged upstairs while I played in the living room. They strolled in the garden while I roasted s'mores. I was sure they would want to be Chelsea's friend too. But the blue lady pointed angrily to the ladder.

Chelsea couldn't see, but she felt them—the blue lady's anger, sadness from somewhere else, another feeling I couldn't pin down. Her teacup rattled in her shaking hands as proof. Then in a blur, I felt arms hook around me and yank me to my feet. Chelsea screamed and scurried down the ladder, and I teetered dizzily for a moment, and then turned furiously to face the blue lady. I threw a teacup to the floor and shattered it. I smashed, stomped, destroyed, until there was nothing left of the set, and there would be no more parties and no friendship between us. My parents were furious. Chelsea cried all night, convinced that I had blown up at her unprovoked.

And in the morning I woke up to a headless Kennedy doll at the foot of the bed.

I didn't know it at the time, but my real mistake wasn't bringing Chelsea to the party. It was getting angry. They don't like anger. It's dangerous to test them on that. They began to fade after that night. I figured out the wine trick eventually, and they faded faster. I knew the blue lady had forgiven me when she began leaving me gifts and doing chores for me again.

But I never did find my doll's head.

"Can we just agree to let it go?" I avoid Chelsea's gaze now as I unpack my socks into the drawer. Tennis socks on the left, whites in the middle, brights on the right. A drawer for delicates, and one for denims, a closet of cottons, a shelf for wools. A place for everything, and everything in its place. Book, puzzle, doll. Eating, sleeping, towel arrangements. There is a harmony to the way we conduct ourselves. A way the hosts of the lake house find acceptable. It falls to me, and it's an intense amount of pressure. I rely on order. The rules. The way we have always done things. The balance that has made everyone happy. I follow routine because if something goes wrong, blood is on my hands. The rules of the house matter. Stick to the familiar. That way I don't forget one little thing and ruin everything.

"No." She folds her arms over her chest. "Not talking about it isn't the same thing as letting it go, and this is your grudge, Kennedy. Not mine."

The cold spills over me as the words vibrate through me. *Your grudge.* I feel ice in my veins, and even through the buzz of my drink, the walls of the room seem to stretch. Chelsea seems to fade backward somehow and I reach for her, but I'm already rewinding. I squeeze my eyes shut. *It isn't my grudge,* I think to myself. *It isn't my grudge.* I keep my eyes clamped shut as I feel layers of the present peel back like the skin of fruit, until I hear footsteps creaking toward me.

"Chelsea?"

"What?" She sounds irritated. Not quite angry. Not yet. They're becoming less forgiving.

The girl on the stairs walks between us as if we aren't there. Chelsea looks straight through her, and every hair on my body stands on end. The girl's long, tangled mess of hair covers her face as it always does, and I watch, spellbound as she pauses in front of the magic mirror for a moment, raising a hand slowly to her face to touch her hair with her pale, slender fingers. Her pinkie is obviously broken, stuck in an awkward, useless position, and I curl my fingers into a fist, phantom pain shooting through my hand. She bends down with a loud, knuckle-cracking sound and reaches for the drawer where I keep my hairbrush, and my breath freezes in my throat. I don't want to see her face. The long, dark hair always seemed like a protective curtain. As a child, I lay awake at night imagining what was beneath. Maybe it was a bare skull, or a mass of worms, or layers of exposed muscle like in an anatomy book. Now I can't imagine anything at all, and that's somehow more frightening than maggots or bones. The unimaginable is always the most horrifying. The thought of parting her hair and seeing nothing, the absence of anything, is the quintessence of my deepest dread. That is my fear of death described in one word: nothing.

This is the first time one of them has appeared to me, actually appeared in person, in years. They're getting stronger. But just as her hand touches the drawer, she suddenly turns to face me and vanishes. I stumble backward into the open balcony door, the handle digging painfully into my back, my heart hammering in my chest.

Chelsea steps between me and my suitcase and folds her arms, her brow furrowed. "Are you okay?"

I rub the small of my back. "Yeah. I'm fine."

She frowns. "Seriously, Kennedy. What was all that about Ryan's secret girlfriends?"

I shrug, deflecting. "Nothing. I was talking him up."

She glares at me. "The whole comment was passive-aggressive."

"You take his side in a conversation he's not even party to. Shocking."

"Because it's not just his side." Her cheeks are beginning to flush pink.

"No, to you, any comment about Ryan is a comment about both of you. Honestly, if I just met us, I'd think you and Ryan were together and I was the outsider." It slips out before I can stop it.

Chelsea's eyes widen and her mouth drops open. "I cannot believe you just said that."

I shrug one shoulder uncomfortably. "You act like you're better than the rest of us. Like our lives are trivial. I know Ryan calls me a spoiled brat. But he's the brat. He isn't as smart as Chase, as clever as Emily, and doesn't have as many friends as I do, and he acts like if he doesn't have something, it's morally deficient."

"And money, right? You and Chase are the stars and we're the nothings. Even Emily." She sits on the bed and pushes her hair back from her flushed face, her eyes bright.

"I didn't say either of those things."

"But they're true. Did it ever occur to you that that's

what Ryan and I have in common? That maybe it's hard being dragged around by special people and being known as the guests all the time?"

"You're not . . ." I trail off. That's exactly what Ryan and Chelsea are. "But you're all guests here." Even me.

"But we're guests at Chase's in the Hamptons, too. And at Emily's art shows. At the games where Ryan is stuck on the bench. We are always the guests. And you know what? I'm not pretending to like Mila anymore. I do like her, and I do think Ryan is a better match. Because I love Chase, but I also love Ryan, and Chase already has Emily."

The words *I also love Ryan* are the only ones that register, and they slap me in the face. I take a moment to gather myself.

"I like her too. I don't know why we play these games, and I don't want to fight. But Chase doesn't like Emily and he's never going to. She's never going to give it up. It's pathetic."

Right then, the door swings open and my stomach drops. Emily and Ryan are standing there. Emily steps in and closes it behind her, leaving a stunned Ryan alone in the hallway. Her eyes are brimming, but she doesn't look sad. She looks absolutely furious. I push the sock drawer closed behind me. I should have locked the door. That's one little thing I could have done to prevent ruining everything. But some things can't be kept out, and an unimaginable cold sweeps into the room with Emily.

She looks at Chelsea and then at me. "I'm pathetic?"

I take a hesitant step toward her. "No. That's not what I meant."

"It's what you said," she hisses in a low, vicious voice. She

takes a breath and lets it out shakily, the ghost of a cloud forming in the air before her lips. "I'll stay here tonight, but I'm
leaving in the morning. But before I go, I want you to know
that I think you are both terrible people. Chelsea, you went
behind Kennedy's back for four months with my brother."

Chelsea's face turns white. "That's not true. Nothing actually happened. You're twisting things."

"You can paint it any way you want. You were together
and you hid it and now you're lying about it. You kept it a
secret, maybe because you were ashamed of my loser family,
maybe because you wanted to wait around for the better catch
and dump him the second she came around. And look what
happened."

I study Chelsea. Her hands are clutching her knees to her
chest, and her lips are trembling.

"That's not true. You have no idea what my personal life
is like."

"Nothing is personal between twins." She turns to me.
"And you lied about the heirloom. You specifically told me it
was stolen, and Chelsea—"

"I never said Chelsea stole it!" I shout over her.

"Yes, you did!" She gets up in my face, and Chelsea scoots
backward on the bed. "You can't change what already happened, Kennedy. You made me do it, and then you punished
me for it because you always get away with everything since
you know everyone is going to believe you over me."

"Liar. You're a liar," I say calmly. But I feel a rage swirling
inside me that terrifies me. She is lying, and nobody should be
allowed to get away with a lie like that. A friendship-breaking

lie, a love-destroying lie. The kind of lie that takes people away from you forever. "Tell Chelsea you're lying right now."

She shakes her head, and the room seems to grow even colder. "No. I'm not letting you win, Kennedy. I'm not the pathetic one."

I place my hands on her shoulders and turn her toward Chelsea, but Emily whips around and shoves me backward into the dresser. It bangs hard against the wall and the mirror topples down, smacking me in the back of the head and shattering. Chelsea screams, and I crouch down under an explosion of pain. I'm afraid to move, afraid that there are shards of glass in my skull and neck, but I don't feel any blood or sharp slices, only the dull ache that you feel when you slam a body part into something hard. Chelsea lifts the mirror off me, the fairy carvings grinning impishly from the intricately carved heavy wooden frame, and helps me onto the bed as my parents rush into the room. The cold lifts, and just like that, our invisible friends have left us. Or maybe stopped caring. It's hard to tell sometimes.

"What happened?" my mother shrieks, combing her hands through my hair. She's a pediatrician and remains calm in every medical situation *except* the ones involving me.

"I fell into the dresser, and the mirror came down on my head," I say.

Chelsea looks at me, surprised, then nods. "It was an accident."

"You should be more careful," Emily says before she slips out the door. Chelsea stares after her, mouth agape.

I don't know why I lied about it. It just came out. I don't

want Emily to get in trouble, but I think the bigger thing is, I don't want World War II. World War I was hard enough. We've already had shots fired, and I want it to stop. If this is what it takes, a little lie, even a lie about a mirror smashed against my head? I guess I didn't even have to think about it. Anything to avoid another battle.

36

After it was determined that I had sustained no major injuries, my parents decided to go out after all, as long as I promised to rest with ice on my head and allow my friends to make dinner and clean up. I thought it would probably be nice to be the guest for once.

Mila and I sit together on the hammock while Chase and Emily warm my mother's patented homemade grill-top pizzas with smoked salmon, red onions, and capers in the kitchen. Ryan picks at his guitar out by the fire pit as the sun begins to lower in the sky, Chelsea brings us gemonades, and we try to avoid the awkwardness between us as we learn a little more about Mila. It actually isn't that hard. It's weird how sickness and injury erase bad feelings, or at least suppress them. My grandmother was the biggest bitch. She cut my father out of her will because she didn't approve of my mom, and then suddenly she got really sick and everyone was devastated because all they could think about were the nice things she did in between emotionally manipulating everyone. P.S. She lied about cutting my father out of her will. One last trick from beyond the grave. Surprise! Here's the money with which I tried to extort you out of true love. These are my last words to you. Remember me fondly.

Chelsea hands us our drinks and hovers over us awkwardly. "One of us should probably go check on Emily."

I nod reluctantly. One of us just had a mirror smashed over our head. But sure. Check on super smash sister. "Go ahead. I'll be fine." She kisses my forehead gingerly, and I grit my teeth as pain radiates through my skull, and then she heads into the kitchen.

Mila eyes my head with a pitying look. "It just fell on you?"

"Pretty much."

She shudders. "That thing looked solid."

"It is." I take a sip of my drink. I know it's not the smartest idea to drink when I've taken a painkiller. But I can't get the image of the girl standing in front of the mirror, inches away from me, close enough to touch, out of my head. I take another sip, desperate to push her away. "So. You're from Islip?"

Mila's expression relaxes and she leans back, dangling one arm over the edge of the hammock lazily. "Not originally. Iowa first, but I was born in Zagreb."

I squint at her, geography class playing on hyperspeed in my head. "Croatia, right?"

"Yep. I don't remember it, though." She draws a heart on the condensation on the side of her glass. "Adopted as a baby. I don't remember too much of Iowa, either, because we moved to the city when I was four. My mom works there. We moved to Islip around fifth grade so I would have a wholesome suburban Long Island childhood."

"And?"

She grins. "And I corrupted them all."

I smile back. "As one must."

She takes another sip and shoots me a sidelong glance. "You realize we're sworn enemies."

I nearly choke on an ice cube. "Why do you say that?"

"Islip and Three Village," she says seriously. "Our sports teams are deadly rivals."

I let out a deep sigh of relief. I would feel so awful at this point if she knew how we'd looked at her when she first walked in the door. Like an intruder. The other woman. What kind of antiquated way of thinking is that anyway? It crosses the line from loyalty to something darker. I'm not sure the kind of loyalty Emily wants from us—or maybe sometimes demands—is right. Maybe loyalty isn't even the right word for it.

"There's no official cheer program for lacrosse," Mila continues animatedly. This is obviously a subject she cares about deeply. "But cheer is immersive, right? Why should one sport be prioritized over another? It's about spirit, not favoritism. So I went to the administration, I petitioned the board, I personally led the effort to expand the program to attend as many games as possible. Win-win, we increased school spirit, it doesn't look terrible on my college apps, and I met Chase."

"Smart. But of course you're just having fun." I study her for a reaction and she blushes.

"Sure. Because watching your boyfriend's ex throw herself at him is a fucking riot. You would know, right?"

I stare at her, taken aback. "I'm sorry."

She blinks. "No, no, I'm sorry. That was completely uncalled for. It's a reflex. Defense mechanism. For a second I thought . . . But you've been really nice." She offers a shaky smile, and I realize she's not completely oblivious to everything that's been going on this weekend. Of course she isn't. Anyone would have noticed Emily throwing herself at Chase. And probably Chelsea and I talking up Ryan. Although maybe—I desperately hope—we were more subtle than that.

"You're really cute together," I say. And I mean it. I really do.

"So are you and Chelsea," she echoes. But she's not smiling. And she's looking over my shoulder.

I turn around with a sinking feeling in my stomach, to see Chelsea sitting next to Ryan in the backyard. Their heads close together, whispering urgently, Ryan's body angled in toward hers in a way that makes me feel nauseous and dizzy that the pain in my head doesn't account for.

I feel anger gathering white-hot in the pit of my stomach, but before I can rise to my feet, there's a loud bang from behind me, and Mila and I whip our heads around in unison to see the cellar door smack against the wall and slam shut on the other side of the living room.

"Who did that?" Mila whispers.

I can hear Chase and Emily in the kitchen, talking and laughing over the sounds of clinking cutlery. Ryan and Chelsea are still outside. "The wind," I say.

But I'm not so sure. I've been making a lot of mistakes this weekend. I made a mistake once, a bad one, and the quiet ones punished me. I'm the only one who knows about them, so I'm the only one who knows the whole story. But everyone knows a fragment or two of what happened.

It was the Summer of Eagles, the first summer I was allowed to bring all of my friends to the lake house for a whole weekend. I wanted everything to be perfect, and I had planned a surprise.

My mother had spoken to Mrs. Oglebie and arranged for us to adopt our class pet, Miss Palindrome, over the summer while our former teacher was studying overseas. My father had driven up a day early with Miss Palindrome, who would be waiting for us when we arrived. For once, I was thrilled to have a secret.

But when we arrived, my father quickly took my mother aside. I tore through the house looking for the cage, but it wasn't there. I eventually found it in the boathouse—my father had apparently moved it there so that we wouldn't be upset to find it empty. So much for that. I wasn't there when the rest of my friends found Miss Palindrome. I was still puzzling over the empty cage in the boathouse.

My father apologized over and over. He insisted that he left the cage in the kitchen, securely locked, and went to sleep. When he awoke, the door was open and Miss Palindrome was gone. He guessed that somehow a raccoon had gotten in through the attic and worked the cage door open, then chased the poor thing down into the cellar and attacked it. I didn't buy that for a second, but exterminators did find some holes that needed mending, so no one gave the matter another thought. The cage was carefully disposed of, and there was another secret for me to keep. None of my friends ever learned what happened to the real Miss Palindrome—how could they, when for all they knew, she was safe at home? We bought Mrs. Oglebie a new rabbit, and she opted to keep the secret and name it Miss Palindrome. Her incoming class was already excited to pet the legendary class bunny.

To this day, I'm not sure what mistake cost Miss Palindrome's life.

Whether it was Miss Palindrome herself that was unacceptable, or something my father did that I will never know, or whether they disapproved of my friends. I don't know if the quiet ones meant to punish me, or Chelsea, or someone else.

Maybe all of us.

I do know that after Miss Palindrome's killing, I never saw a quiet one again. I've felt them for a very long time, but I cannot see them anymore. Not so much as a glimmer of light in the darkness. Not until today.

I don't want to think about what that means.

"How are you feeling?"

I turn around to see Chelsea standing over me. She looks completely innocent. Resentment vibrates through me, but I tamp it down. No more girl on the stairs. No more slamming doors.

"Better."

Mila gives me an odd look as Chelsea settles down on the floor next to me like nothing ever happened. "Everything okay with Emily?" she asks pointedly.

"What?" Chelsea furrows her brow. "Oh. Yes." Her eyes dart out the window toward Ryan just for a split second, and again I have to force myself to stay calm. I press my icy glass against my pounding forehead. I understand that she still cares about him. I don't relate, but I believe he has an important place in her life. What I don't understand is why she would need to lie to me. First about dating him. But at least we weren't technically together then. There's nothing to forgive about that, even if it hurts. But now? The fact that she's still lying to me about anything involving Ryan scares the living hell out of me. But again she turns to Mila like nothing is wrong, the classic Chelsea subject change. "Catch me up? Speed round. Coke or Pepsi?"

Mila looks taken aback. "Water? I hate soda."

"Mets or Yankees?"

"Islanders."

"Fair. Killer or victim?"

"Final girl."

Chelsea leans forward. "And how will the world end? With a bang or a whisper?"

Mila considers. "A series of clicks and chimes from the AI revolution."

"Interesting. Explain."

"The two biggest threats to humanity are artificial intelligence and climate change. But AI wins because it's an economic, security, and potentially mass-weapon threat. And it's the ultimate culmination of humanity's impulse to self-destruct."

Chelsea looks impressed. "All very good points." And like that, Mila wins over Chelsea, too.

Mila might be more interesting than I originally estimated.

She's also kind of cute. Or maybe I'm just pissed off at Chelsea. When I get angry at her, it makes other people automatically more attractive. It shouldn't, but it does. I always wonder whether that's human nature or something that makes me personally evil. Hopefully the former. But I'm too afraid to ask anyone else because I honestly don't want to know if it's just me.

Chelsea sips her gemonade slowly, and my eyes follow

hers out the window again. I can't tell if she's looking at Ryan or the sunset. But I suddenly feel so sad and helpless I want to cry. Nothing feels good anymore. Maybe it's my head. I put my drink down and struggle to rise.

Mila shifts over in the hammock. "Sorry. I'm tangled."

"It's not your fault. It's basically a fishing net. This is how dolphins die and shit." Chelsea reaches over and helps me up, and I lean into her.

"I feel light-headed," I say.

She peers into my eyes as if she knows how to look for a concussion or something. "You should rest. Come on." Chelsea crouches down and slides an arm under my knees.

"Chelsea, no."

She tries to lift me, and we both go sprawling. Chelsea starts giggling uncontrollably, and I realize that she's already buzzed too. She has to be on her second drink. I scowl at her. "You could have just concussed me."

Chelsea laughs harder, her chin bent to her chest, legs tangled in mine. "That's not even a word."

"Yes it is. A person with a concussion is concussed." I try to pick myself up, but she grabs me around the waist and I wonder if this is all it takes to be okay. Laughing like nothing is wrong. Smashing mirrors. Getting drunk. I feel like I'm stuck in a Noël Coward play. But I want it to be okay. I want all of us to be okay. I sigh and sink down to the floor with her.

Mila gazes down at us from the hammock. "I can see it," she says.

"What's that?" I look up at her as Chelsea wraps her arms around me from behind, forming a kind of human armchair.

"Ryan is kind of sexy. In an unexpected way." She takes a thoughtful sip of gemonade. "He did fight Chase for me."

"He *slapped* Chase," I point out. "And I don't know if that was a hundred percent about you. They . . . have unresolved issues."

Mila smiles, almost condescendingly. "It's not the first time two guys have fought over me. Unresolved issues or not, that was about me."

"Well, you're just tumbling right on out of your shell now, aren't you?" Chelsea says.

Mila shrugs. "I'm shy when I first meet people. I know you now."

"Eh," Chelsea says.

"How well do you ever know anyone?" I say, untangling my hair from Chelsea's. Innocuous enough. I think.

"You don't." Mila nods her head toward Chelsea and raises an eyebrow, then tilts her glass up to catch the last piece of ice between her teeth.

37

Dinner is strained, and we gather around a bonfire for s'mores afterward. Seating is trickier than usual. I don't usually bother with seating for something like a bonfire—even I'm not that big of a control freak—but then, we've never been on the brink of a serious group implosion with multiple forces of massive pressure acting upon us.

There's a first time for everything.

I end up placing Emily next to Mila, next to Ryan, across from me, next to Chelsea, next to Chase. That way Emily is farthest from me, and Chase is farthest from Ryan. And, though it's getting pretty damn half-hearted on my part, Emily is across from Chase, and Mila is next to Ryan. So if there's still some remote cosmic possibility that Chase and Emily are meant to be together, let there be magic tonight. It's not really about that, though. It's the gesture. The peace offering.

Because if peace isn't restored soon, what then?

Chase starts the night off with a toast, short and sweet. "To friends, old and new."

We clink branches, and the chill begins to settle like a slow, creeping dread.

I pull my sweater closer around me and gaze around

anxiously, but the night is a beautiful sunset haze. "Tell us a story, Chase."

He lights up. Chase is full of stories, most of them true. Things just happen to him. He'll stroll into the grocery store and run into a celebrity, or stumble onto a movie set on a morning jog and be recruited as an extra. Once he sat on a bus for an hour chatting with a man, only to realize after he got off that it was Stephen King.

"Okay," he says, breaking his bar of chocolate into precise little squares. "I've been saving this one."

Emily twists her hair over her shoulder and leans on her elbow. "Do tell."

Ryan catches Chelsea's eye over the fire and rolls his eyes, and she hides a smirk behind her hand. But she looks tired. Maybe a little sad. I squeeze her hand and she squeezes mine back.

Chase swallows a square of chocolate and then looks around the circle. "I've told you about the hunting cabin up in Phoenicia, right?" He launches into a ghost story, obviously 100 percent pure, unadulterated bullshit. Chase's parents and mine go back to the days before Chase and I were born. I know him better than anyone else sitting in this circle. And Chase doesn't believe in ghosts or know anything about them. This house is too full to just ignore them. If you spend a night in the lake house and don't see a ghost, it's because you can't see them, and you never will.

Emily squeals and grabs his arm, and Mila glares at her openly. I don't blame her.

Ryan cuts him off halfway through the story. "Let me guess. The brother did it."

Chase lifts his glass. "You've been reading my diary, you scoundrel."

Ryan averts his eyes. I guess the "talking shit out" didn't go particularly well. I rise to clean up, but Chelsea tugs me down by the sleeve.

Here's what's messed up about this whole situation. Everyone's acting like nothing's wrong, and at the same time, they're sending out major signals that something really bad is about to happen. Not otherworldly bad. Living bad. It feels like the night before a battle. If you didn't know us and you dropped in, you wouldn't notice a thing. You'd see Chase telling one of his epic stories and Emily and Mila listening like an onstage Greek chorus. Ryan and Chelsea trading knowing looks back and forth over the fire. Me, nodding and smiling, keeping up the conversation, asking questions where appropriate to show that I'm engaged, offering more chocolate and graham crackers at intervals, catching crumbs before they fall.

But it's all wrong.

It's supposed to be Ryan and Chase having an animated discussion, or Chase telling the anecdotes and Ryan constantly interrupting him, not letting him get away with embellishments. Chelsea, Emily, and I discussing the evening plans. And Mila. Mila isn't even supposed to be here.

I blink back to reality, and Chase is already on to another story, really putting on a show without Ryan to keep him in check, and after a while I wonder whether it's to get Ryan's attention. "So the tire's *shredded*, the bus is blocking two of the lanes, and we have no way of getting to the game or home. One hour from the game, three hours from home, nobody's coming to get us. Farmland all around, as far as the eye can see. Semifinals. We gear up, divide into two groups, and play our own game, right there on the cornfield."

"Wow," Emily says, her eyes shining.

"That just shows so much spirit." Mila takes a sip of her wine.

"Well, I mean, some of the guys wanted to give up." Chase takes a bite of his double-decker s'more, his specialty.

I glance at Ryan, wondering if it's a dig at him. He's on the lacrosse team. I wasn't listening to the first half of the story. But Ryan doesn't react. He's using one of my father's knives to sharpen the end of his roasting stick. I *should* tell him that the knife has been used to scale hundreds upon hundreds of fish, that it's the last flavor you'd want to infuse into a chocolate-marshmallow dessert. But I pettily want to see if he notices.

"That's unfortunate," Mila says. "Spirit is kind of my thing. Obviously. It can literally change a tragedy to an uplifting story." She gestures to him, and Emily snorts into her lemonade. I frown at her. This is going too far. Mila looks at her for a moment, and her demeanor completely transforms. It's absolutely stunning. For just a split second, she looks older. Cool, confident, disdainful. But it melts in an instant and she turns back to Chase. "When something bad happens, you *can* let it ruin your day. Or you can use your spirit to make something amazing."

"Yeah, babe, that's what I said." Chase winks at her. "It was a little bit of a downer. We were short a couple of players—"

"I had a sprained neck." Ryan slams his hand down on the table.

Chase laughs. "Whoa. I wasn't specifically talking about you. Of course you couldn't play. You had a sore neck."

"A *sprained* neck."

"Right, that's what I said." He takes a sip of beer and then looks at Emily and shrugs. Emily purses her lips and looks back and forth between Ryan and Chase.

"He wasn't talking about you, Ryan," she says finally.

Ryan looks stung. Even Chase's mouth drops open. Emily and Ryan have always defended each other. Always.

"You weren't there," Ryan says finally. He rises and Chelsea touches his arm.

"Ryan, he was just telling a story." She nods her head toward his seat.

"No, he wasn't." He looks at the rest of us. "You know he wasn't."

Chase studies the fire. "Ryan, why don't you tell the rest."

"I had to lay immobile on the ground for two hours waiting for a tow truck while the rest of the guys alternated between playing a pathetic practice game and bitching about how life isn't fair and they could have been getting laid right now. That's the rest of the story." Ryan taps his fingers on the table. "Did I tell it right?"

Chase sighs. "Whatever."

Ryan heads back toward the house. Chelsea and I exchange a weary look, and she takes my hand.

"Pick out a board game," I call after him with an encouraging smile. I wrap my sweater around me more tightly. It's getting colder by the minute. I put my glass down on the ground. The world is starting to waltz.

"He has no spirit," Chase mutters.

"I don't know if I agree," Mila says.

Emily begins to refill Mila's glass, and it suddenly shatters in her hand.

All four of us stare down in shock at the red wine soaking Mila's skin, the glittering shards of glass catching fragments of moonlight.

"I'm not hurt," Mila says slowly, as if not quite convinced.

It isn't necessarily a sign.

But it feels like one.

38

By the time I've finished cleaning up, a game of Monopoly is well underway. I usually love Monopoly, but tonight I have a headache, and it's no fun jumping in after people have already snatched up property. I linger in the kitchen and mix up a fresh pitcher of sangria. I love the idea of sangria. Wine and juice. It sounds like they wouldn't work together, but they're absolutely perfect. Chelsea wanders in as I'm slicing the apples and hangs her head over my shoulder.

"Careful. Sharp knife." I lay it down and turn around to face her.

She leans into me and sighs. "Everything feels off tonight."

Understatement of the year. "It'll be fine."

"Ryan and Chase got into a fistfight."

"Slapfight." I wipe my hands on a dishcloth and comb her thick, frizzy hair with my fingers.

"Emily literally smashed a mirror on your head."

"She didn't mean to."

Chelsea pulls back and studies my face. Her dark eyes are unreadable. "I think she did."

"She shoved me. That's all."

"Into a pane of glass." She glances over her shoulder at the living room. "Everything is falling apart. I just have a bad feeling. I wish we could read the cards or something."

"The cards are a game." I wish they weren't, though. After Emily's claim about Chelsea and Ryan, there are a few things I'd like to know too.

"They're tools," she insists. She looks so earnest. "They show us what we already know. Instinctively. Knowledge we feel but can't access. I know you're not a believer. But you not believing something doesn't make it not true." Chelsea sighs and looks toward the stairs. Then her eyes light up. "Let's do it," she whispers. "No one will think anything of us going upstairs. They'll think we're going to your room. Which we will. Emily's cards are still in the attic." She nods with big eyes.

I look at my half-finished pitcher of sangria. "I'm busy."

Chelsea lifts the handful of apple slices and dumps them into the pitcher. "Done."

"You didn't wash your hands. Now I have to start over."

"Kennedy, none of us need to be drinking tonight. Come on."

I sigh and follow her up the stairs. "Emily is the reader," I whisper. "You've never done it."

"I have the sight." She closes my bedroom door behind us and locks it. "Remember?"

I remember her as a child again, sitting in the attic with her teacup, looking so lost. Seeing *nothing*. "Of course. How could I forget. Still, isn't there an art to reading tarot cards? Doesn't each one stand for something specific?"

"Yes." Chelsea lowers the stairs to the attic, and I follow her up. "But I remember some of them. We've been watching Emily for years. Haven't you been paying attention?"

"Sort of." Not really. When we were little, it was fun to have

Emily predict who liked us and what we were going to get on our birthdays, and if we were going to be in the same classes. That sort of thing. But why would I bother listening to the drawn-out explanations about what exactly each card meant and *why* it indicated that we'd all end up with Mrs. Oglebie, or that Chase was secretly in love with Emily? This result came up repeatedly, which was mostly why I thought the cards were full of shit. I honestly don't know why Chelsea has any faith in them. Maybe she has her own read on them and thinks Emily's interpretation is skewed by what she wants to see. But when I look at the cards, all I see are pretty pictures. A game.

We tiptoe across the floorboards and arrange ourselves in front of the cards, and Chelsea gathers them and begins to shuffle them carefully, almost reverently.

"They're not going to turn to ash if you bend one," I say as she meticulously slides one half of the deck into the other, making sure to keep the cards perfectly straight. She's touching them like they're made of glass or something.

She glances up at me. "You want Emily to know we were up here messing with them without her?"

I sigh. "Just hurry up."

She presents them to me. "Cut the deck."

I divide the cards twice the way Emily always has us do it. "We haven't thought of a question."

Chelsea chews her lower lip. "Will Emily and Chase end up together?"

"Fair litmus test. The cards always seem consistent on this point."

"One-card draw?"

I nod. "The fewer cards, the less likely we are to get confused."

Chelsea turns over the top card and sets it down between us. It's the Queen of Cups. "Interesting," she says, nodding her head.

"All I remember is that the Queen of Cups is also the Queen of Hearts, and all I remember about her is *Alice in Wonderland*."

Chelsea shakes her head. "No, she comes up over and over. She . . . Something about art? Love. I think Emily gets her a lot. Or was it me?"

"It was you." I do remember the Queen of Cups. Because I always thought it was funny—it made me think of Solo cups, some kind of drinking game. It's so hard for me to take this tarot game seriously. Chelsea always got the Queen of Cups. I wonder if this means Chelsea is supposed to end up with Emily or Chase. But it *is* just a silly game. So I play along to make Chelsea happy. "Maybe it means they'll get together, but only if you help them."

She nods. "Interesting." She looks down at the cards. "What next?"

"Will Ryan and Chase work out their problems?"

"Good one." She flips another card. The Nine of Swords. It's a pretty bleak-looking card. Nine swords hang in the air, pointing down at a woman bent with her head in her hands, apparently heartbroken. "Hmm."

"All signs point to no," I say.

"Well, it's all in your interpretation. Maybe it just means they have to have a painful talk. It obviously goes way beyond

Ryan hitting on Mila. He doesn't want anyone to know this, but Ryan was cut from the team."

I clap a hand over my mouth. "So that's why he was so upset about the lacrosse story at dinner."

Chelsea nods emphatically. "Yeah. It's a lot of things. Losing his place on the team, his grades are slipping, and Chase doesn't get it. Ryan feels like he's just losing everything right now. And honestly, I think Ryan really does feel weird about the Emily/Chase dynamic. I don't know if there's something new that I missed, but . . . he seems *really* fed up with it."

"Right." My legs are starting to cramp under me, and I stretch them out. "I got that sense earlier, too."

Chelsea tilts her head and looks over at me. "You don't think *Ryan* . . . ?"

I burst out laughing and then clap my hand over my mouth, glancing down at the floor. We should wrap this up. "If Ryan ever had any interest in Chase, that ship has definitely sunk. But I don't think so."

"Right." She hesitates. "So what were you implying earlier with the secret-lover thing?"

"Oh my god, Chelsea." I flip my hair over my shoulder uncomfortably. "Look, obviously you and Ryan had some kind of thing while we were broken up."

She shakes her head vehemently. "It's not true."

I stare at her. I don't get it. There are lies that are justified, but right here, right now, I don't understand how she can look at me and lie to my face. Not if she wants everything to go back to the way it was. "Something. Maybe not everything. But something happened."

She pauses. "It's not what you think. I wouldn't betray you."

"Then tell me." I reach for her hand. "If you want us to trust each other, we have to be honest with each other. Screw everyone else. Screw Ryan and Chase and even Emily. We come first, we come last. What happened with Ryan?"

Chelsea meets my eyes for just a flickering second. "Nothing that matters. I love you."

But she's wrong. Everything matters. I gather the cards and set them down, face-up. The devil smiles up at us.

Chelsea slowly turns the card over. "We didn't ask a question."

"That one didn't count," I say.

But his grinning face sticks in my head as we climb back down the ladder, carefully fold it up, and join the rest of the group. The game is still dragging on, but no one seems to be feeling it. Mila is hanging over Chase's shoulder, sipping a glass of the sangria. Chelsea was probably right about the drinking— we've been at it for a while now. I can feel a definite buzz, and it's going to take a while to wear off. Chase is drumming his hands on the table, humming under his breath and rattling the hotels on his side of the board. Emily is glaring unabashedly up at Mila, fanning her money between her fingers, and Ryan is drinking straight brandy, no ice.

"Bored," he says in a monotone.

"Guess I win, then?" Chase sweeps the contents of the board into the box, and Emily swats his arm.

"I didn't concede. I had Park Place. That's a draw."

Mila yawns. "Who cares? This game is the worst. Don't you have any movies or anything?"

"No." I take her glass off the table and place a coaster under it. "This is a lakeside retreat. You don't come here to watch television."

"You sound like a timeshare seller." She smiles lazily, and I try to hide my annoyance.

"Well." I sit down on the leather armchair. "How may I entertain you?"

She falls into Chase's lap and fishes an apple slice out of her glass. "I don't know. What else is there to do?"

"We could go night swimming," Emily says. "Skinny-dipping if you're feeling daring."

"Nope." I begin to gather glasses. "No drinking and swimming. Too dangerous."

"But, Mom," Chase whines.

"House rules," I say. He knows the rules. And they're fair. It's not like I don't allow swimming after a glass of wine or a beer. But all of us have been really going at it tonight. And when that's the case, it's just not safe. There have been tragedies on this lake before. At least a couple every year. A girl drowned not far from our house when I was a baby, and my parents immediately put me in infant swim lessons. And let us not forget my attempted murder via the dripping man. My dad has hammered these rules into my head since I was allowed to step onto the boat. Not only to keep me safe, but because we'd be personally liable if someone else had an accident on our property. My father the lawyer, ladies and gentlemen. But as coldly pragmatic as it may sound, he's right. And if I sound coldly pragmatic, I'm right too.

"I want to see the stars," Mila says. She grabs Chase's hand and tugs him toward the back door. "Come take me."

Chase looks helplessly back at me. "Sorry, guys. I've been claimed."

"I said no." I don't mean to say it so sharply, but all three of them look up at me, a little surprised.

"Sorry." Mila exchanges a bewildered look with Chase.

"She didn't want you here," Emily says.

I stare at her furiously. "That is not true."

Emily shrugs. "I just think we should be honest. You said we should push her out like the lady no one cares about in *The Sound of Music*. The gold digger."

Mila looks so hurt for a second that I want to hug her and shake Emily at the same time. It's true, but it's not *the* truth. Parts of the truth are just as deceitful as blatant lies. But Mila's expression transforms so quickly, so smoothly, that I see my window for forgiveness close forever right before my eyes. "The one who doesn't inherit seven brats? Easy pass."

I turn to Emily, but all that comes out is one word. "Why?" I already know the answer, though. I betrayed her. I chose Mila. And as my punishment, she took Mila away.

39

I link my arm around Chase's. No one is going swimming tonight, regardless of how many people it pisses off. Not after the dripping man's appearance on the dock this afternoon. And the girl on the stairs in my bedroom. And the glass shattering in Mila's hand has me nervous too. And the cellar door slamming. Something is wrong. "Help me in the kitchen, Chay. I need your strong man arms."

Resentment flashes in Mila's eyes, but she holds her tongue and Chase allows me to guide him through the French doors. I shut them behind him and lean against the cool metal of the refrigerator.

He hops onto the counter and looks at me expectantly. "I assume it's my strong man ears you're really interested in."

I hedge for a moment, absently tapping an empty glass with my fingertips. Glasses don't just shatter. It's the sort of thing the dead do when they're upset. It's very hard to dismiss it as an accident. "I'm sorry about what Emily said. It was out of context."

"I figured."

"But you can't go swimming tonight. Or ever without me. I have to be there."

He rolls his eyes. "Yes, Mommy dearest."

"I mean it. No waiting until I'm asleep and sneaking out. It's dangerous." An unsettling feeling creeps over me, and I place the glass quickly back on the drying rack.

Chase sighs heavily. "You used to be fun, Kennedy."

That one hurts. "You used to be nice."

We look at each other awkwardly for a moment.

"I didn't mean that," he says finally.

I should echo him. But I don't. I don't believe him. And I don't believe he's going to listen to me. That scares me more than anything else right now. This secret is wearing me down. It's exhausting. I feel like a hypocrite keeping anything from Chelsea while holding a grudge against her for keeping things from me. She should be the first to know. But at the same time, that's the reason I can't tell her. She won't come clean about Ryan. If only she would just tell me the truth.

But Chase. Chase is my oldest friend. Chase has always had my back. I would trust Chase with my life.

And if I keep this secret any longer, I will break.

I take a deep breath. "How do you feel about ghosts?"

Chase bursts out laughing. "Is my ghost story freaking you out? It was a joke. Dead is dead." He reaches for Mila's purse sitting out on the counter and pulls out a clove cigarette. I shake my head at him, and he shrugs and places the cigarette between his lips without lighting it. "Life is short and then you die."

This is going to be harder than I thought. I close the kitchen window. It's getting cooler outside, and the cold is slowly seeping into the house. "Sure. But after that. More things in heaven and earth. Et cetera."

He flicks his imaginary ash on my nose. "There's a difference between what has yet to be discovered—like the universe beyond what technology allows us to explore—and fairy tales. Infinite things that we can't imagine exist because they're beyond the scope of what we know. But ghosts aren't. We can imagine them. We made them up. They *are* dreamt of in our philosophy. That's all they are. A dream."

"Cool speech."

"But?"

"What if they're more than that?" I feel a warmth surrounding me, *their* warmth. And for a moment I'm filled with hope. They aren't always angry or upset. They used to be my friends. "You're looking at 'your philosophy' as all of human knowledge. But all you really know is what you've seen for yourself. People *have* witnessed things. You *know* I'm an evidence girl. But there are studies documenting cases of people showing cognition while their hearts are stopped, for example. Some scientists theorize our minds live hours after our hearts stop. They used to believe it was seconds. What if the line keeps moving? Science is a process of discovery."

"You know better than to take anecdotes as global fact. And there are scientific explanations for the phenomenon of walking toward the light, life flashing before your eyes—it's the process of the brain dying."

"Well, what about the cross-dimensional theory? Ghosts could be a time-space glitch," I say desperately.

"Maybe if string theory actually held up," he says condescendingly. Then he eyes me curiously. "You've put way too much thought into this." I have. I've spent years of my life researching every possible way to scientifically justify my experiences. But nothing can explain the unexplainable. You can't experience the brain death of another human being. If it were simply a phenomenal crossroads of remarkably similar coexistent universes, why do they look dead? How can there simply be a universe identical to our own in which the dead live? It sounds too similar to traditional notions of the afterlife. A story I'm telling myself to explain the unexplainable. To comfort myself about something truly unsettling. The fact is that I see things that are not there. There is no evidence that what I see and feel is real. People like me are placed in hospitals, given pills, and treated as defective. But I am not defective. I just can't prove what I know to be true.

I draw a deep, shaky breath. It's now or never. "If someone experiences something you can't explain, you have three choices. You can take it on faith, rule it out definitively, or just accept that your reality isn't theirs, and you might not know everything there is to know."

He stares at me. "Okay. What is there to know? What can you personally vouch for? Because I don't buy into stories, but I'll believe anything that comes from you. I trust you, Ken."

Say it. My grandmother's cuckoo clock ticks in the hall. *Say it*. A moth circles the ceiling lamp. *Say*. Time slows down. *Say*. The air in the room grows warm and thick. *Say*.

He's lying. It's the same line my parents and the doctors and the social workers fed me to get me to talk in order to draw their various conclusions. Imaginary friends. Suppressed anxiety. Projections of trauma, the root of which couldn't be weeded out. Everything but the truth. Chase doesn't know what to do with the truth.

The truth is, there's a place at the lake house only two of us know.

Under the boardwalk, in the deep, dark dirt. We dug a little grave, Chase and I, and laid the bones of the rabbit to rest. It didn't seem right to tell Chelsea. She had been so incredibly upset by the discovery of its tiny body in the cellar. I'm not sure whether Emily was actually upset or just mirroring Chelsea. We did that sometimes. It was how we learned to relate. I understand that now. There is so little that we genuinely share anymore.

Anyway.

Something had to be done. I couldn't let my father drop the body into a dumpster or toss it in the woods to be picked over by owls and coyotes. I know that's how nature operates. But people don't. We bury our beloved.

Every year I plant white roses along the path. Every year they die. The ground is much too soft for roses; the shade too gentle.

I hope that's the reason.

Chase has been a good friend. He didn't hesitate when I asked for his help, and he's never spoken a word. He never knew who the rabbit was, only that I felt it deserved a final resting place. And he knew how to dig a grave. Even as a child, his arms were strong. We snuck out after dark and retrieved two spades from the shed, then the body from the trash can. We dug on our hands and knees in the dirt, a deep hole, deep enough that storms wouldn't bring it back to surface. There wasn't much moon that night, and it misted periodically, and by the time we were done, we were covered in mud.

We tucked the garbage bag around the body like a shroud, to protect her for a while, then lowered her carefully, and whispered the Gettysburg Address, which we agreed was the best non-religious text to recite at a funeral and was fresh in our minds from Mrs. Oglebie's class. We washed the mud off ourselves at the edge of the dock and headed back to the house when *they* finally arrived.

They didn't show themselves; that time was over.

Instead, there was the sound of feet, light, quick, beginning from the far end of the boardwalk, by the stone table, gathering speed in the darkness. My heart raced as I stared down the planks, empty and bare. The footsteps grew louder, nearer, as the sound rushed straight through me. It was the oddest feeling, like having an X-ray taken. You search your body for a sensation, and even though you find none, you know something has made contact. The footsteps continued down toward the dock, and my throat squeezed as I realized they were heading toward the lake, toward the dripping man, but before I could cry out, there was a sudden, chilling silence, and then a tremendous splash.

Chase turned toward the water, looking startled. It's the only time he's ever witnessed them, or their wake, anyway, and he hasn't spoken a word about it since.

"Stay away from my house," I whispered.

But it wasn't my house. It's never been my house. The dead always have the upper hand. They see every move we make. They know our darkest secrets.

We buried a body under those boards.

That cannot be undone.

"It's just an old family legend," I say now. I can't tell Chase my secret. What I've seen; what I know. I'll never say it. What's the point? He won't hear me.

He grins, but there's annoyance underneath. "What does that have to do with night swimming? Which, may I add, we do every year?"

"Not without a Hartford. And I'm not going this year." I take his cigarette and toss it into the trash. "Legend or no legend, rules are rules." I look him in the eye. "Right?"

His grin doesn't fade. Neither does the resentment beneath the surface. "You got it."

Back in the living room, Emily is sunk even deeper into the couch. I want to say something comforting, but I don't feel like speaking to her yet. She hasn't apologized, and it strikes me that she never apologizes for anything. I apologize when I mess up, and I do mess up. Chelsea apologizes. Chase, even Ryan. But Emily. Somehow, whenever we fight, it is someone else's fault. She is always the victim, no matter how deeply twisted things get. Like her half-truth to Mila earlier, or to Chelsea about the heirloom. I *never* told her to insinuate that Chelsea stole anything. What I said was that she should throw my mother under the bus. No one would get mad at my mom for banning me from having friends over the way they would hate me for ending our long-standing tradition. Emily twisted that, and I honestly don't know if Chelsea has ever forgiven me. Emily should have apologized then. And she should apologize now. Any real friend would feel horrible for what she did.

Ryan barely glances up when I walk into the room. He tosses a pack of cards to Chelsea. "Texas Hold'em?"

Chelsea looks to me. "What do you want to do?"

I shrug. "Poker sounds fine."

Emily stands abruptly and stalks upstairs. In a moment I can hear stomping footsteps in the attic.

"I think she's waiting for you to apologize," Ryan says as he deals, without meeting my eyes.

"You've got to be kidding me." I snatch my cards off the table. "You saw—" Then I realize that he doesn't know what actually happened. Only Chelsea and Emily know. It's best that way. Contain. Defuse.

"You really hurt her." He darts his eyes to Chelsea as if looking for backup.

Chelsea clears her throat. "Actually, the thing is, maybe we've all been hurting her. By encouraging this thing with Chase that doesn't exist. Or even not actively discouraging it. You know what I mean?"

He looks taken aback. "I would never hurt my sister on purpose."

"Right, not on purpose. But maybe by not being completely clear about how it is." Chelsea places her cards down. "I fold."

"You don't want any cards?" Ryan taps the deck a few times. "Fine."

Ryan deals her a card.

"I call," she says.

He hands me a card. "Kennedy?"

"Raise." I place a chip down, and Chelsea reluctantly matches it. Crap hand.

"We all pretty much agree Chase isn't interested, right? I mean, Emily is so special. She's smart, she's pretty, she's unique, she's talented. Chase appreciates that. There's just no spark on his end. It's no one's fault." It suddenly occurs to me that what Chelsea is saying sounds suspiciously like a breakup speech. And I'm sitting in the middle of it. I try to catch her eye to signal *bad idea*, but she's focused intently on Ryan. I love her to death, but reading the room is not among her strengths.

"Yeah," Ryan says. "I guess that's true."

"False hope is painful," Chelsea says.

Ryan deals her another card, slowly this time, his eyes trained on the deck. "It is."

"Shit. I mean, hmm." She assumes her best poker face, which is terrible. "I call."

I take my next card. Pair of queens. It isn't great, but it doesn't look like she has anything. "Raise you twenty."

"Twenty? I'm out." She tosses her cards down, and I show my hand. "Oh, come on. I had three twos."

Ryan picks up her cards to verify. "Then why did you fold?"

She shrugs. "Kennedy always wins."

Ryan drops his head into his forearm and laughs, and when he raises his head, his face is flushed. "When did you start thinking you were better than me?" His eyes are bright, almost feverish, as he stares desperately at Chelsea. I feel like I've evaporated, an invisible witness.

Chelsea's mouth drops open in dismay. "I never thought that."

I scramble to my feet and make a dash for the kitchen. "The dishes," I mumble incoherently, slamming the doors behind me and collapsing against them, my heart tumbling in my chest. There can't be another fight now, but I'm human and weak, and I need this to end. I need Ryan and Chelsea to be definitively over, and I need to know it for sure. I press my head against the wall, straining to hear over the sound of my racing heart in my ears.

"We used to laugh at them. Golden boy and gossip girl." Ryan's voice is low and difficult to make out. "They have it so easy. They have everything and they still *want*. I've only ever wanted one thing, you know this." I feel dizzy, like I'm having an out-of-body experience. This is a scene from a movie, but in the movies, it's a romance, and the guy gets the girl. In real life, it's horrific. He doesn't deserve her just because he wants her. She doesn't want him. It hits me so hard then, how much I've tortured myself pointlessly with questions. Whatever happened in the past, she doesn't want him, she never did—not while we were together. The only time that matters.

"Everyone wants," she says softly. "It's human."

"I love you, Chelsea." His voice cracks and I close my eyes. This is not happening. Not here. Not now. "You know Kennedy doesn't get you the way I do. You don't have to lie to me, because I know you and I love every bit of who you are. You don't have to live up to any bullshit standard. You're perfect to me, Chelsea. And you know I would do anything for you. I would. You know all of this is true. And I would never, *never* let you go."

"You have to," she snaps. There's an awful, gaping silence.

"Please, Chelsea." His voice goes whisper soft; the house is silent. "You're the only thing that makes sense anymore."

"I know it feels that way." Chelsea's voice is muffled, and I force myself not to look through the glass pane of the door, but I know his arms are around her, her face pressed into his shoulder. I know she's holding on to her friendship, afraid that saying the wrong thing will shatter it, and he's desperate to cling to something else. It hurts to hear.

"Then there's nothing left for me here," he says, bitterness saturating every word.

"I'm still here," she says.

"You are so long gone." He laughs dully. "I've been holding on to a fucking ghost."

I hear the door slam and peek my head back into the room. Chelsea is still sitting cross-legged on the floor, sobbing into her hands.

"I said nothing to make him believe—"

"I know." I put an arm around her.

She leans into me. "It was only a few months." Her voice hitches as she presses her face into my shoulder, and I feel her sob into me, the energy of her sorrow flowing through me like an electric current. "I was sad," she says, sounding so worn down I want to wrap her in layers of blankets and let her sleep for a week. "And I missed you so much." Her body relaxes as if the hurt is flowing out. "And he loved me. I still care about him. I should have told you, shouldn't I? I was so afraid. I couldn't bury the hope that you and I might get back together."

"Neither could I." I kiss her hand. It feels warm and feverish.

"Everyone said if you ever found out, you wouldn't forgive me."

I pull back and look at her. "Everyone said that?"

Chelsea pauses for a moment. "Emily."

Emily.

"Well, she was wrong. I broke up with you. You're allowed to fall for someone else. If you'd just been honest . . . I was afraid it wasn't completely over between you and Ryan."

"It was. It is. He just can't let it go." Her expression darkens.

But before I can answer, there's a huge splash outside.

The wave of cold crashes over me so quickly, so violently, that for a second I'm stunned speechless.

I close my eyes. "Son of a *mother.*"

40

I find Mila perched at the end of the dock, her legs dangling down into the water, Chase splashing below. Chelsea hangs back as Ryan towers above, frowning down at him. "Get out."

I lay a hand on his arm. "I've got it. Thanks. Chase, no swimming drunk. House rules."

He looks up at me with an innocent grin. "You make the rules. You can break the rules."

"I don't want to break the rules. The rules exist for a reason." I give him a meaningful look.

In response, he splashes me in the face. I slowly wipe the water out of my eyes. Mila giggles and I stifle the urge to push her in after Chase. Let them find out for themselves. "It's not up for debate. Get out or go home."

"He can't go home without getting out," Mila says. "It's not a fair choice."

"She has a point, Ken. Give me something to work with." Chase glides back farther from the dock in a relaxed backstroke. He's so arrogant. He may be *like* a brother to me, but he isn't. It isn't his house. He doesn't have the responsibility to make sure everyone is okay all the time. As long as he splashes around like a jerk, I'm obligated to stay out here and babysit him, and really, I'm not in any condition to jump in after him if anything goes wrong. And I am becoming more and more convinced that something is going to go wrong.

"Please just get out," I say, my temper strained.

"You're being an asshole, Chase," Ryan says.

"Stay out of it," Chelsea whispers.

"Seriously, Ryan. You should rest your mouth. You might sprain your neck again, and we'd have to have you airlifted to the Saint Bullshit Hospital for imaginary injuries." Chase treads water, watching Ryan. I can't even believe he started again. Again. I don't know what's wrong with him. With anyone.

But instead of going ballistic like I expect him to, Ryan just says, in this calm, eerie voice, "That's it, Chase."

Chase doesn't answer, but he looks uncertain. He's drunk, really drunk, and I know he's going to regret everything he's said tonight. He loves Ryan. I know he does. I don't know if the feeling is mutual anymore. I don't know how Ryan feels about any of us. Except my girlfriend.

Chelsea steps between him and the edge of the dock. "Okay. Let's all take a deep breath."

It's difficult to tell if Ryan was already in motion at that point or if he just spontaneously shot forward, but somehow his arms are suddenly on Chelsea's shoulders, and then she's in the water. Mila screams and I skid to the edge and reach down to help Chelsea, but when she looks up at me, there's real, actual terror in her eyes. Not hurt—terror.

My heart leaps into my throat, and my lungs seem to empty as I pull her up.

But she's okay. He let her go.

"What the hell is wrong with you," Chase shouts. He cuts through the water and hauls himself up onto the dock.

"I'm so sorry. Chelsea. Chelsea." Ryan pushes his way toward her, but she turns away from him, shivering. "It was an accident." He jumps aboard the boat and comes back with a towel. "Here." Ryan tries to wrap it around Chelsea, but I yank it out of his hands and drape it around her myself, then pull her against me protectively. I am losing control. I cannot protect my friends. This is not supposed to happen.

Chelsea stares at Ryan, wide-eyed. "It was not an accident. You're different. You're changing. Chase, you too. I don't know what's wrong with everyone. Emily, Kennedy, even you."

"Oh, and you're magically exempt?" Mila says.

"You don't know her." I eye her coldly. "You don't get to weigh in."

Mila climbs onto the boat, finds another towel, and hands it to Chase. "Here."

Chase shakes himself off like a dog after a swim and then towel-dries himself vigorously. "Say what you want about me—I don't attack women."

Mila wanders back to the boat and swings a leg over the side, then another.

"Please get off the boat." I turn back to Chelsea. "Are you okay?"

She nods shakily. "Yes. I just need to make some tea or something."

"Okay. The rest of us are going to talk for a moment."

Chelsea gives me a look. "Don't make a bigger deal."

I kiss her hand. "Relax. Seriously. Lavender and chamomile

on the top tea shelf. Make a whole pot. I'll be there in three minutes."

She smiles. "Three minutes." She slicks her hair back, casts Ryan an unforgiving look, and heads back into the house.

"Let's go for a sail," Mila says.

I ignore her. "Guys, this has to stop. Either we all have to get our shit together or we have to go home. Play nice or go home—those are the rules. And no more rule breaking." I look from Ryan to Chase. Ryan looks sullen, his face blistered and burned from a day of overexposure.

Chase points to Ryan. "Talk to him. I'm perfectly fine the way things are."

"I'm not," I say firmly. "Everything's been sloping south for a while, but it's taken a sudden dive. And I'm not okay with it. We only have two more years together. But the way things are going, we're not going to make it through the summer. Chase, you have to stop it with the passive-aggressive comments toward Ryan. I'm not getting in the middle of your drama, but it's got to stop."

Chase side-eyes Ryan. "No drama."

Ryan presses his lips together. "Mm-hmm."

I cross my arms. "You're both terrible liars."

"Mila's leaving," Chase says.

"Good riddance." I can't help it.

"No, she's taking the boat." He points behind me.

I turn around. "Shit. Mila!"

Mila's unfurled the sails while we've been talking, and a steady wind has begun to move her away from the dock. She waves innocently. "Moonlight sail. You can make it if you jump."

I stare, aghast. None of this is remotely acceptable. In the best-case scenario, my father would flip out if he found out that Chase's guest, who for all I know doesn't even know how to sail, took the boat out by herself. Drunk. In the worst, Mila is heading into the darkness to meet the dripping man alone. I back up, take a running leap, and barely make it onto the deck, sliding into the mast and hitting my head for the second time.

"Shit," Mila says. "Are you okay?"

I sit, my forehead throbbing. At least I hit a different *part* of my head. Still, I'll be lucky if there's anything left of my brain by morning.

Chase lands on the deck beside me, and Ryan hits the water a moment later. I can't help a petty grin spreading across my face. Push my girlfriend into the water. Karma. Chase throws him a line and hauls him up.

"Turn around and take us back," I tell Chase. "We're not doing this tonight."

"Pretty pretty please." Mila jumps up and down and presses herself against Chase, swaying against him. "I want to see the stars."

"You can see them from the dock." I massage my forehead. "We all drank way too much to operate a boat. Back it up."

"Come on. It's so romantic out here." She nuzzles up to him.

"Really?" Ryan says in a flat voice. "Is it romantic?" He sits next to me. "How enchanting for all of us."

I stand, but sway on my feet and have to sit again. "Look, I can't sail right now. My head is completely messed up. I need a few minutes for it to clear." But a swift wind has picked up out of nowhere, and we're rapidly moving toward the middle of the lake. Marvelous.

"Give us ten," Chase says. "Fair compromise. Mila gets to see the stars, you get to rest your head, and then we go straight back."

"Please, Mom?" Mila says.

I'm really starting to dislike that girl.

"Fine." I sigh.

"Really?" Ryan looks back toward the house. "This is the moment you choose to start backing down on things?"

"What's the rush, Ry?" I tap my forehead gently. Definitely well on its way to a bruise.

"I'm done with this place. I'm done with all of you. The last thing I want is to spend another minute in that house. Or in my own, for that matter." He goes to the back of the boat and hangs over the edge, trailing his arm into the water.

I look at Chase. "Will you talk to him, please?"

He shrugs uncomfortably. "I don't think anything good is going to come out of talking right now." The wind dies a little, and he spins the steering wheel. "Mila, can you take in that line?"

She tugs at the ratchet and succeeds in tightening the sail a little, but not enough. I look up. The telltale has fallen flat. The night air feels misty and heavy, windless. We rock back and forth, drifting a little, but not really catching any wind. There isn't any to catch. I sigh and bump Mila aside with my hip, straining to tighten the sail as far as I can, but it doesn't help.

"Drop anchor." I let the sail down. "Ryan, get your hand out of the water. Everyone, arms and legs inside the boat."

"Come on," Ryan groans.

"There's no wind. We have to wait it out. Probably just a few minutes. Let Mila look at her freaking stars." I flop down next to him as Mila and Chase snuggle close to each other at the bow of the ship. "Tell me something, Ryan."

"What's that?"

"What's so horrible that you need to get away from?"

He looks down at the water. "Nothing. I'm not running."

"I never used the word *running*." I pause. "I know this has been a shitty year. I'm really sorry, Ryan."

"I bet." He shifts so that his face is in profile. "Some people think they're entitled to everything, don't they?"

"Like who?"

Ryan shrugs, gazing up at the stars. "Off the top of my head? Chase for one."

"He's earned all of it."

"Has he? He was born athletic, I guess, but he also had years of lacrosse camp. He studies, but he also has expensive tutors. Are those things you can really earn, Kennedy? Or do your parents give them to you?"

I shift uncomfortably in my seat. "I guess it's not necessarily earned."

He glances at me, and I feel the accusation in his eyes cutting right down to my core. "What about people? How do you earn people, Kennedy?"

I rest my head on my hand and study his face. I've never paid enough attention to Ryan. He fades into the background too easily. His laid-back posture, his mild expressions, his soft voice. But he's not mild. He's sharp and bitter and angry. "You can't earn people. People like Chase because he's authentic. Friendly and funny. He's a people person."

"No. He's charismatic. He can be friendly. He can also be manipulative. Just like you, Kennedy."

"Well, you can be passive-aggressive and sulky and scary, Ryan. I think that can turn people off."

He smiles. "I guess it would. The nice guys never get the girl."

I laugh in disbelief. "Are you the nice guy?"

"I think so."

"Well, I would disagree with you. I think you've been a dick today."

He looks me in the eye. "Why shouldn't I be? Why should I continue to be a doormat?"

There's a sudden bang and I turn, startled. Chase and Mila have disappeared. I dash across the deck, heart pounding, before realizing they've locked themselves below in the cabin. I kick the door, then sit behind the steering wheel and turn it absently. "You're not a doormat. You're just self-centered. You can't expect someone to love you just because you have feelings for them. That's not how it works, and it doesn't make you a nice guy. I know life feels unfair and it seems like some people get all the wins, but there's no such thing as deserving a person. And you can't take it out on Chelsea, because she cares about you. Way too much."

He whips his head up suddenly. "Why? What did she tell you?"

"Nothing."

Ryan stands, a silhouette against the moon. "Then ask me."

I raise my head wearily. "What?"

"What really happened between Chelsea and me."

A chill runs down my spine. "It's none of my business. All that matters is it's over."

"Nothing stays a secret between friends, though, does it?" He starts walking toward me, and I stand instinctively.

"Sure it docs. I don't want to know."

"Yes, you do. You need to know everything. You always have to be in the center of everything. You're the hostess." He says it mockingly. "You make the seating arrangements. The sleeping arrangements. You decide who eats with who. Who talks to who. Who sleeps with who."

"God, Ryan, stop. I don't want to know." I hold my hands up, but he presses forward like some nightmare zombie creature, and I edge backward until I'm up against the side of the boat and he's pressed against me. I want to scream for Chase, but my voice feels stuck. I'm so thrown off, so taken aback, it feels like the world has turned completely upside down. Ryan is the quiet one. Chelsea's weird-secret-psychic-bond person. He's not the one who pushes you against the side of a boat and says creepy things. I have to be misinterpreting this. I have to.

"Did it ever occur to you that maybe the reason I get so mad at you is because deep down I'm in love with you?" It's so cold I start shivering. I shake my head. "Good," he says. "Because it's bullshit." He grins.

I duck under his arm. "You're an asshole." I try to gather all my anger, bottle and bury it. We're not alone out here. Asshole or not, I can't let my anger put him in danger.

"Now you know how it feels," he says.

But my head aches and my heart pounds, and the cold is already seeping in.

I turn. "How it feels? You're a foot taller than I am, and you cornered me in the dark. On a boat. Far from help. Today you've slapped Chase, given Mila a bloody nose, and pushed Chelsea into the lake, which she's terrified of. You have no idea how it feels."

He nods slowly. "Okay. But Kennedy? I don't care. Because I don't like you."

I feel like the wind has been knocked out of me. It's a stunning thing to hear, especially from someone you've spent so much time with for so many years. It's literally breathtaking.

"You play power games," he goes on. His face is so still, his voice so low and calm. "You control people. It's all a game to you. Everything is a game. Playing house. Playing friends. Playing life. No consequences for golden boy and gossip girl."

"You have no idea what you're talking about." That shit. That ungrateful shit. The amount of terror and isolation and exhaustion I've lived with to protect them. All of them.

But he's not done. "You always win. I hate that, too. Chelsea—"

"Chelsea isn't a fluffy toy at a carnival. She's a person."

"She sees through you," he says with a slanted smile. "Sooner or later, she's going to be gone. Or is she already? It's hard to tell sometimes. When we were—you know." He averts his eyes in an unconvincing display of modesty.

I glare at him, blood beginning to pulse loudly, pounding an angry rhythm in my ears. "I told you, it's none of my business."

He bites his lip and smiles, gazing up. "I'll leave it up to your imagination. She had a lot to say about you. I was pretty shocked when you got back together, I'll put it that way."

"Well. Guess you don't know her very well." I keep my face placid. Now he looks furious.

"I know her better than you ever will."

"Excuse me?"

"Why do you think we got together in the first place? Because neither of us could stand the rest of you. On the surface, sure. We'll always care about each other. But underneath, she resents you every bit as much as I do, because you don't respect her, you treat her like an outsider, and no one, no one in the world, wants to feel like that. You make Chelsea feel bad about herself. So you can drop the smug true-love act. She may not want me, but you're bad for her." He stares at me derisively as my heart goes cold in my chest. The worst words, the ones that cut like knives, are ones dipped in the subtle poison of truth. And I don't want to believe him, but I can see in his eyes that he believes, and I feel in the pit of my stomach that there might be some truth to it. Do the words we use to describe Chelsea—quirky, random, unique—make her feel less special and more like an outsider? When I say offhand things like her ability to silence a room, does it make her feel like she doesn't fit in with the rest of us?

"I'm not bad for her," I whisper. But the squeezing feeling in my chest grows tighter.

"Then why did she come to me when you tossed her aside?"

I try to make sense of what he's saying. "I didn't toss her aside. It was complicated."

Ryan shrugs. "No, it wasn't. You wanted Chelsea at the lake

house, in our little world, where everything was under your control. Back at school you had to deal with the real world. Judgment. Reputation. You don't belong with a Chelsea, do you? You belong with someone like Chase. You can't tell me that never went through your head. Can you?" His eyes meet mine, and they are so devoid of emotion, I want to smack him in the face. No. That's too little. Child's play.

"I don't give a shit what people think."

"But you thought about it."

"Everyone thinks!" I scream, my head pounding. I hate him. I hate myself. Everyone thinks terrible things. Fleeting, wrong things that they regret. They shouldn't come back to haunt you. Not when you keep them silent, bottled inside. Ryan has no right.

"Not me," he snarls back. "I am not like you."

"Well, good for you, Ryan. Good for the nice guys. You're right. You never win."

He tears at his hair and lets out a burst of angry, disbelieving laughter. "Maybe I'm not nice. But I never broke her heart. That's the difference between you and me. You're a heartless, entitled princess. Chase is a spoiled brat. My sister is a manipulative jerk. And Chelsea is just naive. I'm so done with all of you."

I try not to let tears show, but I can't stop them from stinging my eyes. I had no idea how much contempt he had for all of us. Even his own sister. But especially for Chelsea. "I want you out."

"Fine with me. I'm sick of all of you. Your fakeness. Chase's arrogance. The way Chelsea looks at me. It's all so pathetic. *She's* pathetic."

I grit my teeth. "Do not say her name again."

He smiles that infuriating smirk again.

My heart pounds. I have protected him. I may not have liked him always, but I have loved him like family.

"It's your fault, Kennedy," he says. "You threw us together. Your house. Your rules. If it wasn't for you, Chelsea and I never would have fucked."

I push him.

41

It happens so quickly I don't realize it until it's done. The splash is immediately swallowed up in silence. Everything is wrong. Every instinct in my body tells me to rush to the edge of the boat, to throw a line, to shout *Man overboard*, to start the safety protocol I've known by heart since I was six.

But I somehow don't move.

The moonlight hazes down through a light mist that's begun to settle over the lake, my arms look almost iridescent rising up before me, and I listen. Below, Chase and Mila are silent. I look back to the house, my eyes instinctively going straight to the attic window, and I see the silhouette of a head in profile, bent down. Reading. Emily. Maybe with her tarot cards. I see a shadow pass behind her, and frost creeps over my skin.

After Miss Palindrome's murder, the blue lady disappeared along with the others, but they weren't gone. The woman on the stairs always gave me a chill when I had to get something from the cellar, and sometimes I stumbled on the steps. The crushed man bounced around between the living room and garden. He might have been a groundskeeper once—I feel the breeze of his approval when I tend to the roses. Or he might be the one who kills them. I like to think it's the former. No one who hates flowers haunts a garden.

The backward girl is a drifter, sometimes lying in the grass in the warm sunshine, sometimes fluttering a breeze through an open door. And the blue lady is everywhere, but especially the attic. I sometimes feel they're hiding from me. Like they think that since I can't see them anymore, I don't know they're there. Like I can't feel when they draw close to inspect me curiously or allow themselves to treat me like their pet again. I'm pretty sure that's how they've always seen me. Their quaint, living pet.

The problem is that the living and the dead aren't meant to mix.

The problem is that I think the line has begun to blur.

The problem is that I have spent so long in the world of the dead that I am about to lose one of the living and it is entirely my fault.

Oh god, what if that was their plan from the beginning?

What have I done?

Suddenly a sound splits the air and I'm jolted back into the present.

Chelsea. She's standing on the dock, shouting.

I rush to the edge of the boat and look down, the gravity of the situation finally sinking in. He hasn't resurfaced. Ryan, who is an excellent swimmer, who just today jumped in to rescue Mila, is still underwater, and I don't know how long it's been. He is underwater with the dripping man. And the dripping man doesn't let go. I move clumsily, hyperaware of the amount of alcohol in my bloodstream, the possible concussion, the instructions to sit still and rest tonight. My sweater sticks around my neck, and I stumble on my way to the cabin door. I pound my sneaker down on it repeatedly as I wrestle to get my sweater over my head.

Chase finally yanks the door open. "What?"

I pull the sweater off, gasping. "Ryan went overboard. He's gone under. I don't see him. I need you above to watch the water while I go after him."

"No. You stay on board. I'll go in after him." He scales the ladder in an instant and surveys the water uncertainly. "Where?"

Mila climbs up, looking terrified. "I can barely swim."

"Good." I kick my sneakers off. "I need you to stay aboard. Both of you. If you see me in distress, throw me a safety line."

Chase shakes his head. "I'm going in."

At that moment, there is a distant splash, and all three of us turn our heads.

"Was that him?" Mila asks.

"Shit. No." I climb over the edge of the boat and scan the water by the dock, at the figure cutting through the water toward us. "That was Chelsea."

"Chelsea can't swim," Chase says, rising panic in his voice.

"She can," I say. "She just doesn't." The terrible feeling in my gut is beginning to spread throughout my body like frost. There's no time to explain. Or decide. "Chase, if you start to feel cold, get out. It's not worth it. You take that side. I'll take this area. He went in over here." I point to the general area where Ryan hit the water. My heart continues to race faster and faster. What if we can't rescue him? I pushed him. I did it. This isn't happening. It can't. It can't happen. "Mila, keep your eyes on Chelsea."

I dive into the water without wasting another second.

We've wasted too many. No. Organization is vital to rescue. What if we both searched the same spot? What if we both looked for Ryan, but no one looked out for Chelsea, and we lost both of them? The black water surrounds me, and my thoughts overcrowd my mind.

He's down here. One of us will drown tonight.

How did this happen? I swim down as far as I can and spiral my way up in attempt to cover as much area as possible, but I hit nothing. When my head breaks the surface, I have to tread water for a moment to regain my balance. The world is tilting back and forth, sliding in and out of focus. Not now. I'm not going to lose it now.

I see Chase surface and we make eye contact. "Anything?" I shout.

"No. Going a little deeper."

His face is calm, but I hear the panic in his voice. He has no idea what we're up against. He gulps in a lungful of air and dives back down. I glance back up to the house. Emily hasn't moved. I can hear Chelsea still swimming toward us. I fill my lungs and plunge back into the darkness. It's harder this time. I feel out of air almost immediately, my heart drumming a death sentence, my head aching, the Tylenol wearing off, the wine swirling around, driving me up when I mean to swim down. I try again, and again I become disoriented and quickly propel myself straight up to the surface. My eyes sting with tears, and I scream and punch the water.

"What's going on?" Mila shouts.

"Nothing. Just, nothing. Is your eye on Chelsea?" I can't help snapping at her. This isn't a time for being nice.

"I was looking for Ryan." She falters.

My blood runs cold. "Stop looking. Where is she now?" I swing my head around, but I don't see her. Then I hear a splash about fifty yards away, no voice. I immediately begin to swim toward it, slowed by tears and shivering and my body beginning to shut down from panic.

I collide with Chelsea before I see her. She grabs onto my neck and the weight pulls me under, water flooding into my nostrils, intense pain filling my head. I can't breathe. I'm a fish out of water. No. The other. I kick away from her and grasp for the surface, pulling, pulling up. "Stop. Chelsea. Stop swimming. Just stop. Let go. Trust me."

She spits out a mouthful of water, coughs. "I'm drowning."

"Just relax, and I'll get you to the boat."

"I can't."

"You can." It takes everything in me to mask my own panic. But I do, long enough for her to roll onto her stomach in a dead man's float, her head turned to the side, shivering. I grasp her carefully and begin to sidestroke slowly toward the boat.

"Someone fell off the boat. They went straight under and didn't come back up. It was like something grabbed them or something," she says.

"I know. Chase is getting them."

"Who was it?"

"Ryan."

She starts crying, and I feel the last part of my heart that was intact rip in two. "Chase is taking care of it," I say.

"There was something in the water. Something grabbed him."

"It's a lake," I say. "Nothing grabbed him." *But it did. He did. Stop. Protect.*

"Then how did he disappear like that? People don't just sink."

I don't answer. Instead, I focus my strength on closing the distance between us and the boat. When I reach it, Mila helps pull Chelsea up onto the deck, but she doesn't look at either of us. Her face looks completely drained of blood and her eyes are wide open, fixed on the water. Her hair is wild and messed up, her shirt thrown on backward. She looks like a figure from a horror movie, like someone who just stepped through a mirror in a haunted house or something. As soon as Chelsea is safely on board, Mila turns from us as if in a trance and leans over the side of the boat, watching. I try to help Chelsea sit down, but she drapes herself next to Mila, shaking hard, shuddering breaths, blinking tears down her face.

"We have to do something," Chelsea says.

I stand behind her, afraid to do or say anything. It's been minutes. There is nothing else to do. Chase resurfaces yet again, takes another determined breath, and goes back under. Mila inhales sharply, as if each dive is another stab of a needle. That's what it's beginning to feel like. My eyes go back to the house. Emily is still in the window, her head down. She doesn't know.

I turn to Chelsea. "You're right, you know. People don't just sink. He probably swam away to freak us all out."

She looks at me with contempt. "He wouldn't do that. He's not cruel."

I look at her. I love her. I really do. "Of course he isn't."

Chase reappears. He floats on the surface for a moment, a shadow in the water. Then he slowly makes his way to us and silently climbs the ladder, dripping water on the already-soaked deck. Mila continues to stare at the water, and Chelsea covers her face with her hands, but I look at Chase.

"I can't do it anymore," he whispers. "I'm exhausted." I want to cry. Those words are everything.

"He probably swam for shore," I say in an even voice. "People aren't stones. They're filled with air."

"Not when they drown." Chelsea looks at me. "I saw him fall."

A shiver runs down my spine. "So, what did happen?"

She shakes her head. "It was far away. He fell in and never came back up. I told you, it was like something pulled him down."

Chase glances at me. "Where were you when it happened?"

"I got tired waiting for the wind. I closed my eyes for just a second. At least it felt like just a second. Then I heard the splash and . . ." I shrug. "I got you right away."

He nods. "But you definitely saw where he went in?"

"I saw the splash." I steal a look at Chelsea. She's pacing back and forth, biting her nails.

"It's my fault. I should have stayed with you." She points at me. "You never would have gone out on the boat. I never would have tried to swim to the boat and then panicked, and you never would have had to rescue me, and you might have rescued him."

"It's not your fault," I say, a little sharper than I mean to.

"It is." Chelsea sits, her knees bouncing rapidly.

"I was the one who brought out the sangria," Mila says. "I

got him drunk. He wouldn't have fallen without me. He would have been able to swim."

"I'm sure he did swim," I say.

"No." Mila shakes her head. "I'm bad luck. I wanted to see the stars. I'm the whole reason we're out here on the boat." She finally turns and looks at us, and there's an odd expression on her face. "I'm cursed. I'm a siren. People follow me to their doom."

"No one is doomed." I eye Chase carefully. "I really think Ryan is fine."

He looks between me and the radio. "Well, you didn't seem to think so a few minutes ago. We should call for help right now. We should have done that first."

"I know." I close my eyes. "Just wait. Let me think."

"Where's Emily?" Chelsea looks back at the house. "What are we going to say to her? What are we going to say to her parents?"

"Nothing. We're not going to say anything. Ryan is fine." I retrieve a stack of towels and hand them out. "We got into a fight, he did one of those *You'll be sorry* things, and he dove in. The more I think about it, the more sure I am that he's doing this to get back at me. At us. Chase, he was fighting with you all night. Chelsea. Don't you think he might have some little passive-aggressive motive to Tom Sawyer you?"

"What do you mean?"

"Tom Sawyer fakes his own death and goes to his funeral to see how much everyone really cares about him. Also just to be an asshole," Chase says. "I guess I could see that? But it's fucked up."

"This day has been fucked up, Chase. Right?" I look to Chelsea first and she nods.

"I can't believe he would do that," she says softly. "I just thought he was the one person who didn't play mind games."

"Everyone plays mind games," Mila says. "We can't help it. It's in our wiring." She looks a little comforted already. The power of a good lie is inestimable.

"We're going to get back and find him waiting for us and laughing so hard," I say. But that won't work. Because they'll know immediately that he's still out here. If he is. Maybe he's not. Maybe he was just messing with me. Maybe there's no dripping man and my entire life has been one big delusion. Everything I've said makes perfect sense. People don't sink. "You know, though . . . He was honestly upset. About us. Emily. Chelsea. Chase. Even you, Mila. His parents. The last thing he said was that he wanted to be as far away from us as possible." I cringe as the words come out of my mouth.

Chase doesn't buy it for a second either. He knows me too well. "Ryan wasn't going to suddenly take off, no matter how pissed he was."

"But we all heard him," Mila says hesitantly. "When the wind died. Before Chase and I went below. He said he didn't want to be here *or* at home anymore. We all heard him say it."

"Why does it sound like we're standing here constructing an alibi?" Chelsea glares at us one by one.

"My cousin was in prison for six years," Mila says quietly. "I would basically do anything to avoid going through that. Anything."

Chelsea stares at me. "Kennedy. Don't make me go along with this."

I swallow, my throat tight. "No one is making anyone do

anything. He said what he said. He's probably back at the house."

"And if he isn't?" Her voice edges up in pitch.

"Then we can look for him, or wait it out, or call the police," I say. "Unless you think some sort of supernatural being pulled him under. Does anyone believe that?"

Not for one second.

Chase looks at the radio again. "They're going to ask why we didn't call right away."

I meet his gaze evenly. "*If* that were to happen, which it won't, we'd tell them the truth. He threatened to run away, told me I'd miss him, and swam off." My mouth and throat burn every time I spit out another lie. I may not have taken the time to think it through in the moment, but I knew exactly what would happen when I pushed Ryan into the water. There's no question. Whether Ryan miraculously made it back to the house or not, I'm going to hell for this. The only thing that remains to be seen is whether my life is ruined before that happens or not.

And I already know before we get back to the house, before we face Emily, patiently studying her cards in the attic. I know it in my bones.

No one is ever going to find him.

SUMMER OF SWANS

Last Year

Emily

42

It's been one year, and the house has the nerve not to change one bit. One full year of missing days. Stark and unforgiving, endless mileposts. But this is. This will be. The longest night.

I took extra care in the car to paint on my face exactly the way it should be. The way I have every day for a year. The day since Ryan disappeared. No note. No funeral. No closure.

I paint strength for my mother, humming along with the radio in the front seat. I still sit in the back, the passenger seat a placeholder, like Ryan is suddenly going to appear at the side of the road and hitch back into our lives.

Wouldn't that be just like him?

I paint a layer of quiet suffering for my friends, and determined resilience over that, a dab of mad genius under my eyes, a twist of mischief on my lips, so they know it's me underneath. I dust a shimmer of wonder over it all. I'm still here. I'm still me. I haven't faded under all of it. Nothing is going to break me.

They have nothing to worry about.

Not me.

We pull up in the driveway and the house rises above us like a demon waiting to swallow up our remains. The remains of my family. My father is already gone. His body is still here. But what use is a body? He doesn't speak. He doesn't hear. He just wanders through the rooms, looking. Looking at pictures. Examining artifacts. Staring at us. At my mother, accusing her for letting us run wild with Kennedy and Chase. He never liked them. He held their families in contempt. Entitled rich folks.

Maybe it had nothing to do with the fact that Chase's family had more than we did. But I doubt it.

Maybe he didn't think Kennedy would turn me into a lesbian.

But my dad isn't a good person.

None of us, any of us, are good people.

We don't deserve a happy ending.

Ryan isn't going to come back.

Chase isn't going to fall in love with me.

Chelsea isn't going to get over her nightmare.

Kennedy isn't going to have her fairy tale.

None are pardoned; all are punished.

I step out of the car and lug my suitcases behind me. Usually Ryan does this part for me. I don't pack light. I never have. I strain my face into a smile as Kennedy rushes down the stairs and gathers me into an embrace. Chelsea watches from the porch, leaning against the railing, her hands hanging loosely at her sides. I haven't seen her for almost a month. Not since the incident.

The other incident. When Chelsea hit a point break.

I'm getting sick of incidents.

"How *are* you?" Kennedy holds me at arm's length and examines me, like it's been months since we last saw each other, instead of a few days. This is how people treat me now. Is it sick that part of me enjoys the attention? I don't think so. I think it's warranted. I think it's the least they can do. After all, I've lost my twin. A twin is more than a brother. It's a part of you. I'm half missing. It's difficult to reconcile.

I allow Kennedy to struggle under the weight of my suitcases as I turn and wave my mother off, trying not to look too dismissive or impatient for her to go. If my father has faded into a ghost in the past year, my mother has become the opposite. Too tangible, an unsculpted lump of clay. Always parked in the same spot in front of the TV in the living room, equidistant between the landline in the kitchen and the front door in case the phone rings with good news or the police show up with bad news. How it must feel to be suspended in that awful state of flux.

I don't know exactly where Ryan is or what happened to him, but I do know one thing.

My friends know more than they're telling me.

I turn as Chase pulls up in his SUV and my throat tightens. He grins and waves as he bounds toward us and throws Kennedy over his shoulder. Which one of them was the last to see Ryan that night? It's so hard to tell. Their stories are so vague. Night swimming off the boat. After Kennedy shot me down when I had suggested we do the exact same thing. All of them exhausted from searching for him. But Mila returned to shore bone-dry. And she doesn't swim. Neither does Chelsea, for that matter, and *she* was wet. None of it adds up.

But Chase. He looks down at me with that look he's been giving me since last summer. The mix of sadness, regret, and something I can't put my finger on. Something that edges beyond the way everyone else looks at me now. Something that makes it okay for me to slip into the empty locker room with him, shut his mouth with mine to prevent a confession from falling out.

He slips a casual arm around my shoulder now, and I lean into him and smile, giving nothing away. I was angry when he left. The days melting into weeks blurred by police reports, interviews, silent moments waiting, my father turning to stone, my mother flickering like a candle, Chelsea quarantined supposedly with mono, Kennedy studying nonstop. I needed Chase. I've always needed Chase. This was his chance to finally be there for me. And he failed.

Until suddenly it was September. And he was mine, in secret, all mine. No one knows. No one can. It's a delicate balance, a tightrope walk. Guilt and suspicion and desire and loathing.

I loathe myself. This was never the way it was supposed to be.

It was never supposed to be a secret.

I was never supposed to be an obligation. Atonement. I look up at Chase, the sounds of Kennedy's voice blending in with the birds. He's smiling, but it's his new smile. Thin. Elastic. Ready to snap. My head floats down and I look at Chelsea. She's lost weight over the past year. After the note incident, she stopped eating lunch with the rest of us. She just disappears at lunchtime and reappears for English. Maybe she's in guidance, or maybe she's crying in the bathroom. I don't really care. I blame her most of all. She could have stopped whatever happened, whether he really did run away, or got himself into worse trouble. She always had some strange power over Ryan. I hated her for it, a little.

Just a little.

"Shall we?" Kennedy nods toward the door, and Chase takes my suitcases from her.

"Are your parents here?" I don't see their fancy-ass BMW in the driveway.

"I came up with Chelsea." Kennedy smiles over her shoulder. "We're on our own. But I have our entire weekend planned. No need to worry about a thing. We stopped at the cutest farm stand."

I tune her out as I step inside the house. The smell makes me shudder, dry and hot and wooden, like the inside of a coffin. Everything about this house is a rotten piece of history that should be buried. Kennedy and Chelsea head into the kitchen, and Chase begins to carry my bags upstairs, but I stop him.

"Leave the green one down here. I have some of my art things in it."

He places it down carefully and leans against the wall. "How are you doing?" He darts an eye out the window and quickly looks away.

"Okay. I mean, I think it'll be good to be here. For all of us. To get closure or something." Answers. To get answers.

Chase nods, a stiff jerk of his head. "Right, but he's out there somewhere. He'll turn up when we least expect it. You know Ry." He grins, a lightning flash that illuminates those irresistible eyes. Dark and beautiful and so naive. Every day is summer, Chase.

I lean toward him and he bends down and pulls me close, pressing his lips against mine. He tastes like sweat, sweetness, salt. I want to drink him down and drown in him. I want to erase every second of the past year except these moments where we're together and the world is obliterated. But he pulls away the second Kennedy calls his name.

"I'm gonna get the rest of the bags, 'kay?" He runs his hand along my collarbone and I tug him toward me, but he drifts away.

"Later?"

"For sure." He smiles and taps my nose with his forefinger. It leaves me feeling cold and hollow.

I gaze out the window at the lake, the grave formed by some shifting rocks or pounded out by a falling star millions of years ago, filled by endless years of rain. I pull the glass down and bolt it shut tightly, then fix my eyes on the placid water.

Ryan.

Can you hear me?

I hope so.

I've been so lonely this past year.

Kennedy makes tuna sandwiches for lunch, and we eat them out by the lake. I literally hate her for how good they are. The bread is crusty and she uses olive oil, freshly ground pepper, lemon juice, and some other shit I can't identify instead of mayo and celery like any normal person. Who does she think she is? This isn't *Top Chef.* It's life. My brother's body could be decomposing in the lake.

I feel like I'm desecrating him by continuing to eat, but

it's good and I'm starving. So I hate Kennedy for making me.

"So." As if she can hear me thinking her name, Kennedy brushes her shining hair out of her eyes and smiles at me. A soft, tentative smile. *Sorry Ryan's gone, but let's make the best of it.* That's the implication embedded in the slight downturn at the left corner of her lips. "What's the plan after lunch?"

I chew on the crusty bread, even more annoyed. It's delicious, but it takes forever to shred into pieces small enough to swallow. I take an enormous gulp of icy lemonade. "Whatever. You're the hostess. Do your thing."

Kennedy chews the side of her mouth. "I thought maybe you had something specific in mind when you wanted to come back up here." She looks at Chelsea, but Chelsea is off in wonderland, gazing distractedly at the lake, one leg swung over the stone bench, as if being beckoned to it by sirens the rest of us can't hear. Maybe that's what happened to Ryan.

"You said you had the whole weekend planned out," I say, putting my sandwich down.

"I meant food," Kennedy says. "I thought that was implied." She drums her fingers on the table rapidly. "We can just hang out. It's fine. I didn't know if there was some special spiritual thing you wanted to say or do to honor Ryan, or something?" She trails off, an eyebrow raised.

I can feel my face go from white to red in an instant. "I'm not my mom." I grab my glass and head for the kitchen, heart pounding in my ears. My eyes burn and my body buzzes with adrenaline. I want to turn right around and smack the condescension off her face. Instead I slam the door behind me, drain half of my glass, and fill the rest with gin. My mother never spoke to the Hartfords before Ryan went missing. It wasn't the same as with my dad. It was a pride thing. She thought they looked down on her. Maybe they did. I don't know. They were always nice to me. But they may have felt sorry for the poor kid whose mother was a mall psychic and whose father worked at the country club where they played their charity tennis matches and lounged by pristine infinity pools.

She spoke to them after Ryan disappeared, though. Constantly. She called them nonstop. First with questions. What did they know? Did they remember anything else? Did a detective thoroughly examine the property? Then with requests. Could she have a private investigator speak to Kennedy? Could she speak to Kennedy alone? And finally, the kicker—could she have a medium, a ghost whisperer, walk through the house with her?

They got a restraining order.

The back door swings open, and I hide the gin bottle guiltily. It's not like we don't drink sometimes, especially up here. But it's early, and without permission, and I grabbed a lot.

Chelsea wanders up to me and pulls a blood orange–flavored soda from the refrigerator. "Kennedy didn't mean anything by it." She pops the top of the can and gives me a reproachful look. Like I'm the unreasonable one here.

"It sounded like she meant something very specific." I pick a sprig of mint off a potted plant and stick it in my mouth. Hopefully that will mask the smell a little.

"She didn't. And no one thinks anything bad about your mom, either."

I nod, but I feel the rage beginning to spread throughout

my body again. Chelsea has no idea. She has no clue what it was like to have Ryan go missing, to know all of my friends were with him when he disappeared and have them insist to my face that they knew nothing. To know that *I could have been there* if I hadn't been so stubborn that night. I could have been there. I can't get over that. I never will. She'll never know what it was like to have my family collapse around the black hole my brother's absence gave birth to, to see my father fade like a ghost, to have my mother in hysterics and not be able to offer her closure, and then to have *her* treated like there was something wrong with her. Quite the inconvenience, that tasteless woman. Get her out of our sight.

"I should have stopped by." Chelsea takes a sip of her drink, and the tattered hospital band slides out from her wispy linen shirt. This is what Chelsea has become. This is how I know she knows something. The note. The bracelet. All of the little clues.

What do they imply?

Guilt.

"You had your own shit to deal with," I say, trying on a sympathetic smile.

She nods. "It was a rough year for all of us."

But Chelsea didn't die or disappear. She's right here, in the flesh, heart pumping buckets of blood through her veins, just two feet from the knife drawer. I blink the thought away.

"I'll be right out."

She gives me an awkward, clinging hug, then wanders back out the door, and I exhale shakily.

It's odd, being back together like this.

Horrible and odd and revolting.

They shouldn't be here. It's a sacred site. To ignore that is a special kind of violence.

They should know better.

I have waited, checked my phone a thousand times, watched the door with my mother, knowing that hope is a coward's drug. Because I *know* there is a better way. Someone knows where Ryan is. Someone is lying to my face. Four some-ones. And they've had a whole year to come clean. It may just be time for a little nudge.

I head back outside and smile brightly. "You're absolutely right, Kennedy. I think we should try to communicate with Ryan's spirit."

43

Everyone stares at me.

"I meant more like if you wanted to say a few words to remember him or tell some stories," Kennedy says in a halting voice.

"An Irish wake?" Chase lifts his empty glass, and Kennedy refills it with lemonade. She looks nauseous. If they're so sure he's coming back, why are they acting like he's dead?

I shake my head. "No. I think we should hold a séance. That's what my mother wanted. Unfortunately, her request was denied."

Kennedy blushes. "I—I didn't have anything to do with—I don't really have any say—"

"It is your house, though." I raise an eyebrow.

"Yes. But it would be a legal violation for your mother to come here," she says quietly. "Even her dropping you off was kind of over the line."

Bitch. I pause. "I never said anything about inviting her. I just said it was what she wanted."

Chase pushes his plate around in a circle. "Hey, why not? We can do that, right?" He shoots Kennedy a look. "Closure for Emily. For everyone."

"But Ryan's not dead," Kennedy says. She looks pale. Nervous.

"Then what were you alluding to with the whole 'say a few words' thing?" he says, smiling in the way Kennedy's parents do when they're pretending not to fight. My parents don't do that kind of thing. They turn it straight up to eleven and start throwing *fuckwad* and *shithead* back and forth across the dinner table. Ryan and I were the cool kids who taught the other kids at school all the best words. Thinking back, that was probably our initial in with Kennedy and Chase. We knew the best curse words.

Now my parents never talk at all. The quiet is nice, except when it's not.

Kennedy sucks in a controlled breath. "I was just talking about remembering. We can remember him, wherever he is. Until he comes back."

Chelsea takes my hand with her warm, sweaty one. "Whatever you feel like, Em. We can light candles, close our eyes, and just open our minds to the possibilities. Right, Ken?"

Her earnestness is the most awful thing about her. She knows. She's always known. The old soul. Swooping in with her innate little ghost-whispery suggestions. I wouldn't really know the first thing about contacting the dead. That's my mother's area, and it's beyond what she does, even. But Chelsea. Mom has always idolized wildflower, dreamy-eyed, no-filter Chelsea. I always wanted to scream at my mother that there is nothing special about Chelsea. She's just weird. Everyone else at school sees it. She's awkward and random and has no sense of taste or style or the art of kissing ass. People only like her because she's Kennedy's best friend. I've always had to put in effort to stay in Kennedy's good graces. It's more exhausting than studying. It is like studying, in a way. A new exam every day, every time

I open my mouth. Always being silently judged. I wonder if that's what happened to Ryan. Maybe he finally said no to Kennedy.

But I bet that wasn't it. She would have kicked him out of Camelot. I bet it was a bigger sin. I bet he crossed Chelsea. The Queen of Cups herself.

There's only one way to find out.

I pick up my plate and begin to stack the other plates on top of it. Kennedy stares at me like I've just started peeing on the table or something. "I'll clean up. You've done so much."

She quickly jumps to her feet and starts gathering napkins and glasses, but I grab the silverware before she can get her hands on it. "Really, Emily, just sit back and relax."

"I've got it, Kennedy. Let me."

She presses her lips together and makes an odd strangled noise, and we carry our armloads into the kitchen silently. I can't help but note the pained expression on her face with satisfaction. It's killing her that I'm stealing her role. Kennedy is all about role-playing. Everything in its place. Everyone in their place. No one ever stepping out of line. Even to help anyone out. To save a friend from drowning? Maybe. We'll find out soon enough.

Chase follows me upstairs, and I pull him into Kennedy's room and lock the door behind us.

"Are you sure this is a good idea?" He twists his baseball cap in his hands, and I take it and toss it on the dresser and pull him onto the bed. "Whoa. I thought we were doing an 'Earth to Ryan' thing."

I kiss him quickly and urgently, the way we always kiss, rolling over on my side and sliding my hands up and down his body until he moves on top of me, tightening his grip on me and starting on my buttons.

"Here?" he whispers into my ear. "Right now?"

"Got anything in your pocket?"

"Always. Be prepared."

"Yes, here."

I can't help the way I feel about Chase. I don't know if I love him. I don't think it's possible to love someone and want to hide them, and I know that feeling is mutual. I don't know if it's possible to love someone and hate them too, though songs and movies seem to urge that possibility. It can't be healthy, but most of the relationships I've witnessed in my life aren't. I don't know what he saw that night, what he knows, and the fact that he won't tell me is unforgivable. But I've been wanting Chase so long, I can't turn it off. I don't want to be his girlfriend. I don't want to marry him. I just desire him. The messed-up part is that before Ryan disappeared, I think part of that desire had just a tiny, tiny, tiny bit to do with his pointless rivalry with Chase and the fact that Ryan is/was the Joiner family golden boy. I can't really explain it. But every time Prince Ryan was lavished with some unearned praise, I fantasized about having Chase. It would kill Ryan. It sounds more twisted than it is. It's a question of loyalty. Switching sides is the cruelest betrayal. I think all people have these thoughts but don't articulate them. I'm very in touch with my feelings. My mother doesn't see that about me. Maybe if she did, she would have said I was the one with the sight.

Anyway. After Ryan disappeared, it just intensified. Like being with Chase brought me closer to Ryan. Again. It sounds more twisted than it is, I think. I think. Because I think it's the same for Chase somehow. He never paid that much attention to me before. Not in a sexual way. Now it's like we can't get enough of each other. Only the second it's over, we have nothing to say and I feel like a traitor. No. I have everything to say, but it's all extremely unsayable.

Like, *I know you're lying to me, Chase. Just tell me the truth and I'll forgive you. Just you.* I can't say it, because I can't forgive him unless he tells me on his own. But he hasn't. He's had a whole year and we've been alone together many times. And if he hasn't done it by now, he never will.

"Tell me something, Chase."

He rolls away from me a little. "What?"

"Something I would never guess."

"I'm not afraid of clowns."

"What?" I laugh unexpectedly. It happens so rarely these days.

"It seems like most people are afraid of clowns. I don't get it. They're just actors with bad taste in clothing and really dramatic makeup. I feel sorry for clowns."

"What about killer clowns?"

"Well, I'm afraid of killers, period. I'm also afraid of killer farmers. But people don't go around saying they're afraid of farmers. They say they're afraid of clowns. It's clownist."

"What else are you afraid of?"

He furrows his brow, narrowing his bright eyes. "Being tantalized."

I sit up and try to look sexy. I think. "Like, tempted?"

"Oh no. Like Tantalus. He tried to trick the gods by serving them human flesh in a stew—his own son, actually. As punishment, Zeus killed him, and made him stand forever in a lake surrounded by water underneath a tree of fruit. But whenever he tried to drink or eat, the water would recede and the fruit went just out of his reach. That's being tantalized. Surrounded by what you need, but you can't have it." He pauses. "People use the word in relation to desire, but when you think about Tantalus, even if he was already dead, that's food and drink we're talking about. Hunger and thirst are more than desire. You need some things so much that if you don't have them, you change." He looks at me quickly and then off the bed. "Maybe that's silly."

"No. It makes sense. Like trust."

"Companionship."

We neaten ourselves up and leave the room one at a time, me first. When I get downstairs, I find Kennedy standing stiffly at the back door, biting her nails. I tap my fingers on her shoulder. "Everything okay?" I ask. I kind of hope she did hear us a little.

She turns to me, her dismay unconcealed. "Extra guest. I hope you don't mind. I really didn't know Chase was planning . . . I don't . . ." She trails off and I push the door open.

My heart drops into my stomach. Chelsea is perched on the table, peeling green grapes and babbling on about wormholes. Beneath her, smoking a cigarette and picking at an heirloom tomato salad, is Mila.

Mila.

Onetime Mila. Mila of the past. Mila, who has no business in the lake house or my life.

Or with Chase.

With Chase.

I turn around, light-headed, and sit on the large green suit-case Chase left by the cellar door. "Was Chase planning this?"

Kennedy throws her hands up. "It's his girlfriend. Trust me. She was not invited." She rushes to my side. "Emily, I'm so, so sorry about this. Say the word and I will pull the plug on this whole weekend."

The word *girlfriend* sends an electric current through my body, and I feel my heart flicker out. I tap it. He wouldn't do that. Of course he would. He betrayed Ryan; he betrayed me. None of these people, my friends, have any redeeming quali-ties. They do what they want, when they want. "I thought they were over. Ages ago."

Kennedy's forehead creases, and if you didn't know her like I do, you would fall for the act, believe that she cares one bit how I feel. Like dirt. A single, crumbling grain of dirt. "They were. But you know Chase. I'm sure it's not serious." She hesi-tates. "At least I don't think it is."

I take a deep breath and purse my lips, letting my cheeks fill like a sail as I exhale. "Whatever. He can do what he wants."

She scrutinizes me. "You don't care?"

"Why would I?"

She shakes her head. "If you don't, I don't."

Look at us, lying like a couple of besties. Like last year never happened.

Kennedy crouches next to me and lays a cool hand on my knee. "Is there anything I can do to help you set up for the, um. The talk?"

She can't even bring herself to say the word *séance*. It's a party game to her. Everything is a game to Kennedy.

"No. Do you have any candles?"

"Tons. Any special colors?"

"Black and white are best."

"I doubt we have any black candles. But I'll check." She disappears into the kitchen, and I open the cellar door and lug my suitcase down. It's ridiculously heavy. When I get back up to the first floor, Kennedy looks annoyed again. Chase is standing awkwardly by Kennedy's side. Avoiding my eyes. I stare straight at him. No get out of jail free. Not anymore.

Kennedy shoves him toward me with her hip. "Mila wants to go for a swim."

Of course she does. "Okay," I say. "Let her. That's why we're here, right? It's the lake house. There's the lake."

"Come with." Chase offers his usual dazzling smile, but he won't meet my eye.

"Why?" I blurt out.

"I didn't know she was coming," he mumbles, his face flushed. "I told her I'd be here and it would be fun. I didn't mean it as an invitation. It was a misunderstanding."

Kennedy slowly begins to back away into the kitchen.

"Fun?" He can do better. I demand better. It does not have to end this way. I suddenly feel more alone than I have this entire year. These entire seventeen years. "Chase?" I despise the pleading in my voice.

"I'm so sorry." But he says it while walking away from me. And that is not an apology.

Kennedy waits for him to leave and then flutters back to my side. "I don't know what's wrong with him." She furrows her brow.

"Are you okay with this? We can go do your ritual right now."

"I'll start setting up." I take a box of white candles from her. "You guys go ahead. Have fun."

She looks uncertain. "We're here for you, Emily."

I wave a hand. "Not at all. Go."

She spins gracefully, and her skirt whirls up around her. "Give a shout if you need anything."

Not at all.

I watch them out the window as they gather on the dock. Chelsea sits aside with her book, as usual. Kennedy dips one foot into the water, kicks back and forth for a moment or so, and then arranges herself on her towel to sunbathe, a watchful eye on the lake. Chase splashes in the water like a kid, and Mila lets him hold her and throw her around. She's not shy like she was at the beginning of last year. She's grown teeth. Sharp ones. Chase is different around her than he is with me. Lighter. Bouncier. More like the old Chase. Maybe he's been this way all along, and he only changes when I walk into the room. Or maybe it's all a performance for my benefit. I don't know which is worse. It makes my stomach turn.

I run upstairs and tear through Mila's suitcase, looking for clues that I should have known this was going on all along. All I find are clothes, toiletries, two packs of clove cigarettes (for one weekend?!), a fancy lighter, a packet of sangria mix, and birth control pills. Shit.

Mila.

You know . . . I hadn't planned on her. But she came. And look what she brought.

The murder weapon.

44

I fill every room in the house with candles, from cellar to attic, though I can't light them or I'll have a house fire on my hands in minutes. Then I retrieve my art supplies and begin to paint. I've been working on a custom set of tarot cards for weeks now. Over time, the theme has morphed from an idyllic nature setting to one specific to the lake house. Right now I can't get that night out of my head. I start with the lake in rich, sapphire blue, the boat on top framed by a velvet sky. Anxiety begins to build up in my chest as I look for a place to paint Ryan. Because I don't *know* where he was. I add Kennedy and try to imagine once more, but my mother is right about me. I see nothing. I paint thick, ruby red over the water in turbulent waves, add violent stitches into the sky, all the unfairness of not knowing, of the worst that could be. And then I paint a card for Chelsea—who didn't go out on the boat either, but came back with the others—on the dock, watching. *She came back with the others.* I scrawl an inscription at the bottom of each and set them neatly in a corner to dry, then wait up in the attic for the others in a circle of candles, Mila's lighter in my pocket, a single candle lit to light the rest. After everyone has gathered in the circle, I walk the perimeter and light each one.

"Should we join hands?" Mila asks. She snaps her gum. Nerves maybe. Or maybe she's just bored.

Kennedy glares at her, a scolding, motherly look.

"Yes. Unbroken circle." I've placed myself between Kennedy and Chelsea so that I don't have to deal with Chase. I can't even wrap my head around the fact that we just slept together and he has a date here with him. He's been avoiding my eyes. I think that's the worst part. He owes me a real explanation. More than that. But at the very least he owes me the truth.

I try to wipe it all out of my head. This is more important.

"So, what's next? We chant or burn a goat or what?" Mila bounces her knees up and down.

I remember hating her, but I don't remember her being this obnoxious. "No, we don't burn a fucking goat. Do you see any goats?"

She shrugs. "I don't see any ghosts, either."

This close. I'm this close to punching her. But I don't. "Why don't you start?"

That wipes the smirk off her face. "What?"

"Call to Ryan. Ask him to come back and speak to us."

She pulls her knees into her chest. "I didn't really know him." Her voice is small now; she is small.

"But you saw him the night he disappeared. If he died, you saw him closer to his last moments than I did. Right?" I hand my candle to her.

"He didn't die." The words snap off Chase's tongue like a rubber band. Reflexive. That doesn't mean much.

Mila stares down at the flame, and her face lights up and darkens in the flickering glow. "Ryan, will you please come talk to us?" she mumbles. She shoves the candle into Chase's hand.

He holds it far away from his body like a stick of dynamite in a cartoon. "Hey, buddy. I'm here. Speak up if you want to. We all miss you."

He nudges Kennedy with his elbow and she takes the candle, holding one hand underneath to catch any dripping wax. "Ryan, sweetie, we're all here waiting for you to come back. Whenever you're ready, you know the door is open." She passes the candle to me, then casts her eyes down to the floor.

"Ryan, I know you're out there. I feel it. At home, at school, everywhere I go. I feel it stronger in this house, and I won't leave until I hear from you. Talk to me." I wait. But nothing happens. I reluctantly hand the candle to Chelsea.

She heaves a big sigh and concentrates on the flames. She is so fake. Chelsea and her sight. Instead of saying anything coherent, though, she whispers something so softly it's impossible to make out, her lips barely moving, her eyes narrowed, so focused on the candle it looks like she's intent on moving it with her mind or something. I try to read her lips, but I can't.

"Share it with the class," Mila finally says.

Chelsea startles. "Sorry. I can't really think of anything good." She hands the candle back to me.

She did, though. She thought of something good. It just wasn't something she felt like sharing. Just like Chelsea to keep her precious little Ryan secrets from me, even now, after she's played her part in silencing him, maybe forever.

I place the candle back in the center of the circle, and we join hands again.

"Now what?" Chase whispers.

"We wait. Open your mind and wait." I know that if the worst did happen, Ryan will speak to me. I may not have been the favorite in life. Chelsea may have been his chosen one while I was left to gather clues and put on a show of knowing, of twin closeness. But it's my turn now. I'm all he has left.

He wasn't the perfect brother. The favorite child doesn't have to be. He can think mostly of himself and his wants, and Ryan had many, and toss around little kindnesses like favors. I was always running after him for approval somehow, ever since we were little, because if he approved, so did Mom and Dad. It was the opposite with our friends. I was the one everyone liked. It was a confusing balancing act. The portrait of the unbreakable bond for all our friends, because if I faltered, he would be alone. And if I lost his approval, my parents would be relentless. Why couldn't I be practical like Ryan? Play sports. Focus on school instead of art. Stop dressing like a hooker and talking like a truck driver. Be a lady. They were such hypocrites. They hated the Hartfords, but they wanted us to become them.

But I'm getting distracted.

Clear my mind. Clear as crystal. I picture running water. Pure, untainted, fresh water. It pools and stills and I see Ryan reflected in it, underneath the surface. Eyes open, mouth open, smiling. Speaking.

"Come out," I whisper.

He looks at me, then looks away. The moonlight washes over him. He begins to fade.

"No," I say sharply. I feel Chelsea squeezing my hand.

"He's so close," she says in a breathy voice. Bitch. *Bitch.* She's faking. Taking him. Even now.

"Shut up." I yank my hand out of hers and squeeze my eyes tighter, trying to conjure him back. His image slowly reappears beneath the water, and I float to him until I'm hovering just above, gazing at him like he's on the other side of a mirror. *Where are you?* I ask him silently.

"He's here," Chelsea says. "Kennedy, do you feel it?"

"No," Kennedy says softly. With pity.

Ryan shakes his head and I understand.

She doesn't see him because he doesn't want her to.

"Do this for me." Chelsea's voice is distant. Barely a whisper. Not meant for my ears. But I don't have time for her pity or Kennedy's stubbornness. Because it *is* real. He *is* here. And I don't need my friends to play along anymore. We're not reading cards for luck or romance. I'm tracking my brother's killer.

Ryan just gazes at me. *What happened to you?* I ask in my mind, my lips forming the words soundlessly.

"We should stop," Chelsea says. I feel her climbing to her feet, and I grab her hand and yank her back down.

Ryan points to the side. To Chelsea.

"Chelsea?" I say aloud.

"What?"

Careful. No sound. Lips motionless. *Chelsea did this? Chelsea killed you?*

He shrugs and grins.

"I don't want to do this anymore." Chelsea rushes past me and down the attic stairs.

I open an eye. Kennedy, Chase, and Mila are still sitting, looking uncomfortable.

"Is that enough?" Kennedy asks.

"Almost." I take Mila's hand reluctantly. *Chelsea killed you?*

He waves his hand around the circle.

Mila, Chase, Kennedy?

He nods at every name. *All of them.* He continues nodding, his head bobbing all the way back and all the way down, unnaturally far. Smooth, current-like motion.

Where is your body?

He spreads his arms wide.

What am I supposed to do?

He points to me. *It's your turn.* Bubbles erupt out of his mouth, and his voice echoes in my ears, snapping and popping like lava.

A chill runs down my spine. *My turn?*

You're next. They know you know. That's why you're here. You're a goner, Emily.

I look around the circle. Kennedy is watching me carefully, her expression unreadable. Chase is digging his fingernails into his palms. Mila is biting her lips, suppressing a yawn. She winks and I turn away. She's at the heart of it too. She and Chelsea. Mila was the instigator. The new element. She fell into our happy little family like a lit match onto a short fuse. You can't blame the match entirely, but that fuse would have been fine for a long time.

"We're done," I say abruptly.

Kennedy blinks. "Are you sure? No rush. We have all day."

"Nonsense." I blow the candles out, leaving only the dim light from the single window on the other side of the ladder. "I have to clean up, you have to make dinner, Chase and Mila probably want to spend some time alone together."

Chase clears his throat, but Mila grabs his hand and pulls him up.

"She has a point. Sorry Ryan didn't show up. Well. Not sorry." Mila squints for a moment, as if there's something in her eye. "I mean because he's going to be okay, Emily," she says quickly. "Just try not to think about it too much."

"Yeah. Good advice."

She shakes her head and climbs down the stairs. Chase jumps down after her without a word to me.

Kennedy begins to pick up the candles.

"Leave them."

She hesitates, her fingers wrapped around one. "It gets so hot up here."

"I know. I'll get them later. I just—I'm not completely sure I'm done. Can we leave them up for now?"

She raises her eyebrows. "Around the entire house? Until when?"

I sigh. "I just don't feel like this was the right time. It doesn't work if there's a single nonbeliever in the group."

Her gaze doesn't waver. "Who's the nonbeliever?"

"All of you."

She laughs. Actually laughs. At me. Nervous laughter, maybe, laughter of disbelief, but it slices through me just the same. "Because we choose to hold on to hope?"

I feel the last remnants of friendliness slide off my face. "No. I don't think you do. I think you know just as well as I do that he's dead. But you won't admit it. That's the difference."

Kennedy's hand goes right to her mouth, like I knew it would. She has no more nails to bite. That's how I know *she* did it. Every one of them has a sign, a tell. It's like playing poker with the devil.

It suddenly occurs to me that I must have a tell too. That every moment I spend with them, they're figuring out what I know. That maybe I did reach Ryan. Maybe it wasn't wishful thinking. A warning. A sign. *Don't let them know you see. You're next. A goner.*

"Do you really think he's dead?" Kennedy says. Her eyes cut through me.

"You know what I know," I say.

"I know that the dead don't wait for rituals and they don't care about believers," she says. "If he was gone, and he wanted you to know, he'd have done it by now." Kennedy closes her eyes. "Sorry. Emily, I'm so sorry."

I stare at her, speechless, then escape down the stairs, my heart pounding.

Kennedy. Chelsea. Chase. Mila. It's not that I blame one more than the others.

All of them are at fault. They share the blame.

Perhaps if any of them had stayed home last year, it would never have happened.

But no one ever stays home. They always come.

Nothing keeps them away.

Not even an inconvenient little death.

I creep down the hallway to the master bedroom and push the door gently open. Chelsea is lying on the bed with the lights off and the shades drawn, a damp washcloth over her eyes. She gets migraines now. It's one of her vague, unspecific symptoms. Migraines, nausea, insomnia. Exhaustion, paranoia, depression.

"What did you see?" she asks in a dull voice.

I step softly into the room. "What did *you* see?"

She presses her palms into the cloth, but she doesn't answer me.

"I don't have the sight," I remind her. The words sting my throat, my tongue, my lips.

She slowly peels the washcloth off her face, but her eyes remain closed. "I saw myself."

"Bullshit."

Chelsea opens her eyes. Bloodshot, rimmed with red. "When you do a tarot reading, you tell us that we see a reflection of what's inside us. I think this is the same. We see what we believe. That's why it doesn't work for nonbelievers. They don't expect to see anything, so they don't."

No. "He was here."

"He's still out there, Em."

I feel uncertain for a moment. Just a split second. Because she looks like she believes it. "Not like us."

Chelsea hugs her knees to her chest. "Well, what do we know? Maybe no one ever does leave. Every night we go to sleep and dream. Our minds untangle the parts of our waking lives our brains can't make sense of. Maybe that's the part that goes on when we die. Or maybe some people get caught in the transition, like the falling between wake and sleep. The lucid in-between. Maybe they stay forever where—"

"Where they died?"

She's silent for a moment. "I was going to say where they were happiest. But I do believe he's still out there, Emily. We *will* see him again."

Liar. I turn to leave, and she collapses back onto the bed.

The waiting.

The waiting is the trick.

I waited a year for this moment.

I waited to gather with my friends, murderers all.

The awful thing about waiting is that if you wait too long, you start to disappear.

I thought if I waited long enough, there would be some dramatic moment when one of them would scream, "I can't take it anymore! I killed Ryan!" A telltale-heart type of revelation. I was almost certain it would be Chelsea. But it never happened. There was just the phantom illness and the vague little hint in the note, and now she's kind of semi-Chelsea. I still keep thinking if I do or say the right thing to freak her out, I'll get some kind of confession. Chelsea plays the best innocence game, but she knows.

If she didn't kill him herself, she watched him die, and she didn't lift a finger to save him.

I won't let them do it twice.

45

I paint some more while Kennedy makes dinner. My last
memory of Mila on the night of the murder, her standing on
the dock, beckoning for the others to follow her out to the
starlit lake. It was such a small, meaningless moment at the
time. Now it feels like a puzzle piece, one I just can't place.
Ominous, foreboding. Only hours left until they came back
without him.

Chelsea lies upstairs in her little make-believe headache
cocoon. Go ahead, get your rest. Close your eyes and drift
away. I'll be right here beside you. After everything you've
done, I'm still here. Chase and Mila are outside at the dock,
but I don't hear splashing. Instead, their voices rise and lower
sharply. It rather sounds like they're fighting. It lightens my
mood considerably. But the sound of Kennedy in the kitchen
unnerves me. A thick, sharp knife; precise, staccato beats on a
chopping block. Ryan's warning hovers over me. *You're next.
A goner.* She dices tomatoes, cuts thick slices of buffalo moz-
zarella, and soon the house is filled with the aroma of sizzling
garlic cooking in rosemary-infused olive oil, but all I can think
of is the blood red of the sauce she's making, the gleaming edge
of the blade. She's really gone all out this weekend with five
individual flatbreads, each with different toppings, and there's

something about the extravagance that makes me feel uneasy. No one plans a feast for an ordinary gathering of friends. Feasts are for weddings and funerals, greetings and goodbyes.

I'm packing my paints away when Kennedy asks for a hand bringing the flatbreads outside to the grill, and I rise reluctantly to help.

"How do you feel?" Kennedy asks as we balance the flatbreads between us on a baking sheet and attempt to fit it through the back door.

"About?" I try to kick the door open with my foot, but it's stuck. I balance the pan precariously on my shoulder and run my hand over the door behind me, finding the heavy lock bolted. I turn it. "Door was locked." I push the door open and carefully pick up the flatbreads again.

Kennedy frowns. "It shouldn't be. I didn't lock it. We never lock it. Chase and Mila are outside . . ." She trails off and her eyes float up toward the attic as she steps out onto the grass.

And Chelsea's upstairs. Which means she's implying that I lied. Or she's lying to me and playing mind games. I eye the flatbreads. There's something about them that just doesn't sit right. This was my favorite food, back when I had an appetite, but Kennedy hated the messiness. Maybe the food is an apology. But maybe it's an expression of guilt. What did we eat at Ryan's last supper? Did Kennedy know that's what it was?

"I'm lactose intolerant," I say.

"Since when?" She pauses for a second, bent over the grill, like a weird, modern-day Hansel and Gretel witch, and a little voice in the back of my mind says, *Push her and eat the house.* But that would only result in Kennedy having striped grill burns on her hands and me getting sent to juvie with splinters in my gums.

"Trauma-induced," I lie.

The back door swings shut and Chelsea steps out, shielding her eyes from the sun. "I'm starving."

Kennedy stretches her lips into a smile. "Fifteen minutes." I can see her brain basically hovering on the edge of explosion.

Chase returns from the dock, Mila trailing behind him, an unlit cigarette dangling between her lips.

"Chelsea, do you mind eating the chicken flatbread? Emily's lactose intolerant, and yours is the only one without cheese."

Chelsea hugs her stomach and makes a face. "I'm not eating meat these days. I can't take a bite without picturing the slaughterhouse."

You don't belong here. I stare at Mila, willing the words from my brain to hers. *Nobody wants you.* She casually leans her head to the grill, lighting her cigarette. The sun is beginning to set, and a sudden chill settles over us. I shiver, my eyes trained on the warm glow of the fire as Mila tilts her face close to the flames.

"Please be careful," Kennedy says, pulling her back.

Mila rolls her eyes. "It's not a volcano." We all stand there uncomfortably for a moment. "Jesus Christ. You people got a lot less fun in the past year."

"Maybe you just got a lot more fun, and we seem less fun in comparison," Chelsea says, deadpan. It sounds like the old Chelsea, and it stings me to hear for some reason. I like the drifting Chelsea better. She deserves to be lost. And never return.

Mila makes a face at her. "I've always been fun."

"Eh. Fun is subjective." Again, old Chelsea seems to be making an appearance. Out of nowhere. For the first time in forever. I don't like it. She slides into her seat, across from Mila.

Chase grins at Chelsea over the table, then sits down beside Mila. "She's just being difficult. Let's all agree that we've never been any fun and that Mila needs a new lighter. That grill thing? Lose your eyebrows that way. And your eyebrows are exactly right." He puts his arm around her, and she reluctantly smiles.

"I'm fun."

"No." He shakes his head. "You're calculus."

"I saw myself as more like anatomy," she says, snuggling up against him. He looks uncomfortable.

Kennedy slides the flatbreads out of the grill and arranges them on the table. "Mila, yours is the tomato and cheese."

Mila makes a face. "I don't like—"

"They're flatbreads, not trading cards," Kennedy snaps wearily.

"I'll take that one," Chelsea says.

Kennedy smiles tautly and hands her the plate. I glare at Chelsea. What the hell is going on? An hour ago she was freaking out in the attic. Now everything is fine? We're back to the good old days, minus Ryan?

"I'll get drinks," I volunteer. "Kennedy, please. Sit."

"Chianti on the counter," she instructs. "Right next to the basil plant. Not the one by the spice rack."

"I got it." I go inside and grab the bottle, then hesitate. Why was she so insistent that I take the one by the basil plant? I

examine the two bottles side by side. The one Kennedy wants
is a twist cap. I turn it and it opens easily. Did she specify
this one because she was sipping from it all afternoon? Or did
she request it specifically for me because there's something
wrong with it? I stare at the bottles for another minute and
decide that I can't take chances. I have to switch the bottles.
She'll look, so I pour the wine into a decanter before bringing
it out. The slow, steady stream of crimson into the smooth,
serene glass is mesmerizing, and the sound of the wine flowing,
swishing, dripping, calms my nerves. The cold seems to have
followed me inside, and little crystals bloom on the surface,
like snowflakes falling in pools of blood. I stir them with my
pinkie and they vanish. The moment they're gone, I'm sure I
imagined them. But it is cold, almost unbearably. The Hartfords must have had central air installed. Just as I'm funneling
the second bottle of chianti into the first, the door swings open
and Chelsea leans back against it.

"What are you doing?"

I stand there for a moment shivering violently, a decanter of
wine next to me on the counter, a half-empty bottle in one hand,
the damning funnel swirling the contents away into the other.

An expression of disbelief crosses her face. "Did you do
something to the wine?"

"It's a joke. You know how Kennedy is. I'm switching the
bottles. To see if she notices. Two chiantis." I show her the
labels. "No poison." I take a sip from each. "See?" It *is* a joke.
I'm not the one who makes people disappear.

She gives me an odd look but nods. "Okay. Do you want
to talk, Em?"

I shake my head. "Starving." But I couldn't eat if it were my last meal. I imagine the two sips trailing down my throat, one innocent and one wicked, and I feel the vomit rising.

"All right. I'm going to run to the bathroom." Chelsea jogs upstairs, and I immediately throw up into the sink. I have to stand there for a moment to allow my heart to stop racing. Why did her mind immediately go there? As if she knew there was something in one of the bottles that shouldn't be there? Her sudden change of mood. I tiptoe up the stairs and into the master bedroom and unzip her bag. She packs light; there are only a couple of T-shirts, a dress, a light sweater, and some toiletries, including—bingo—an orange bottle filled to the brim with little pills, plastered with warning stickers. Controlled substance. Do not mix with alcohol. A dozen other warnings. The temperature is even colder in the bedroom than in the kitchen, and I grab a sweater from my suitcase after pocketing the pills. Then I head back downstairs and carry the decanter outside.

"I bring the gift of wine," I say, filling everyone's glasses.

But Chelsea comes out of the house with a six-pack of soda, which she conspicuously places at the center of the table. She pops one open without looking at me and doesn't touch the wine even after Kennedy begs her to.

Mother always used to say Kennedy was a young soul. Born from the blue, no previous lives, everything so new. An excuse for ignorance, selfishness, the mercurial lack of focus that people mistake for passion.

What's Chelsea's excuse? She's died over and over and never learned a thing.

Every time the same mistake—the cards never lie: She *is*

the Queen of Cups. She *loves* a fool. She's crossed by the Ten of Swords. And she falls from the tower.

But she is not the innocent girl my brother believed.

Why was she allowed to survive last year?

Why wasn't she the sacrifice?

I don't think it's fair.

"So." Kennedy saws at her flatbread with her fork and knife. The rest of us usually eat it with our hands, like a pizza, but Kennedy has her way. "What's the after-dinner plan? Emily? You wanted to leave the candles up."

I chew and swallow my food before speaking. It's like rubber in my mouth. Fake. "I did. I do. But I can't ask all of you to join me again. I don't think Ryan will be able to communicate with everyone here."

"Oh?" Chelsea says.

"Well, many people believe that even one nonbeliever in the room will break the connection," I say.

No one looks at me.

"That's okay. I know Chelsea's the only one who thinks it's possible. So I think the rest of you should go out on the lake tonight. Exactly like you did last year."

Chase, Mila, and Kennedy all stop eating.

Chase speaks first. "I don't think I can do that."

"The boat isn't even ready," Kennedy says.

"I thought your dad was up last weekend." I peer over her shoulder to the dock. The sailboat tilts back and forth in the blazing early-evening sun.

"He was, but . . ." She hedges. "It's possible to sail the boat—I just haven't in a long time."

"You did last year," I point out.

She makes a pained expression. "Please don't make me."

"What if that's the only way to reach him? We have to recreate the conditions as perfectly as possible." I'm making all of this up. I want to see them squirm. I want to burn it out of them like a bug under a magnifying glass. I'm going to telltale-heart the truth out of them.

"Fine." Kennedy folds her napkin. "I can do it after we clear up. For whoever wants to go."

"I don't want to," Chase says. "But if that's what you need, Em." He looks at me, pleading in his eyes.

No mercy.

"That's what I need."

"Then that's what I'll do."

I look at Mila, not expecting much.

"Me? God, no. I'm not stepping foot back on that thing. It's cursed. You should have sunk it."

"Maybe it's not cursed. Maybe you're cursed," I say.

Mila flinches. "Fine. I'll go, and nothing bad will happen." She pauses. "You'll feel better?"

"So much." A light breeze lifts my hair off my shoulders, and I twirl it into a bun and wrap an elastic around it. The air is beginning to cool nicely. "So we're agreed? Kennedy, Chase, and Mila out on the lake. Chelsea and I will make one last attempt to reach Ryan."

There are a series of nods around the table, and we clean up without much conversation. Kennedy changes and goes down to the dock while Chase and Mila have another whispered fight in the guest room. I go from room to room, inspecting, feeling the air, picking up objects and putting them down, repositioning the candles. This time I light them all. It will take some time for them to burn all the way down, and everyone will be gone for a while. I do have to be careful, though. The place is so old and the wood so dry that if there was an accident, the house wouldn't stand a chance for very long. Nearly everything in it is made of wood. There are old books everywhere, artwork on the walls, and my painting supplies, which are highly combustible. And if that weren't enough, Mr. Hartford keeps extra cans of gasoline in the cellar for the boat. But I am careful. I set each candle firmly in place. And to keep them from blowing over, I close all of the windows tightly, fastening them with a wrench. They're not opening anytime soon.

46

Chelsea and I sit facing each other in the attic. Everyone is gone and the house is empty. The cold from earlier has dissipated. Heat from the closed windows and doors has begun to accumulate in the house, and it's concentrating itself in this room. Beads of sweat cover Chelsea's face, and she pulls off her sweater and scratches the linen tank she's wearing underneath.

My eyes go to the band around her wrist that she never takes off, the worn hospital bracelet. "Why are you still wearing that?"

"As a reminder," she says.

"Of what?"

"Of what happens when you're not careful." She plays with it, slides it up and down her forearm.

"What weren't you careful about?"

She smiles with her mouth only. "Words. Friends. Trust."

"You mean the note." I rest my chin on my knees. Let her say it.

"It wasn't a suicide note."

"You wrote that you weren't sure how you could live with yourselves anymore. Those were your exact words."

"It's a phrase," she whispers.

I believe her. It was never a suicide note. It was an admission of guilt. That's why I turned it in when I found it in Chase's jacket pocket. I don't know how no one else saw it that way. But people believe what they want to believe. See what they want to see.

"I guess the 'live anymore' part made people worried, you know?" I paint my concern. Thick, with deep lines of chiaroscuro. I want her to keep talking.

"But who?" She takes me in. My colors and strokes. My effort.

"Guidance, obviously. Your parents."

"No." Her expression tightens. "Which one of you passed that note to the school? It was a betrayal."

It's almost too much to handle. The idea that of all things, *this* was the betrayal. "Chelsea, none of us would have betrayed your confidence. It probably fell out of one of our pockets."

"It wasn't an accident." Her voice is sharp and severe. "One of you didn't trust me. They made me leave school, Emily. They told me I was suicidal, and when I told them it was a mistake, they didn't believe me. They made me see a therapist, and when I told him it was a mistake, he didn't believe me either. They locked me in a hospital for *two weeks*, forced chemicals into my body without my consent, and every hour of every day was filled with questions that weren't really questions because no one ever believed a word I said."

"Questions about what?"

She stops abruptly and stares at me. We both know about what. Come on, Chelsea. Now or never. Why couldn't you live with yourselves?

But her face goes blank, then smooth. "It was a nightmare.

I was the only one who knew the truth, and they didn't believe me. They looked right through me like I wasn't there. Like a criminal. And they started taking things. School, and then home, and then my clothes and phone and privacy." She's shaking, and for a second I forget what Chelsea did and I start to feel horrible. "It was a mistake." Her voice is flat, hollow. "That's the truth."

I stare at her, breathless. "Whoever turned you in probably knows that. She wanted to make sure you were okay." Keep talking, Chelsea. Don't stop now.

Her shoulders drop. "She. Kennedy did it?"

"I have no idea. But I did wonder. What was the mistake? Why did you write the note? If everyone is so convinced Ryan ran away." I pause. "Dove into the water, faked his own death. If he's really okay, why would it be hard to live with yourselves?"

She picks up a candle and lets a drop of wax fall onto her shoe, then presses her fingertip into it. "I don't know. I guess part of me feels responsible."

"How?"

She raises her eyes. "You don't remember last year?"

I nod. "Sure. Chase and Ryan were at each other's throats. So?"

"It was more than that. Things were falling apart. You were fighting with Kennedy, too. Mila was . . . there. Ryan said he wanted to be with me, and I told him it couldn't happen."

"So? Why would that drive him to fake his own death? That's ridiculously extreme."

Chelsea drips a drop of wax straight onto her hand, and I cringe. "Maybe he didn't fake it."

My heart begins to pound. "Why do you say that?"

"Forget it." Her voice goes quiet, distant.

"Chelsea." I inch closer to her, my hands shaking a little from the sudden jolt of adrenaline. "You've been lying to me for a year. Everyone has been lying to me for a year. Your note wasn't the mistake and you know it. You wrote that note *about* a mistake. That's why you still wear the bracelet. That's why you can't sleep. No one is supposed to carry this kind of secret. It's poisoning you, Chelsea."

She drips more wax onto her hand and then seems to suddenly realize what she's doing and cries out and drops the candle, the flame flickering out as it hits the floor. I pick it up quickly and relight it with another. She peels the wax off her skin. "I need to run this under cold water," she says.

"Tell me what happened." I block the door.

She looks exhausted. "It was a mistake. Okay? I wasn't there, Em. I wasn't on the boat. They all went out together like tonight. I saw him go into the water. It didn't look like he jumped in. It looked like he fell. Or maybe . . ."

"What?" I can barely breathe. In my ears, there is a pounding beat, a warning. A terrible warning.

"Maybe he was pushed." She covers her mouth with her unburned hand. The words are electric. They stop my heart. A beat. Restart.

"Who?" My voice is scratchy and dry. Heat damaged.

Panic flares like a wildfire in her eyes. "I don't know. I don't want to know. I probably imagined it. I don't believe it." She takes a step forward, but I grab her wrists and force her to stay, to face me, to face the truth.

"Then why are you telling me?"

"In case it's true!" She tries to push past me, but I shove her backward. No backing out. Not now.

"I need to know the rest. All of it." My head is throbbing. My heart is pounding, offbeat, arrhythmic. Stop. A beat. Restart. But faster. And faster. He's dead. They lied. They killed him and lied.

Tears glisten in Chelsea's eyes. "I swear, that's all I know. I was on the dock. I jumped in and swam after him. But I didn't make it. I panicked and couldn't breathe, and Kennedy had to come for me."

I try to make sense of it. He's dead. "Who came for Ryan?"

"Chase tried. Kennedy tried. I tried. No one could find him."

"So you pushed him in, and then had second thoughts." My brain is pulsing in my skull. They lied.

"No. No. I didn't push him. I wasn't even on the boat." She grabs my hand. "Emily, I'm probably being paranoid. Chase swears he's getting emails from Ryan."

Lightning flashes. I don't know whether it's through the sky or in my brain. I don't care. They killed him and lied. "When? Why didn't he—anyone—tell me?"

"He said Ry didn't want it getting back to your parents. He doesn't want to be tracked down. Chase only told me after the note incident because he was worried." Her voice falters. She's lying. Or Chase was lying and she knows it. I can't trust anyone anymore. He's dead and they lied; they killed him and lied.

My mind is too busy. I have no time for arguing. Chelsea is not my friend. I look her up and down, too overwhelmed by all of this information to think clearly, then shove her hard, run down the ladder, and lock her in the attic. Attics are places for secrets. Attics are places to hide. Attics are places to set traps.

For creatures that creep inside.

I walk downstairs in a fog and pace back and forth in the kitchen, waiting for the others to return.

I can hear Chelsea in the attic, stomping around and shouting. That's going to be an obvious problem. I'll never hear the other sides of the story if they immediately come in and find that I've locked Chelsea in the attic like Mrs. Rochester. Shit. What did I do? I think back to last year. Sangria. I slice the fruit with shaky fingers, use the second bottle of chianti, try to remember the way Kennedy does it. Brandy. Ryan was drinking brandy too. I pour myself a glass and begin to feel warm and steady.

My eyes fall on the glass decanter, and Chelsea's words swirl around my head. Someone pushed him. I pour half of the sangria into the decanter and mix up a little more, so I have a full pitcher and a full decanter. Then I dump half of the bottle of Chelsea's pills into the decanter and begin stirring before I can change my mind. They dissolve slowly, turning from pill to powder to nothing. It's impossible to tell the difference by looking at the two pitchers. I take a sip. You almost can't taste it, but there is a tiny sweetness to it, like saccharin. I dump in a little more brandy and taste it again. Perfect. I carry the pitcher and the decanter outside and set them on the stone table along with four glasses. Then I go inside, down to the cellar, and turn off the power in the attic. That way there will be much less of a chance that anyone will glance up and see Chelsea in the window. The candles will give off some light, but the light in the rest of the rooms will draw the eye downward. No one will even glance up at the attic, and the single tiny window doesn't open. But as a final touch, I scroll through my playlists, and choose Ryan's favorite album, *Kid A*. All of that banging and stomping fades into the sounds of the forest out here, anyway. But under the sound of warm synth bleeding out of the speakers, it's no more discernable than someone else's heartbeat.

I wait at the table as the boat returns just at sundown and watch as Kennedy, Chase, and Mila step off *Summer's Edge* one by one. There is a glass set out for each of us, the pitcher and decanter at the center of the table. Every place setting is identical. Everyone will start out with a glass from the pitcher. The decanter is reserved for the person who pushed Ryan. Four glasses, four settings.

Chelsea likes to think she has a place among them, that she could get away with being the odd one and somehow not be the odd one out. That I was always the extra chair at the table.

A twin is never the extra chair.

Now there's only room for one of us. Mila has taken Chelsea's place, and I drink for Ryan and for me.

Let the game begin.

Kennedy begins to walk past me toward the house, but I whistle and wave her over. She looks less than enthused, shoulders sagging and hair tangled in knots, but she slides into the seat next to me and reaches for the decanter. I study her, copper hair gleaming in the dying light, the lake almost the color of blood behind her, and last year comes rushing back to me, the moment the mirror smashed against her skull and all of those beautiful silvery fragments glittered around her like a crown. If this were an ordinary night, I would add those finishing touches to my tarot card. But I can't. Another day. I place my hand on top of hers to stop her from drinking the decanter wine—that wine is reserved—and pour her a glass from the pitcher instead.

"I thought it would be nice to have sunset cocktails," I say.

"We missed it by a few minutes." She takes a sip. "Mmm. Did you use tomato juice or something?"

"Does it taste like tomato juice?"

She takes another sip. "It's fabulous."

Chase downs one glass immediately. "Definitely needed that."

I eye the pitcher. I hope he doesn't drain it too quickly. I pour him half of a second glass, and make Mila's three-quarters full. "So how was the sail?"

"Fine," Kennedy says flatly. "Good wind."

"How was your séance?" Mila asks. She plays with a cigarette.

"I thought you were quitting?" Chase asks her.

"It's a nervous habit." Mila taps it against the table. "Everyone has one. Don't judge me. Sitting is the new smoking. We're all doing it right now." She sighs. "My cousin got out of prison, and my mother forced me to hang out with her. She doesn't do anything but smoke, play Scrabble, and tell prison stories. That place scares the shit out of me."

"Sorry I asked." Chase takes another long sip.

"Did the sail bring back any memories?" I ask.

Kennedy's eyes go to me briefly. "Of?"

"Last year. Ryan."

"No one wants to remember that." Mila stands. "You keep obsessing. It's not healthy." But Mila was the one who wanted to go out on the boat in the first place. If it hadn't been for Mila, Ryan would still be here. My last glimpses of my brother are like a slideshow, snapshots from the attic window. Mila on the boardwalk, running out to the boat. Turning back toward the house, beckoning. To follow her, into the darkness, the uncertain depths of the lake at night. Ryan sprinting after, a little while later. He never turned to look back. I saw him run, a swift pale figure darting down the boardwalk, from the safety of the lake house to *Summer's Edge*, and then he was gone. I'll add a final touch, an inscription, a warning, to Mila's card too. To all of the crucial moments. The puzzle pieces.

"He's my brother."

"That doesn't make it healthy."

"Says the chain-smoker." I grab the cigarette out of her hand and throw it on the ground. Kennedy covers her mouth with her hand. "Don't you laugh about it. I want answers."

Kennedy puts a hand on my arm, and I try not to visibly cringe. "Emily. Did you really think we were going to get on the boat and go out there and suddenly have some kind of epiphany about what happened to Ryan? It's not logical." I can't stand the look of pity. It makes me want to scream. "It's out of our control."

"What about last summer? When you pushed Ryan into the water and watched him drown, and then lied about it for an entire year. Was all of that out of your control, too?" The album ends, and I was right. You can't hear Chelsea at all out here. Time slows down. A chill descends. The last of the sunlight is drowned in the dark, the sun sinking into the lake with a swift and silent sense of finality. The windows of the house glow with the light of the dozens of candles. I place the last unlit one at the center of the table and light it, and each of us becomes a flickering glow in the dark.

"That never happened," Kennedy says with a practiced calm.

But at the exact same time, Chase blurts, "It was an accident."

And Mila says, "Kennedy did it."

I refill Kennedy's cup with the decanter, a low buzz beginning to hum in my ear. We face one another, a circle of players—a killer, a liar, an accomplice, and half a twin.

She takes a nervous gulp. "That's bullshit. You weren't even there, Mila. You were belowdeck."

"How else?" Mila's voice shakes. "How else did he just disappear? He didn't randomly go for a swim fully clothed. Chase, you know it's true. Why do we keep lying to protect her?"

"Because it's impossible! Kennedy is not a killer." He looks at me. "Emily, you know that. We're not monsters. People don't just kill their friends."

Mila looks at him sharply. "But we did. Own up to it. Every one of us was an accessory when we covered it up, because we knew what happened. She did it. And we went along with it because there are no consequences for people like Kennedy or you, and that made it feel like if we didn't say it, it didn't happen. But that's your world, not ours. Chelsea isn't okay. I'm not okay. You should not be okay with this."

"I'm not," he shouts.

I stare at him, taken aback for a moment. Kennedy sits silently, her lips pressed tightly together. She looks like she's holding in a scream. A long, high-pitched, endless scream. I can hear it in my head, a mourning, keening wail. I need to hear it. I need to know that she cares about what she did. That she mourns Ryan, that every day the knowledge of what she did to him is a howl in her throat begging to be released. That she regrets killing him.

But she says nothing. Nothing.

"Pushing someone into the lake isn't necessarily intending to kill them," I say, my voice blending with the hum. "We used to do it all the time. Accidents happen." I look at Kennedy, her pale, frozen expression. "Did you push him?"

She shakes her head jerkily. "I didn't mean to. I don't know. I was startled. Why does it matter? We all know he ended up in the lake. We all tried to pull him out. We tried everything."

Lies. Always more lies.

"The only thing you tried to do was cover your tracks. You made us believe he ran away. My parents are convinced—I half believed—he's going to walk through the door any minute. They're torn in half, believing he's alive and dead at the same time. It's destroyed them."

"It wasn't malice," Chase says. "We were trying to protect you." And right there it hits me. That thing between us. That I haven't been able to put my finger on. It's not guilt after all. It's a lie. And it's not to protect me.

"You were trying to protect yourselves." I fill his glass from the decanter. Because I no longer believe that Ryan was killed with a mere push. In a hit and run, it isn't the hit that's the crime. It's the *run*. The crucial moment when people—bad, twisted people—choose not to do the right thing. Choose to preserve the convenience of their lives over the hope of saving someone they were supposed to care about. Ryan wasn't killed by a little shove. He was killed by abandonment. Betrayal. Lies. Because the push wasn't the end of the story. There was a world of potential paths that branched out from the push. The path where Chase dove in after Ryan right away, and he was saved. The one where Kennedy radioed in for help. The one where Chelsea held me while I cried because there was a terrible accident and we didn't know what was going to happen, but I wasn't alone in this. She wasn't going to let me go through it alone. None of them were going to abandon me to go through this alone. But that's not what happened. None of it is. And Ryan wasn't the only victim. All of my friends are equally guilty, because they all watched Ryan die, then looked me in the eye and *lied* to me. And whatever happened that night, it's clear that they all made a conscious choice to go all in on it together. All of them vs. Ryan and me. No, I don't believe I care who did the pushing anymore at all. They're all guilty as hell.

Chase downs his glass all in one long gulp, and I refill it.

"We were scared," Mila says. "We didn't see what happened, we wanted to believe, and yes, we wanted to protect ourselves. There was no time to think. And then Kennedy told us what to say, and it was that or dive headfirst into a nightmare, and we didn't know. At least, I told myself I didn't know. But every second that passed, I was more sure that Kennedy pushed Ryan into the water."

"I didn't—" Kennedy protests.

"I think you did," Mila says. "Chase and Kennedy tried to go after him. Even Chelsea tried to swim all the way from the dock." I wonder if I've been too hard on Chelsea. But she played her part too. It's too late to take any of it back. "I was the one who wanted to take the boat out. I've been blaming myself for a year. But there's nothing we can do about any of it now. That's the truth. Do what you want with it."

I fill her glass from the decanter.

She takes it and heads back toward the house. "I need a cigarette."

Kennedy's face flushes crimson. No. Blood red. "Chase is the one who hid the body."

The silence is stunning. Chase turns to her, his lips twitching, stuck between laughing and crying, perfectly cubist. Mila freezes, her bare shoulders tense, like all the world has turned to ice.

"You did." Kennedy's voice is steady, but her glass shudders in her hand. "You went back on the lifeboat that night. I saw you."

"So?" Chase whispers.

"So if you had nothing to hide, why didn't you tell us?" Tears glisten in Kennedy's eyes, and I want to smash her into the earth. How dare she cry.

Chase looks at me helplessly, and his silence says everything.

I run after Mila, leaving the others behind. "Is all of that true?"

"Of course it is. My part anyway."

I try to block the door into the house. "Stay. We can talk some more. It's not your fault. Accidents do happen. You couldn't have foreseen any of it. Don't worry."

She shakes her head. "I have to go to the bathroom."

"Go in a bush."

Mila looks at me out of the side of her eye. "What are you hiding?"

"Nothing." I shrug, but it's unconvincing; I can hear the rising panic in my voice.

I have to let go. They say letting go is hard. That it will come with time. That forgiveness is key. Forgiving the others for surviving, and most of all, forgiving myself. For remaining. But I don't buy it.

Because the others didn't just survive. Survival is passive. It implies clean hands and a clear conscience. It implies innocence. It assumes that survival is something they earned, or were destined for, or just happened upon. That they deserved life more.

And that would be a lie.

Survival is something they stole.

Because Chelsea and Kennedy and the others created the tragedy they survived. They're killers. And I can't wait any longer.

She opens the door into the house and I hold my breath and walk in behind her, leaning back against the door and locking it behind me. *Please, Chelsea, be quiet.* I realize, though, with a sinking feeling, that Chelsea has to come down sooner or later. I haven't thought any of this through. I've just poisoned four people with a drug I know nothing about. My eyes go to the cellar door.

Mila follows my gaze curiously. "What's down there?"

"Paintings. I made portraits of everyone." It slips out on its own. "It was a surprise."

She hesitates. "That's so nice. It's too nice."

"It was before." I pause. "Maybe you should carry them up. It's the least you can do."

She draws closer, reluctantly. "Now?"

"No. A year ago, before you slept with my boyfriend and watched my brother drown." I watch her bite back a sharp response. *He was never your boyfriend.* No. He sure as hell wasn't.

She approaches the door cautiously. "I just want you to know, Emily. None of this is who I am." The living room is lit up with candles, and the effect is dazzling. It's like Christmas in summertime.

"But it is. You did it."

"We had no choice." Mila places a hand on the lock. Slowly her fingers twist the metal. A soft click. A draw of the doorknob.

I stare down into the darkness, remembering. This is where we found the rabbit. I had nightmares for months afterward. It was the first time death forced its way into my life, and Ryan was the one to make me look away. I would have stared for hours. I was helpless not to. It was like the whole world stopped. It stuck in my head during sleepless nights, during summer swims, over breakfasts and during class. It never really went away. It's never left me. I had some hope that Ryan was still out there, some hope that death was not all that there was. But it's never left my side. And now I don't think I'm going to fight it anymore.

"You had a choice." I go to Mila slowly. Breathe in and out. Imagine Ryan by my side. But he isn't here to hold my hand, to make me look away.

Mila flicks the light on and peers down. There's nothing down there, and she hesitates. "I don't see any paintings."

"They're there."

She turns to me, a deeply unsettled look on her face. "I feel like there's something you're not telling me," she says.

I pause at her side. "Trust me, I know the feeling."

I take a deep breath and shove her down the stairs.

She lies motionless at the bottom. I don't look away. There's no going back now. If it weren't for her, Ryan would still be alive.

And as I stare down at the broken body at the bottom of the stairs, my heart pounding, I have a moment of clarity. This house. The house is poisoning me. The house has to go. And everyone in it.

47

Here are my rules:
1. You may run.
2. You may hide.
3. You may apologize.

Oh, who are we kidding? None of you think you've done anything wrong.

4. You may attempt to escape.
5. But you will not.

I run down the cellar stairs and grasp the railing with numb fingers. Mila lies like a broken doll in the eerie beam of light spilling down from the top of the staircase, a dark halo pooling around her head. For a moment, I'm stuck in time, struck by her terrible beauty, and then the reality of what I've done begins to prick at me. Little cuts all over. An overwhelming wave of panic numbs me again, and I tear the cover off the circuit breaker and flip every switch, my hands shaking. The gasoline can is heavy, but I lug it up two flights of stairs, and then another can, along with a large bottle of paint thinner. I coat the solid oak floors of the guest room and master bedroom with one can and close the doors, then hide the other in the upstairs closet with the paint thinner. I rescue my beautiful tarot cards, tucking them gently into my shirt pocket, next to my heart. Then I run back down the stairs and fling open the back door.

"Kennedy! Chelsea's locked in the attic!" I wait in the downstairs bathroom, saturated in darkness, but I know every inch of it. I know the family portraits that cover the walls, and the precise location of the group photo of *our* family, the five of us in the Summer of Swallows, arranged on the dock. Chelsea and Ryan deep in conversation, Chase attempting to lift Kennedy over his head, Mila laughing. Me in the background, a smile plastered on my face, staring straight at the camera. Camera smiles are always fake. I pull the photo off the wall and smash it against the toilet, then turn to the sink and grab a bar of soap. Even after scrubbing my hands with lavender-scented soap, though, I smell too much like gasoline to go near her. It's almost absurd, the delicate guest towels and handcrafted soaps, and my hands all filthy and coated with accelerant.

I hear the back door open and footsteps slowly walking up the stairs. "Something smells!" Kennedy shouts from the loft.

"Yeah, I don't know!" I yell back. I open the back door again and wave to Chase. Chase, who buried a body. Who buried my brother's body. And lied, and lied, and lied to me, with me, beside me. No more, Chase. No more Chase. "Hey, can you help me with something?"

He jogs inside and looks me up and down, scrunching his nose. "What did you do?"

I shrug and try to grin helplessly. "I spilled a bunch of crap from the cellar all over myself."

He crosses the living room toward the cellar, and I bolt the back door shut and seal it with one of the combination locks the Hartfords use during the off-season. I don't know the combination, and neither does Chase. Nobody but Kennedy does.

Chase whips around and stares at me. "What did you do? Where's Mila?"

I back against the door, out of breath.

His eyes fall to the floor, slick with gasoline, and rise to the flickering candles, the masses and masses of candles, filling the room with a gorgeous, brilliant glow. Heaven on earth, the sky fallen down on us. I hear music in the chaos, the thumping of footsteps above, Kennedy screaming, Chase saying my name over and over, making no sense, no sense at all. He grabs my wrists.

"What did you do to her?"

Laughter spills out. I can't help it. The question is nonsense. A *year* of lying and hiding what they did to Ryan, and he expects me to tell him about Mila after five fucking seconds?

"It's much too early for answers," I tell him. "Don't you think? What's the statute of secrets? One year. In one year, you'll find out. You made the rules, not me."

He stares at me in horror. "Emily."

I push him away with all of my strength, and he stumbles to avoid a row of candles lining the windowsill by the front door. "You buried my brother?"

"No. Kennedy doesn't know shit." He begins blowing out candles. That's fine. It's fine. He won't get to all of them. He couldn't possibly. There are too many.

"What did you do, Chase?" I pick up one of the taller

candles carefully and begin to relight the ones he's blown out.

"I went looking for him. Anyone would. I couldn't accept—you couldn't either." He turns to me, pleading in his eyes. "I wanted to know what happened, just not like that. I didn't want him to be dead."

"But he was." Every step he takes, I follow. Every candle he extinguishes, I relight.

"There was nothing I could do about that!" He gives up on the candles and takes me by the elbows.

I would have fallen for it once, melted into him and disappeared. Instead I hold the lit candle between us, a warning. "You could have told me. You could have saved my family a year of torture."

He shakes his head, and I feel his hands trembling against my skin. Vibrating his fear straight through me. "It would have ruined our lives," he whispers.

"So you chose you," I whisper back. "How did you do it? Bodies don't bury themselves."

"I made a phone call," he says, his voice thick with shame. Of course he did. Boys like Chase can make phone calls. There were always whispers about his father. Entanglements with the sort of people who make problems disappear. Just like in the movies. Isn't it glamorous? I picture him deep in the woods, all alone at the cell spot, desperate to catch a single bar of cell service, his phone glowing in his hand. He made a phone call. That's all. With a phone call, he buried a body. One more puzzle piece. Another snapshot. Another image to immortalize. The last tarot card, and the rest writes itself.

I run back upstairs just as he's discovering Mila. Who led

my brother to his death, and kept the secret like a promise. No more. His scream is exquisite.

I wait outside Kennedy's room, the princess tower, pink gauze and wood carvings and the memory of shattered glass. Someone should have told the Hartfords to read the Grimm brothers. Fairy tales never end without bloody revenge or haunting defeat. The mermaid dissolves. The stepsisters are savaged by birds.

The witch in the woods is burned in her own enchanted home.

Kennedy is halfway up the attic stairs to a panicked Chelsea, a mistake, but not her first. I pull her down and push the stairs back up.

She stares at me, stunned, from the floor. Untouchable Kennedy. Kennedy, who will always come out on top. Looking up at me. Even now she doesn't look afraid. Just desperate. Searching. What to say to get out of this mess. I almost enjoy it.

"Don't do this," she says. Calm. Measured. "Everything will be different. We'll go to the police. We'll tell the truth."

But I don't think any of them know the whole truth anymore. They're so tangled up in their own lies. The only thing left to do is destroy it all and start over.

"Is this what it was like?"

She shakes her head. Playing stupid. As if she didn't know. I grit my teeth. "When you killed him."

A hard, cold burst of air escapes her lips. It's not a gasp. It isn't shocking, what she did. Not to her. She's just cornered. Every breath she takes is stalling. "Emily. Please think. None of us would kill a friend. We had ups and downs. Sometimes small ones." She almost shows an emotion and it disgusts me. "Sometimes bigger. But our history was bigger than that."

"Bullshit. You didn't like him."

She looks at me accusingly. Me. Like I'm the bad one for saying it out loud, for seeing the ugliness in her. "People grow apart. That's life. It doesn't mean he wasn't important to me or that I stopped caring about him. Or that I haven't relived that day over and over and over in my mind, trying to figure out what any of us would have done differently if we had a second chance. You were there too. Would you have been nicer to Mila? Because if you had, maybe she wouldn't have felt like she had to leave the house. Would you still have smashed my head with a mirror? Because if I hadn't been stuffed full of drugs, maybe I could have saved him. And if you hadn't held us to that unforgiving standard of loyalty, you might have been there on the boat, and maybe he wouldn't have gone into the water. But every second of our lives led to that moment. We have always been doomed for this. There was no other way, and Emily, you played your part too. You pushed."

And that's it. Kennedy Ellis Hartford has played her last card. I step past her wordlessly and pull down the attic door. She looks at me distrustfully and then turns and rushes up the stairs to Chelsea. There are sounds of joy. Reunion. Love. Chelsea rushes down the stairs first, and the relief on her face is palpable. Then her eyes fall on me.

My eyes trail up the ladder. Kennedy is still up there. Extinguishing candles. Breathing a massive sigh of relief. She should be leaving. Protecting herself and the one she loves. But she protects the house. I fold the ladder back up, push the trapdoor closed again, then grab the hair-trimming scissors off Kennedy's neat, meticulously organized vanity, and snip the pull string off.

Chelsea stares at me with a look of mixed horror and betrayal. "Why would you do that?" She jumps, straining to reach the lock on the attic door as Kennedy calls down to us in vain, but we both know it's too high up.

"You know why." I turn away from her, but she blocks my way out of the room. "If you don't get it now, you're never going to."

"I loved him too, Em." She pushes past me and positions herself behind the bed, throwing her weight against it. But with its heavy oak frame, it's not going to move an inch. "You know why I wrote that note."

"Because you didn't save him. You didn't call for help. You didn't even admit he was gone. You may not have pushed him, but your silence *held him under*, Chelsea. You killed Ryan too."

"I still loved him."

"But you chose Kennedy." I can't say her name without bile rising to my tongue, venom.

She tries the vanity, straining from the effort, then pauses, gasping for breath. "I loved her more."

I glare at her. I know she loved Ryan. Anyone knew who saw them together. And it hurts more that she let him die. That she buried him even before that. That she wouldn't admit that she loved him until he was dead, because she wouldn't dare risk Kennedy finding out. Wouldn't risk losing the bigger prize.

"You kept him a secret," I whisper. "That's not real love. Loyalty doesn't have two sides."

She tries the last piece of furniture, the heaviest, the

bureau, and starts to cry. I want to break her in half. "You were the one who convinced me I had to keep Ryan a secret or lose Kennedy. You always want us to choose sides. You don't understand loyalty, Emily. I don't think you understand love. All of us have loved you. You made the rules too strict. I'm sorry I broke Ryan's heart, and I can't forgive myself for not saving him. But we don't deserve this. No one does. We've fought and made mistakes, but it's still love that ties all of us together. Not Ryan's death." She believes all of this. I know she does, truly. But Chelsea lives in a fantasy. It is a murder that ties the rest of them together. And I have no love left in me.

She looks at me imploringly. "Let Kennedy go."

"I am. I just wish you had." I flee the bedroom, slamming the door behind me and pushing a decorative table in front of it. Chelsea screams, kicks the door, pummels the wood with her fists. I ignore her.

Chelsea. The willing witness. No more. Kennedy, the executioner, no more, sealed in with the melted wax and locked in with a cut cord. Your turn, Kennedy.

When I flipped the switches on the circuit breaker, I turned off the power to every room in the house. If they do blow out the candles, they'll be in almost total darkness.

Power is a funny thing.

When you have it, you take it for granted. When you don't, it's the only thing you think about. I'm going to take yours before you die.

It's the least I can do. Maybe not the least. But I *can* do it. That's the whole point of power.

Every one of them will be stuck in a different place. Every

one of them will die alone, like Ryan did. Kennedy is in the attic, and there's no way out. Mila will never leave the cellar. Chase will be in the living room when he realizes there's no saving Mila, and Chelsea is in the bedroom. If I know my friends, and by now, I think I can say without a shadow of a doubt that I do, Chelsea will panic and run for it, like she did while my brother drowned. But there's only one way out for her, and that's straight down from the balcony. Chase will play the hero, like he did when he covered up Kennedy's inconvenient little murder. But I won't let either of them get far. I can't. It's already gone too far. We have all gone too far.

Six candles burning in the dark
Find them fast before they spark
One is in the living room
One in the garden where the flowers bloom
One on the boat that bobs on the lake
One in the room where we sleep and wake
One in the attic over your head
One in the cellar where you'll find one dead.

It occurs to me that I haven't thought of a way out. There are still pills in my pocket. But I didn't come here to die. I didn't come here to kill, either.

I came here to learn the truth.

But the truth was murder.

The truth was lies.

So I leave Kennedy's room. One last time before I go. There's a sudden flare of light from downstairs, and I run to the balcony overlooking the loft. The candles on the living room table have finally burned to the bottom, and I watch in fascination as the cards from the board game ignite as if made of some hyperflammable substance. A sudden wind blows the front door open, and the cards go swirling into the air like leaves lifted from a bonfire. As each card makes contact with a surface, a brilliant blaze blooms, spreading with almost supernatural speed. Everything is light and heat. Everything is sick and strange. The smoke is poison, the fire is ruin, but the house is dying. There is nothing left to save. I focus on the door, the one I was sure I locked. This is the one chance to turn back. Chase is still in the cellar, administering CPR like the Boy Scout he is. He has a shot at escape, if he were smart enough to take it. By some miracle or act of god, almost a supernatural force, the fire hasn't come into contact with a gasoline-coated surface. But I find myself running, unable to stop myself, down the stairs, to the front door, padlocking it, and sprinting back up again, my lungs bursting, out of breath. I lift the can of gasoline and spill the rest over the side of the balcony. There is no turning back.

Chase runs back up from the cellar and stares up at me from the living room. "What did you do?" He looks at me like a stranger. But he's the stranger.

"Don't ask me that." I don't like the way it makes me feel. I don't like the way he's looking at me. Like I'm the villain.

He looks around helplessly. "The fire extinguisher's missing."

"Bad luck."

A wall of fire rises behind him, and he backs away from it. "You killed Mila."

"You killed Ryan."

"It was an accident. This is so fucked up, Emily. This is so fucked." He whips his head around, looking for an out.

It's almost comical, like a cartoon. But he's smart. Smart-guy Chase. If there is a way out, he will find it. So I search the room too, surveying the scene from above. "You planned this."

Remain calm. Focus. Look. There's still room for him to edge sideways to the bookcase. He could possibly climb it and pull himself up to where I'm watching him from the loft, or it could fall over and crush him. Flatten him like a pancake. I don't see another way. Two walls of fire are now blocking his exit, and there are no windows in the cellar.

"Only a little." I hold Mila's unlit lighter over the railing. It's going to burn my fingers, and if I'm not careful, it could set the rest of me on fire. I have to do it quickly or not at all. There's pure terror in his eyes, but I see sedation there too. The pills work quickly.

"Emily. Em. You don't need to do this." His eyes focus on the bookcase, and he flattens against the wall and begins to inch toward it. It was only a matter of time. He begins tearing books off the shelf, leaving the bottom row filled. Clever. That will weigh it down, make it less likely to topple over as he climbs.

"Why do people always say that?" It irritates me. Does he think I don't know that? Like I'm a child with no sense of agency? "I choose to do it. You made your choices, I get to make mine. And you made a *lot* of bad choices, Chase. Let's be honest, this isn't just about Ryan. You ignored me for years. You brought Mila to *our* place not once but twice, you had sex with her behind my back, and then you paraded her in front of me after . . ." I can't even say it. The words stick in my throat like something rotten.

I watch little sparks of hope die in his eyes as he begins to climb, looking up at me, stricken, reaching one arm over his head and finding his footing. "Jesus Christ, what is wrong with you?"

I open my mouth but swallow a cloud of smoke and choke for a moment, gasping for breath. "Nothing is wrong with me, Chase," I gasp. "You are a toxic friend. All of you are toxic friends. I am cleansing my life of toxic friends. Like I should have years and years ago." I double over, coughing, as he continues to climb. I shouldn't let him. But I'm angry. He shouldn't be allowed to say these things to me.

I can hardly make out his words at first through the sound of the fire, but I lean over the side of the balcony, straining. He's coming closer. "Not like this."

I struggle to see him through the smoke. It's getting harder and harder to breathe. Chase is an athlete, but I don't see how he can climb through this. I can barely stand. My head is beginning to swirl. The smoke is poisoning my senses, pouring in through my eyes, ears, and nose. And then his hands sweep out toward me, grasping only air. Again, embracing nothingness. Once more, so close, and I can't breathe, and then his fingertips brush against the balcony, and my heart stops. Chase, who I loved. Chase, who I adored. Who I spent summer after summer, year after year, reaching and grasping and longing for, to have him slip through my fingers. I grab his hands, lace my fingers through his, feel the electricity surge through them, the warmth, the *need*. He needs me. In the most fundamental sense. But I don't need him. Not anymore. I let go, gently, lovingly, pushing him firmly away, feeling his weight shift back and over, into the thick, poisonous air, feeling the crunch of his bones as sharply as I hear it.

There's something I should tell you, before it's too late.

"I really do love you," I whisper. "Every last, damned one of you."

And you are all damned.

Every last one of you.

I kick the bookcase over, just to be sure. Goodbye, love. Goodbye.

I ignite the lighter, and it burns my fingers. I snap it shut. Chase is quiet now. Chelsea is kicking the door. The smoke is so thick, I couldn't find my way back downstairs if I wanted to. But I know what would be waiting for me. Rivers of fire. Blood red, electric. The heat is incredible. It scorches and comforts me at once. It will burn out all the parts in me that don't belong anymore. The soft parts, the decay. The sadness and longing. It burns. The longing burns. It's almost gone. I know now where my brother is, and how it happened. I'm finally done with Chase. I'll never be second in Kennedy's eyes, or third in Chelsea's. I'm ready to let go. I grasp the railing dizzily and nudge the can of gasoline over the edge with my foot.

This is how I'll say goodbye:

Not with words.

Not with a kiss.

But with a promise.

You will remember me forever.

I light the lighter one more time and drop it.

Flames leap up and I step back, humbled by their strength. The desire to not die hits me so hard it takes my breath away, and I run to the one place I haven't been able to secure, the balcony in Kennedy's room. I stagger to the table that's blocking Kennedy's room and push it aside to find Chelsea tearing the room apart, searching for a tool to open the attic.

She turns to me frantically, weak and coughing. "Help me."

I smile. "The only way out is down." It's not a friendly drop, but it's my only shot. I slide my legs over the railing and drop down, landing safely, then look up at the house.

Goodbye, friends.

I'll leave you with this thought.

Before you ask about second chances,

Remember the Summer of Swallows.

Remember.

Remember.

Because it's never, ever, ever going away.

Not after what you did.

So if you think this is over?

Think again.

And again.

And again.

Your very best friend,

Emily Joiner

SUMMER OF EGRETS
Present
Kennedy

48

The attic door closes behind me, and with the slam of wood against wood, the last pieces fall into place.

I feel him behind me before he speaks my name.

"Kennedy." His voice is hard and jagged, and I know my time is up. I feel him drifting behind me like an errant tide. I feel his presence like heartbreak, like something loved and lost, like a thousand past summers fading into photographs in dusty albums. Like something trying desperately not to be forgotten.

I know I've failed again.

I didn't save Ryan. I lied to Chelsea. She was better than us. She couldn't live with the guilt. So we tried to erase it.

It was one little lie.

We all tell little lies.

Chelsea tells them all the time. She lied about her relationship with Ryan. I'll probably never know the truth about what happened between them, but it doesn't matter. It was never any of my business. It was over and done the moment we became each other's worlds.

Mila lies. She lies with every cutting word she says. She pretends to be harder, colder, than she is. She deserved better from us from day one. We could have been friends. We should have been friends. I should have taken her side.

Chase lies. He lied about helping Ryan run away. He faked all those letters from Ryan, proving he was still alive out there, spinning stories to ease our guilt. He lied to Chelsea's face with his half-truths. He lied to Emily with his silence. It wasn't malicious. None of our lies have ever been malicious. They were benevolent lies. Lies in service to friendship. Lies to keep us from falling apart.

We did what we had to, Chase and me.

We buried a body.

Ryan lied. He lied on the boat that night. He pushed me and I pushed him. He lied when he came back year after year, when all that remained between him and us was history and longing. He let us believe we could go back to the way things were. That every day could be summer. That our friendship was more than a ghost following me, waiting for the final cut.

I lie. I lie by omission. I lie every time I open my mouth and speak any words to Chelsea that are not *I still love you.* I lie to myself as often as I lie to my girlfriend. I have never been more frightened, with heat rising below, with smoke clouding my lungs, because there is love in the world, filling me, there are ghosts behind and before, all around me now, and I love her. There have always been ghosts, fires, death, distractions, lies, but the one that destroys us is the pain of not knowing we are loved, not telling. Not telling Chelsea. I press my palms against the scorching floorboards below and push, knowing they won't give way.

I turn to Ryan, resigned. He stands over me silently, stale lake water soaking his clothes, matting his hair to his skull, dripping

dripping

dripping

and I finally understand.

"I was just a kid," I say. "You tried to kill me."

"You killed me first." He stares at me dully. "It took me a while to understand. Why I was still here and you were all gone. And then I realized that *here*, there is no time. Not the way there used to be. It was like being everywhere at once. Only it was everywhen, not everywhere. Because this is the only place left now, Kennedy. You did that to me. You trapped me in the one place I never wanted to see again. So yes. I did try to kill you. A dead three-year-old can't grow up to be a murderer, can she?"

"But it doesn't work that way."

"No. I've lived that moment over and over. I've even watched you die. It doesn't change what happened to me. Maybe in some other reality. But all that matters is what we know, doesn't it? What we live through. Or don't. I'm stuck in some kind of loop with you, Kennedy. I always come back. And I always regret it."

"I'm sorry," I whisper, then begin to cough as smoke fills my lungs.

He turns to the window and begins to draw in the dust. When he turns around, the words *too late* are revealed. He grins at me, a cold, wet grin. I can't feel sorry for him. I don't.

He settles himself down on the floor with his hands folded behind his head. "It's just you and me, Kennedy. Can you think of anyone more fitting to spend your last moments with?" He aims a piercing stare at me. "Because I can't."

I slam my fists against the wood, shout Chelsea's name, silently pray to space and time to bend for me. I want to go back. I want a redo.

It can't end this way.

I reach Kennedy's room and throw the balcony doors open, but as I'm about to slide my leg over the railing, I hear a familiar, horrible, crushing sound.

Hands knocking.

Emily screaming.

From the attic.

Chase was right.

It's happening again.

Exactly the same way.

I turn and face the monster. The crushing heat, the smoke, the fire creeping closer and closer, Emily's panicked voice above me, the pounding in the attic. Not this time. I'm not leaving her this time. I position myself behind the bed and force it across the room, agonizingly slowly, throwing all of my weight, my heart, my terror, behind it. In a nightmare, you get second chances. This doesn't feel like a nightmare. It feels unbearably real. But I can't live with the guilt of killing her twice.

I step up on the bed and stand on tiptoe, and my fingers just graze the latch of the attic door. It's scorching hot.

"I'm here!" I shout up to her.

She doesn't answer, and the thumps are growing fainter and further apart. I steel myself and go for the latch again, and this time it comes open. I yank the door down, and a wave of shock runs through me. It's not her. It's not Emily. Kennedy is crouched at the top of the ladder, her face pressed low, taking short, shallow breaths. She reaches for me, and I pull her down into my arms. We land on the bed in a swirl of smoke, and she coughs and drops onto the floor.

I try to pull her up, toward the balcony, but she stops me, grabbing my arm.

"Chelsea, wait." She looks into my eyes, dread radiating out of them. "Ryan is dead."

I stare at her, my mind spinning like a music box. But then I see it. The shadowy figure comes into view. The panicked swim to the boat, the alibi, the doomed walk back to the lake house, Emily's silhouette in the attic. The Summer of Swallows. "When did you remember?"

"The boat brought some of it back. When I first woke on the deck, I thought it was a dream. You were so sure you saw someone fall, but it didn't make sense. Ryan left. How could he have . . . But then when I was alone on the water, it came back. He followed me. I lived it, like a waking nightmare. I knew what we did."

I try to comprehend. "Mila figured it out when she went back out on the water too. Chase saw it in the clearing in the tarot card. That's what you were hiding from me. Not who set the fire. Mila tried to tell me, but Chase wouldn't let her."

"The guilt almost destroyed you, Chelsea. Of course he was afraid to tell you."

"Ryan never came back." I crawl over to her and we huddle together.

"We saw what we wanted to believe." Kennedy coughs violently. "I didn't mean to kill him, Chelsea." She coughs again and buries her head in my shoulder. "We've been lying so long, some parts begin to feel like the truth. But I didn't mean to do it. I didn't."

I take her hand, cold and smooth, and press it to my lips. "I know, Kennedy." I feel my insides turning from numbness to nausea. The smoke is killing my lungs. "But we have to get out of here." I start to climb to my feet.

"Wait," she says again, and pulls me away from the balcony. "When I was a little girl, I used to see ghosts. Especially in this house."

"But you don't believe," I whisper.

She sits, steadying herself on the bed. "I learned long ago to keep it a secret. It scares people. They sent me away once and I never said another word. But this house is special. The ghosts. There was one in the lake that was always angry. The dripping man. But the others looked after me like family. Like one of their own." Her eyes drift up to the attic, and a sense of dread fills me.

"The tea party," I whisper.

She nods. "They've always been here. It's like time doesn't work the same in their world. They're living every day at once. Reliving. Every moment of my life that I spent at this house, they were there. They don't leave. They don't change. To me they looked grotesque—like corpses. But to each other, they look exactly like they did the day they died."

I look to the balcony anxiously. The fire is burning through the house, devouring the walls, creeping closer. "Kennedy, we have to go."

"One minute," she begs. "There are five ghosts in the lake house. The dripping man, the blue lady, the backward girl, the woman on the stairs, and the crushed man."

I pull her to her feet. "I want to hear this. I do. But we need to get out before the floor collapses." My bigger fear, though, is that the smoke is making her delirious. Smoke kills more people than fire does.

She pulls back wearily and sinks back onto the bed. "I can't."

There's a loud boom from somewhere within the house, and I begin to panic. "Six feet. I'll carry you. You don't even have to get up."

Kennedy coughs and braces herself against the bed to steady herself. "I wouldn't make it to the ground."

I get on my hands and knees and begin to pull her toward the balcony, but she's dead weight and, struggling with every ounce of strength in my body, I still can't make her move. "The smoke is messing with your head. You don't remember how fast this place went up before."

"Chelsea," she says in the softest voice imaginable. "*You* don't remember."

Her hand breaks out of mine, and I crash through the balcony doors. I catch myself on the railing and press my face against the bars to get a breath of untainted air. For one sweet moment I close my eyes and feel a cool lake breeze sweep over my face, breathing life, hope, faith into me. Then I open my eyes and they travel down toward the ground.

It's the strangest thing.

A body lies there, lifeless, drained. I know she's dead with

just a glance. The angles of her bones are sharp and unforgiving. It wasn't necessarily a deadly drop from the balcony, but
it was a harsh fall, an unlucky fall. She just didn't make it. Her
neck is twisted in such a way that although her chest is pressed
into the grass, her face is wrenched around over her shoulder.
Backward. She gazes up, her eyes wide open, fixed at the sky,
clear and questioning. Not peaceful. You couldn't say peaceful
or at rest. She looks searching, hopeful, afraid, but determined.

I died determined.

No.

No.

"You have to understand why we can't leave," Kennedy
says quietly.

"But we did leave. I was at the hospital—"

"After Ryan died," she says firmly. "For weeks, not a year.
Remember—"

"No." I back away, from the balcony, from Kennedy. I don't
remember. I don't want to remember.

But she advances toward me, and I push it away, the memory of the hospital, the note, last summer. The fire and the fall.
Emily. The stories we told ourselves, dreams in the in-between,
blurred into the buried horror of that dark night.

"We saw what we wanted to believe," Kennedy echoes herself. "We saw ourselves survive."

"But Emily was the one in the attic."

Kennedy nods. "She was, the night Ryan died. But not the
night of the fire."

I run to the attic ladder and climb it, and when I reach
the top, the whole world falls away. I stare at the figure lying

airless, drowning in smoke, her skin tinged with sky. Kennedy. Lifeless, lost, alone. Gone. I climb back down numbly. "You were the blue lady."

"You're the backward girl." She smiles, her eyes glistening. "Ryan was the dripping man, Mila was the woman on the stairs. Chase . . . was crushed. I finally understand."

Fear grips me, and I grasp the ladder for balance. "Is this hell? We killed someone, then woke to our worst nightmares."

"I don't think so. We've been working through parts of our lives that puzzled or frightened us. Like in dreams. I think those places we thought we went last year were like a smoke-screen because none of us were ready to face the truth. That's what we've been doing tonight, isn't it? The invitation, the game, the boat—all of that came from within. We all betrayed someone in the room. We all kissed a killer. And we all killed a best friend."

It is true. There was always something worse than each of the places we imagined we were last year, something harder to face.

What we did.

We killed a friend and covered it up. And we've been lying to ourselves and everyone else since the day his body was swallowed up by the lake.

"We never left this house, Chelsea." She holds on to me tightly.

The realization creeps over me slowly, like goose bumps. "It was never rebuilt. We're just stuck in time." There's another explosion, and flames begin to move inside the room. "We have to go."

"Why? I've seen us here since I was a baby," she says. "You, me, Mila, and Chase. We go on. I don't know whether it's a punishment or a gift or a scientific anomaly. But we do go on. We get to watch us grow and fight and fall in love and die, again and again and again. We've always been here."

It isn't possible. We did those things. That's our past. The future is nothing. But Kennedy looks so sure. "It's not a gift. We stole a person's life. We kept the truth from his parents."

"And Emily stole ours. We'll have to carry both of those things with us forever. No more lies." She sounds relieved, and for the first time since I can remember, she looks like herself again. Her shoulders relax. A calm settles over her. She takes my hand, and I feel warmth, a new warmth I don't know how to understand. "This is where we belong," she says. "Where all our best memories are. Every day is summer here. This is our house." Her hair is brilliant in the glow of the blaze, her eyes feverish, her cheeks flushed. She looks like a goddess.

I want to run away and I want to stay. There is love here and pain here. "I can't do it. It hurts."

"We remember pain," she says. "Maybe someday we won't."

But we will, at times. At the tea party, it will hurt to see my young self for the first time and to know the price of coming to the lake house. In the Summer of Thrashers it will hurt to see Emily walk through the door. It will hurt to let that raccoon kill our beloved pet. It will always hurt to see our younger selves grow angry and estranged, because that is what led to our downfall, our death. But what happened happened and we can't change the past.

"We made it through the fire," she says. "We survived death itself. What do we have to be afraid of anymore?"

I take a deep breath, and the memory of smoke evaporates inside the memory of my body. It's beginning to fade already. "This was the last puzzle. The biggest fear. We faced the truth and broke the spell. What we did to Ryan. What Emily did to us. We could be done with all of it, Kennedy. Leave the lake house."

"And what? Disappear? Cease to exist?"

"Or something better."

"But not together."

"You don't know that."

"I know I choose forever in a burning house if it means I'll wake up and see your face every day. I don't want something better. I don't know that there is something better, and neither do you." Flames surround us, but the heat has dulled to a gentle warmth. Kennedy's hands close around my face, and I remember heat. I remember salt and fear and sadness and longing. "Chelsea. Stay." She kisses me and I remember stars and fireworks, laughter. I kiss her back and remember rain, hope, beauty.

We remain until the world is gone.

We cannot go forward, or backward, or remain, alone. We have played dolls and demons, fire and first love, blood and betrayal. We have kissed and killed and broken hearts and bones and promises and trust. But we have done these things together, always. We always come back. We *are* the invitation. We came to the lake house, to live and to love and to die. To the Hartford Cabin, our grave and our home. We come one last time, every time, before we all go. June 17, the day we die, every day, forever. We will always come to the lake house. We will no longer burn. Time will move backward, sputter, spin on its axis. The house will rise and fall and rise again, and still we will remain. It lives on, and so do we. No one can make us leave.

How could they?

We are the lake house.

NO.

They do not get a happy ending.

I returned to the lake house, to the leveled charred remains, because I had to, to leave a tribute, my finished tarot cards. One in the cellar, the only real remaining room. One in the garden, a fertile ground for bones. One in the place I imagine the attic fell. And one where my beloved Chase lay for a while.

They say it was a mistake, that maybe if I didn't keep returning, I wouldn't have looked so guilty. But I had to. I still have to. I'm not done.

So I rebuilt the lake house in my mind, log by log and wire by wire. I painstakingly painted the walls, matching shades of color to my memory, carving fairy tales into Princess Kennedy's walls. I snaked plumbing through the innards of the house, flushing the scent of sawdust through the attic and mold in the cellar, tinged with rot, infusing the garden with dew. I resurrected the souls of my brother and his killers and filled their minds with fractured memories, and wound them like dolls to relive the night I killed them over and over again.

My little dollhouse by the lake. Not bad for a plain Jane who lacks the sight.

Revenge doesn't come to you in a moment.

It has to be repeated again and again and again until it sticks.

I haven't perfected it yet.

Because they're all still here in my head.

The dead don't sleep, and neither do I.

My mother's last words to me, after the trial and before the sentencing, were this: *Do you feel any shred of remorse for what you've done?*

Mine to her: *They never did.*

They never did.

She took a hard look at me, and I knew what she was thinking. *You will.*

But it's true. They never did.

It's just as simple as that. They killed Ryan, they felt no remorse, and no one held them to account. They never faced a trial, never had their story picked apart with all the world watching.

Of course it wouldn't be the same for me. I will serve four consecutive sentences for second-degree murder. But there you have it.

I am held to account every day. Every time I close my eyes. My visions are no longer in my control. My friends no longer burn. They walk through fire like rays of sunlight. They play board games while billows of smoke swirl around them. Time seems to move backward.

The house lives on, and I'm the only one who knows. My wicked, unforgivable friends, buried but not gone, dead and awake. In my mind, in dreams and daylight, I am forced to watch them in that house I burned. Ryan hovering at the edge of the lake. Me a world away, and still so close I can smell the charred wood. I've spent so long reliving my revenge that I cannot escape it. The house is lodged inside me now. I don't think I could ever pry it out. No matter how many times I burn it to the ground, it rebuilds itself, and they return. Like it never happened, and I am not done.

I wish my mother would come back so I could ask her if this is how it feels to see.

Or if it's just the ghost of a dozen odd summers haunting me, twisting things up. Making me see things and feel things I shouldn't.

Because the more the house visits me, the stronger my need to return to it grows. It calls me to it night after night in a voice as soft as ash, whispering an invitation. I long to return to its empty rooms, its echoing walls, to my phantom friends. I wish I could make them listen, make them understand what they did to me, why I had to do what I did to them. Maybe then I would be allowed to come back. I know that there is a price for what I've done. The house decides its own fate, and the fate of all whose lives it touches. And as long as I live and forever after, when my body is dust and dirt, it will hold me as it does now, powerless to stay, powerless to leave. I can never return to the lake house, but it will not let me go. It will never, ever let me go.

ACKNOWLEDGMENTS

First and foremost, thank you to my editor, Deeba Zargarpur, for your faith in this book, for breathing life into it and pouring your time, energy, and passion into making it real. Thank you for seeing what the book could be and pushing me to take it to the sharpest, most brutal places. For giving me a chance to tell this story and making it about a hundred times better than what it was.

Thank you to my agent, Elana Roth Parker. This book could not exist without your encouragement, support, and advocacy. For puzzling through plot holes, championing the living daylights out of it, and riding a roller coaster of emotion alongside me, I am so grateful. Heartfelt thanks to everyone at Laura Dail Literary Agency for your unwavering support.

Many thanks to the entire team at Simon & Schuster Books for Young Readers, to Dainese Santos, Charlton Villavelez, Justin Chanda, Anne Zafian, Kendra Levin, Morgan York, and Amy Beaudoin. An awed thank-you to Lizzy Bromley for designing, and to Nicole Rifkin for illustrating, a stunning cover, and grateful thanks to Jen Strada and Kayley Hoffman.

Thousands of thanks to everyone who read, gave feedback, and supported this book, especially Chelsea Ichaso and Jessica Bayliss, who read the earliest draft as I was writing it and did not tell me to flush it down the toilet; Madeline Dyer; Alexa Donne, who convinced me not to let this manuscript die a lonely death in my "bad first drafts" folder; my most fabulous writer group, Rebecca Sky, Kim Chance, Tiffany Case, and Jess

Pennington; a shout-out to the Spooky Book Club for forcing me to balance my writing with reading; and the Electric Eighteens. A special thank-you to Allison Varnes for being a most excellent brainstormer and friend.

Writing is sometimes joyful, often fulfilling, occasionally devastating, and always demanding, and I couldn't do it without the support of my family, friends, and support people, especially David and Benji, Deb, Mike, Chris, Steph, Julia, Frankie, and every member of my gigantic, wonderful family who has always been a source of comfort, help, humor, and support. Thanks always to Jan Simon, and to WAJ.

This book is as much about grief and loss as it is about ghosts, murder, and dysfunctional group dynamics. I would be remiss if I did not acknowledge those I've lost who have remained with me in spirit, including my grandmother Michelina Mele, who passed away as I was revising this book. The networks of family, friends, and sometime strangers who keep us nourished and help us to continue moving along in the routines of our lives when we are grieving. We are all guests here, ultimately, and leaving time is fiercely sad. To my friends, present and past, I am grateful to have known you all.